WHISPERS IN EMPTY ROOMS

LES POBJIE

Whispers in Empty Rooms
Copyright © 2024 by Les Pobjie

All rights reserved. No part of this publication may be reproduced, distributed, or transmitted in any form or by any means, including photocopying, recording, or other electronic or mechanical methods, without the prior written permission of the author, except in the case of brief quotations embodied in critical reviews and certain other non-commercial uses permitted by copyright law.

tellwell

Tellwell Talent
www.tellwell.ca

ISBN
978-1-77941-562-2 (Hardcover)
978-1-77941-561-5 (Paperback)
978-1-77941-563-9 (eBook)

To Helen my constant light

Rage, rage against the dying of the light
-*Dylan Thomas*

CHAPTER

1

The pages fluttered in the detective's hand as his head turned, gazing into every corner of the room. The untidy home office was dusty, dark. If any secrets hid in the jumble of books and magazines, they were safe under the dangling globe's feeble light.

The young detective, Sergeant Peter York, standing near the desk, watched his superior in silence. Detective Inspector Mitchell Cleary was a tall, solidly built man. His dark grey suit fitted snugly over his shoulders, but the lower front buttons gave the impression of being under pressure. The staid blue tie was a shade darker than his eyes. Short fair hair topped a face that if not for a crooked nose, gained from Rugby playing days, and a scar near his right ear, would have been described as handsome rather than 'not bad looking'.

Detective Sergeant Peter York was a contrast with a smaller frame and a shock of red hair that seemed to be combed in different directions sideways and backwards. At twenty-eight, he was nine years younger than his superior.

Experience had taught Peter not to interrupt Cleary when he was mulling over a crime scene. But, in Peter's view, this was clearly an open-and-shut suicide. Eventually, he could contain himself no longer.

"So, something's bothering you, sir?"

For a few more seconds, the Inspector kept his gaze on the big hook in the ceiling from which a rope had tautly stretched down to go around the neck of a man who had been hanging there when they arrived an hour or so earlier. The body was gone now. Cleary dropped his face and looked into his colleague's eyes. This always disconcerted Peter, making him feel he had asked a silly question. Perhaps he had. He was new to this detective business having transferred from uniform to plainclothes only six months ago. He had undertaken the usual training courses but hadn't read any books about how to spot clues at crime scenes. He squinted and tried to gaze intelligently around the room. The bookshelf next to the door almost filled the wall opposite the desk. As big as it was, it was too small for the number of books that were stuffed haphazardly into every space available.

The second shelf from the top, however, stood out, not just because it was dust free but because all the covers were of varying shades of green. With the titles and author's name in brown ink, Peter thought it looked like a stretch of forest with thin branches hanging down. The titles were different, but the author was the same: George Martin, the man who had recently died here. The neat row of books was topped by a blue feather duster. A long white cane with a ball at the tip was leaning up against the bookshelf.

Peter turned and studied the rest of the room.

"This place is so dirty," he said. "Dust everywhere. Doesn't anyone clean in here?"

"It seems that his wife and daughter left it to the blind man to look after."

Peter swiped his hand across the top of the filing cabinet, sending a small cloud of dust into the air. Individual particles glittered as they floated through the sunbeam from the window. Their brief time in the spotlight ended abruptly in the shadow, as if cut off by a switch, finally settling into the anonymity of the carpet never to be individually seen again.

He looked through the window into the bright day, the sunshine unhindered by falling dust, across the valley to the ranges. He sighed and turned back to the reality of his job.

Cleary was looking at him. "See any answers out there, Sergeant?"

"Umm, I was just..."

He was sure there was no question that needed an answer here. His face reddened. He felt as he had when his father caught him reading a Phantom comic hidden under his homework book.

"Are we missing something, Sir?"

"I am missing a couple of things that are missing."

Peter looked at the Inspector without speaking. Cleary said: "I am puzzled that there is no coffee mug on the desk or a voice recorder in this room."

Peter had no answer to that, so he changed the subject. He pointed at the bookshelf with its one sparkling clean shelf of George Martin books.

"He looked after his own books, I reckon," Peter said.

Cleary gestured towards the desk and said: "And also, at least part of his desk, around where the laptop and printer were before our guys took them away, and the small radio behind it."

Peter said: "He might have wiped this end of the desk, too, Sir." There was a large rounded clean area at the other end of the desk. Cleary studied the clean shape.

"No, Peter, it looks more like somebody was sitting there, at least temporarily."

Peter wondered if maybe…something about the victim worried Cleary. The look on his face? Had the man changed his mind at the last moment?

Cleary blinked and said: "Yes, Peter. Something is worrying me. But the question is what is that something. The fellow was blind, so how did he get up there to hang himself?"

Peter nodded and then said: "He might've tied it around his neck first and then threw the other end up over the hook…and…" His voice trailed off.

Inspector Cleary nodded without any conviction. "You'd have to be a bloody good shot, wouldn't you? I couldn't do it and he was shorter than me." He paused. "And another thing, who put the hook up there?

"You don't usually find big hooks like that in the ceiling of home offices. It looks new."

"If someone else put it there," Peter said, "they would've had to do it while Mr Martin was out and he, being blind, would not have known it was there when he returned."

Cleary said: "Yes, or Martin would have had to get someone else to do it while the others were out."

Peter opened his mouth to speak, and he stopped at the sight of the slender manuscript the Inspector was waving at him. "And there is this. He was writing a book, for God's sake. Why would he do this in the middle?"

"It might not have been working out, Sir."

"Peter, I'm not really satisfied that this is all that it seems. I'm gonna poke around a bit, talk to Mr Martin's wife and daughter and that Nagle fellow.

"And I want you to take this." He pushed the pages which were stapled together into Peter's hand.

"Just go through this. You read a lot, don't you?" Peter nodded, wondering what that had to do with investigating a crime — or probably not even a crime.

"You'll see some odd things and I have only just flipped through it. It is strange."

Peter looked at the first few pages, flipping briskly through them, stopping briefly to read a particular paragraph.

He thought he saw a clue. A flimsy one. He said nothing.

"Must be just first draft." He looked at some more pages. "It's full of typos or things I don't think belong in the book.

"It hasn't been proofread or obviously revised."

Cleary frowned. "Didn't Hemingway say all first drafts are shit?"

"That certainly describes this." Peter grinned at the Inspector. "Messy, uncorrected."

"Just rubbish then?"

Peter looked up at his boss, hesitated, then said: "Needs tidying up, of course. It could offer hints to his state of mind and how he related to others in this household. I may be wrong, Sir, but I think it's worth having a deeper look."

Inspector Cleary looked unconvinced.

"So all waiting to be proofread, corrected, revised. I wonder who was going to help him with that. Who was going to be the eyes for a blind man's book – now dead man's book?"

"Maybe his wife or daughter would do that for him."

Cleary held up his hands.

"Okay, go through it Peter. I know it's a long shot. But you may glean something from it. About his state of mind when he was writing. Was he considering suicide? I noticed a bit about suicide on one of his pages. But does that mean anything?"

Peter didn't answer. He was only half listening, engrossed in reading. Cleary put his hand out over the pages.

"Not now, Peter. Take it home: consider it homework."

"I will, Sir. Yes. Definitely. I'll give it my full attention tonight."

"Good lad." Cleary walked around the room. Peter followed. Expected they would be there for another hour or so acting like Sherlock Holmes. Peter was satisfied it was a wasted effort. The man hanged himself. But they would talk to the wife, daughter and the chauffeur.

Cleary locked the door of the office and gave instructions to the uniformed constable to make sure nobody entered while they were away.

The detectives went down the wide, slightly curved staircase and into the main lounge where Mrs Margot Martin sat in a brown, leather sofa chair. Cleary apologised for keeping her so long. The look she gave them indicated it hadn't been a patient wait.

Her dark brown hair was cut to just above shoulder length. A string of what Peter thought might be pearls hung from her neck.

Her arm stretched along the arm rest, fingers tapping impatiently. An open magazine lay on her lap, the vivid colours of a fashion spread contrasting with the sedate autumn-floral of her dress.

Peter guessed that she had not assumed her annoyed position until she heard them coming down the stairs.

Cleary apologised again for keeping her waiting. Her expression didn't change as she nodded — possibly in acknowledgement, certainly not in acceptance. He asked if they could sit. They took the silent answer and nod to mean they could sit on the lounge opposite. Peter took out his notebook and placed his pen over an open page. She looked at the notebook and up at Peter's face. She turned her eyes onto Cleary.

"Is this going to be an interrogation? Don't you accept the evidence you have seen with your own eyes? So, your boy there must write all this down? I suppose you say that's all routine, too."

"Detective Sergeant York is an experienced officer. He is assisting me now by doing what is required at this moment,"

Cleary said. He paused. "I understand that you found your husband's body this morning."

"Yes, it was a shock. Not something one comes across every day." She looked at Cleary. "Or is it part of your daily routine, Inspector Cleary?"

"A violent death is never routine, Mrs Martin. It would've been terrible for you and your daughter. You have our sympathy."

"And yet," she interrupted, "here I am, the grieving widow, forced to answer inane questions a few hours after my husband killed himself."

Watching her, Peter wondered if the 'grieving' adjective might be a tad exaggerated.

"Nevertheless," Cleary said, "I must ask each of you a few questions for the record. Once they are all cleared up, we'll be on our way and out of your hair."

"And then, after all your intrusive questions and our grief-filled answers are written in your little notebook, then can you leave us to grieve? How kind of you, Inspector."

Peter lifted his pen off the paper and studied the tip, touched it with his thumb, then looked at his thumb as if being very interested in learning whether the ballpoint would write on human skin. After a few seconds, when Cleary began to speak, Peter lost all interest in that line of inquiry and put the pen back on the page ready to write.

"Now Mrs Martin, I must ask, do you know of anyone who might have wanted to harm your husband?"

"Of course, I do," she said.

Peter was poised to write something in his notebook, but Mrs Martin's face made him suspect that she was not going to say anything helpful.

"Can you tell me who that is?" Cleary asked.

"It was George Martin." She sat back in the chair, her eyes going from one detective to the other. Cleary sighed at his junior colleague who was scribbling wildly.

"You are saying your husband was responsible for his own death, then?"

"Yes. I am surprised you both missed the clues with poor George hanging there. Case closed."

She sharply smacked her hands together and began to stand. The Inspector raised his right hand.

"Not quite. It's not closed until I say it is."

Mrs Martin began to protest. Peter smiled but quickly stopped when he saw Cleary glaring at him.

Mrs Martin started to protest again but Cleary spoke over her. She plopped down.

"Has anybody seen a suicide note?"

"Spent all his time on stories for his precious readers …" She licked her lips. "He couldn't even write a few words to his loved ones."

"Okay, so no note." Cleary persevered. "Excuse me, Mrs Martin, but had you noticed any change in his mood or behaviour in the last few weeks or months? Was there anything worrying him that you knew of?"

"Well, George kept a lot close to his chest. I don't know if anything was particularly worrying him. If there was, I would probably be the last one to know." She paused. "Except for his obsession with the idea that he could write a book of short stories."

Peter said: "He was such a success as a novelist, but I understand that he took up the short story idea after his last novel wasn't a success."

Margot made a scoffing sound. "Ridiculous. How can a blind man write a book?"

Cleary said: "Do you think that was causing him stress?"

"He was causing stress to all of us. He had a deadline from the publisher, and I couldn't see him meeting that. And he didn't, did he?"

A loud noise at the door distracted them. Constable Brandon moved into the room. He seemed to be stopping somebody from entering.

Cleary said, "What's the trouble, Constable?"

"It's Ms Martin and Mr Nagle, Sir," Brandon said. "They say they got sick of waiting around and insist on coming in."

Nagle pushed his way into the room and said: "We are fed up waiting around, wasting our time. Cut and dried case and yet you cops want to make a federal case out of it." The man was obviously angry.

"Alright, Constable," Cleary said, "I'll have a word with them."

Peter wondered how Cleary could have had any other choice. The man and the woman were standing there glaring, feet planted firmly as if they had no intention of moving from that spot. She was pretty with long flowing blonde hair and was wearing brown trousers and a caramel-coloured shirt. In contrast, Nagle, however, was not attractive. His hair was not blond and flowing, it was dark and sparse. His face was much grimmer than Nola's.

Peter thought she was about his age while he guessed Nagle was in his early forties.

"Hoy," Nagle shouted, "you can't keep us locked up like this. I've got work to do. You don't have any right to—"

The constable held out his right arm to block their further progress into the room.

Peter moved towards them. Cleary stood where he was, waiting for the clamour to die down. When he spoke, his voice was louder than usual. "Mr Nagle, you are interfering with the lawful investigation of a suspicious death." Nagle snorted, Mrs Martin shook her head, her daughter's eyes widened.

"I think that you would all agree that this death, of a well-known and talented man, was unexpected. He seemed to have had many good reasons to live. There are a few questions my colleague and I would like answered. Once that is done, I expect that we will close the case."

Nagle shouted something that Peter didn't understand. He didn't think it was worth asking him to repeat it. Cleary put up two hands and called upon everyone to be quiet. They shuffled their feet but kept their mouths closed.

"I understand how difficult it is for each of you," the Detective Inspector said, "however, it is essential that we gather all the information available about this tragic event."

Mrs Martin said: "Event? Is that all my husband's death is to you, Inspector?"

"No, Mrs Martin, it is much more than that. But we must ensure that his death was at his own volition. We must not allow someone who may have caused it to escape punishment. You may have your own idea of what this is all about, but this case will not be closed until I say it is. We have to get the facts. We may both agree with your own thoughts, however, I am wondering why you are so keen to make sure we walk away from this incident and wrap it up as a clear case of suicide."

"Which it is." Nola said.

"You may well be right, Ms Martin," Cleary said, "We shall soon see, I believe. In the meantime, go back to where you were waiting and relax until I ask each of you to come in."

He turned to Mrs Martin and said: "I expect we will wrap it up in a few days."

Margot looked at him but didn't comment.

"Thank you, Inspector," Nola said, "I don't get the mystery about Dad's death. But I will help you in any way I can."

Cleary nodded. Peter smiled encouragingly at the young woman.

"Thank you, Ms Martin. There is one thing I would like to ask you now if you don't mind." Without waiting for her agreement Cleary said: "Had you noticed any change in your Dad's mood?"

"No... I..." She began to cry and wiped across her eye with the back of her hand. Constable Brandon offered her his handkerchief.

She shook her head and gazed back at the Inspector. "He is... was, a writer. They go through many moods, ups and downs."

Nagle shouted: "You're talking rubbish."

Margot pointed to the manuscript under the open notebook on Peter's knee.

"If you want to see rubbish, look in there. That load of junk will get you nowhere in this so-called investigation."

"Mum," Nola shouted. She moved further into the room. Brandon picked up a small nod from Cleary and didn't move after her.

"You know how Dad worked. He is... was, blind. He relied on me to revise it, to cut out the irrelevant stuff."

"It's all irrelevant," Margot shouted back at her daughter.

"He was a mad man, that's what I reckon," Nagle said. You're well rid of him, Margot."

"If you were able to read," Nola said, you would know what a brilliant writer he was."

She swung around and asked Cleary if she could be allowed to leave the room until he wanted her. Cleary nodded and she brushed past Nagle and left.

Nagle glared at the detectives and said: "Your experts need all day to determine that rope marks around a man's neck means he was hanged?" He walked out.

"She's a bit emotional," Margot said, unnecessarily. "You must understand, Inspector, what was going on here."

Peter hoped that he could get to know what was going on.

"George didn't just dictate stories. He took that blasted recorder with him all over the place. He jabbered away sounding like he was thinking aloud. It was–"

Cleary interrupted her. "Do you have that recorder, Mrs Martin?"

She seemed surprised.

"No. Why would I?"

"The recorder was not in the office or on Mr Martin. The scene of crime officer confirmed it was nowhere to be found. That seems odd to me, considering he always had it with him.'

'It must be somewhere, Inspector. I'll look for it later. I don't see that being of any use to you now," Margot said. "Or to George, for that matter. He maintained it was a great way to get ideas for new stories." She laughed, apparently scoffing at the idea.

"We won't keep you much longer, Mrs Martin," Cleary said.

Cleary asked her how long she and George had been married. At first, she didn't seem to want to answer that question. She crossed her legs and pulled the skirt over her knees before looking up at Cleary.

"I think it would be thirty-three years. A long time, anyway." Pause. "Yes, thirty-three years."

Cleary said: "How would you describe your marriage? In the past few years, I mean."

"I don't see how any of this nonsense can be of value," Margot said. "Isn't it just prurient curiosity, Detective Inspector? My husband killed himself. You know, it's like talking to slow learners with you two. Not enough real crimes to while away your time?"

"I would appreciate it, Mrs Martin, if you would answer my questions. I'm trying to build a full picture of your marriage and this household. As to considering it to be a clear case of suicide, I am uneasy about that. There are some snags that I must straighten out." He looked at her again. He waited for an answer to his question.

"Well, if it will help get you off my back, our marriage over the last few years has not been a happy one." She paused. "It all began in a wonderful love affair but drizzled out as we… I guess, lost interest in all the romantic stuff… we had the business of life to attend to and one day we… I, at any rate, discovered there was no love there anymore."

Peter said: "When I skimmed through the manuscript, I noted that your husband wrote that he still loved you –"

She snorted. "In that rubbish that you persist in calling a manuscript? His mind was wandering, surely. He just rambled on and on into that recorder. And, I believe, he stored in it things that we said. Surely that's against the privacy laws, isn't it?"

Peter thought, the woman's husband was found dead this morning and she's going on about privacy laws.

Cleary persisted. "And in later years you were living more like a couple who had separated? In separate rooms?"

"If I thought that was any business of yours, Inspector, I would say yes. But as it's not any of your business, but nevertheless true, I will say yes, anyway."

"Was that hard on your husband? I mean, he was going blind over the last couple of years, so I imagine your separation would have added to his distress."

She fluttered her dress again with both hands and looked around as if searching for the magazine she usually had on her lap but had slipped to the floor.

"I know it distressed him. At times I think he cried. Not in front of me, of course, but sometimes when I looked at him his eyes were wet." She glanced at the detectives in turn. "I believe you think I am an evil woman." She paused and looked impassively at Cleary, as if hoping he would negate her comment. Her gaze was met with blank eyes: strikingly blue but non- committal.

"I am not," she said. "It is not easy for a woman to have dreams of the future taken away so dramatically, so horribly, when her husband becomes disabled… I'm sorry if that shocks you, gentlemen, but I am speaking frankly."

Peter thought that she wanted to talk and saw that Cleary was content to let her express what was inside her. Who knows? It may be a breakthrough.

She said: "I have so many things I want to continue to do with my life, going to the theatre, long drives in the country, travel within Australia and travel overseas again. You know, George and I went overseas quite a lot in our early days." She started another sentence but stopped suddenly. She looked across the room as if reimagining those holidays in faraway places.

Cleary was about to bring her back to the present when she abruptly shook her head and spoke again. "But how could I do those things after my husband went blind? I would have to travel around all those places as a carer." She spat out the word as if it was distasteful to her.

"We couldn't do any of those things together the way we used to. He couldn't even eat properly in public. He couldn't see to cut his food up to the portion size required. He couldn't tell if he was dressed properly."

She looked, this time, at Peter and said: "Does that sound unfair of me? Would you like to have to watch your spouse struggling, food dripping off forks, spoons, onto his clothes? Would you like to have to wipe his shirt or... her blouse... in public?"

Embarrassed by the question, Peter turned his eyes away. She turned to the Inspector. "You know," she said, "I couldn't even invite friends to dinner."

Cleary said: "I understand that it has been difficult for you, Mrs Martin, but –"

She laughed bitterly, without humour. "Difficult isn't half of it, Inspector. I hated it all. I know how dreadful that must sound. But I am sure you want honest answers. How could I go on like that? I am only fifty-three years old. I have a lot of life ahead of me, God willing. And I saw it stretching into blackness, like a tunnel with no exit, caring for the needs of a man who was once the love of my life. He had become a burden."

"Mrs Martin, I can understand what your husband's loss of sight has meant to you. It took so much away from your life."

"You reckon, Inspector? You think that it might have been difficult even for me, the bitch of a wife?"

Cleary said: "Mrs Martin, we do not come here seeking evil in anyone. We are quite neutral. My only bias is against whoever killed your husband –" Margot started to speak but stopped when

Cleary raised his hand. "No, I mean that. We do not want to allow a killer to get away with it. If it should turn out to be your husband, then, he will have got away with it. Got away with what I consider to be murder, even if it is of himself."

Margot was silent for a moment. She picked up the magazine, flicked pages over and for a while Peter thought she was going to ignore them as she began reading.

"It may be hard for you gentlemen to understand that George and I were once very much in love as most young people are in the months and years after their marriage. We enjoyed our lives, we did so much: we travelled, we entertained, we planned – and we loved living in this beautiful big home.

"It is, at heart, a romantic place. At least, it was once. Now it is the home of sudden death. Death that you think is murder."

Peter said: "I think this is… this was, a lovely place for you and Mr Martin to live in. I would love to have this as my home, the home for me and my wife and… I hope one day children. What a place."

Margot gazed at Peter silently for a minute. She looked from one detective to the other, finally focusing on Peter. "The big room upstairs, the lounge room with the open fire in winter…it has such lovely memories for…" She paused as if lost in memory herself. "We would often sit cosy and warm and cuddle and…" She stopped for a moment then began again. "Now those big picture windows looking out over this valley and the ranges in the distance have different meanings for me. Different meanings for George.

"He would stand there looking out and I knew he was seeing our past. I go there and walk away saddened. Because I don't see our past, I see our future. I saw our future." She stopped, seemingly done.

Peter began, "That is just so –"

Margot interrupted him. "But now there is no future anywhere I look in this house, in the spaciousness, in the big rooms, not even in the small details of the kitchen, the cutting board and the food in the fridge, in the pantry... there is nothing for my future life in any room or outside in the garden. There is..." She paused, and the detectives waited for her to begin again, but this time she didn't. Peter could see she was done.

The three of them were silent for a long time. At last, Cleary ended her thoughts: "I know I must appear cruel, Mrs Martin, but I have to ask this: did you hate your husband enough to want him dead?"

"Yes, Detective Inspector, yes, it grew to where I would have preferred him dead." Pause. "And I truly believe that at times George would have wanted that, too. And now, he is dead. By his own hand, his own wishes. His own actions. And yet he had the temerity to claim that he wanted to resurrect his writing career. It's clear to me that he accepted what we had all tried to tell him. His career was over and that's why he hanged himself."

"We may well find that is the truth, Mrs Martin, but in the meantime, for the next day or maybe more, we shall try to discover what is truth and what is fiction. We may have a preliminary forensic report by then."

After another brief silence, Cleary thanked Margot for her honesty and said she could go. Shortly after she left the room, Constable Brandon opened the door and ushered Nola Martin in.

*The wrong answer is the right answer
to a different question*
-Paul Sloane

CHAPTER

2

Nola sat in a single chair facing the detectives.
"Your guys are busy. What are they looking for?"
Cleary told her they were looking for the recorder.
Peter said: "Ms Martin, what do you make of the manuscript your father left behind?"
She gave a side-long glance at Cleary before staring into Peter's eyes for a moment.
"My best guess would be that he had no way to take it with him." When Peter didn't respond, she added: "Another reason— he might not have thought it was worth taking anywhere."
Cleary said: "Don't you think it was any good?"
She shrugged, shook her head. "Sorry. I get it from my Mum. I don't know what Dad's mental state was like at all. I have been

proofreading it and correcting it and doing all things necessary to get rid of superfluous stuff he recorded."

Peter wondered if Nola was deleting things that could be critical to the investigation – or adding things.

"There was a lot of it," Peter said. Nola looked around the room for a few seconds then said: "Oh, heaps. That little recorder took down everything he said. I can't believe that any of that talking-to-himself stuff could be any use in a book of stories."

"Do you think your Dad had come to believe this?" Cleary said. "That his career as a successful author was ending?"

Nola shrugged but didn't answer. She brushed a wisp of blonde hair from her forehead and gazed at the closed door as if considering her chances of making a break for it. She jerked her head around to focus on the detectives again, appearing to be dragging her mind back from a different world. Cleary was about to repeat the question when Nola spoke.

"My father was a very talented man, Inspector. He sold a lot of books. Thousands of people love his work."

Peter said: "Not so many with his last book."

"But he was going blind while writing that book –"

Cleary interrupted her. "What I am trying to discover is whether your father was deeply depressed in the weeks leading up to his death.

"You do realise, don't you, Ms Martin, the possible importance of this information?"

"I am not a psychiatrist, Inspector."

"We realise that, Ms Martin," Peter said.

Cleary began: "Did you notice any drastic changes in his mood or attitude?"

"I think he was excited about his new work. It was a whole new ball game to him."

"So, no sign of depression or even sadness or worries?" Peter said.

"Well, he was worried about meeting the publisher's deadline for his book of short stories. He had not written short stories before this, but he generally seemed upbeat about the progress of this new project."

"Do you think he was being realistic? Did you believe that he could write a book of short stories?"

"I'm sure he had the talent to do that." She paused. "From what I saw, Dad was confident of achieving that. And no, I don't believe he was depressed."

Cleary changed the subject. "Mr Nagle. What is his position in this household?"

Nola laughed in a non-humorous way. "He is not what he thinks he is."

"What does he think he is?" Peter asked.

"God. He is a long way from that. Way down below"

Peter smiled. "More like a devil? Is that what you mean?"

"Yes, that's a good assumption." She reached across to the coffee table and idly flicked the pages of the magazine her mother had been reading earlier.

Cleary continued: "Well, Ms Martin, can you tell us where his loyalties lie? That is, what is his position?"

"My mother thinks he is a chauffeur."

This is like pulling teeth, Peter thought.

"But you don't think he is a chauffeur?"

"I don't think he knows anything much about cars. He can drive, sure. But who can't?"

"Does Mr Nagle do any other work around here besides being the chauffeur?"

She shook her head. "Not that I know of. I think he is a lazy bugger. I'm sure my mother would praise him more than that."

"Ms Martin, does anyone else work here or live here?" Cleary asked.

"We have a gardener, Jeremy, he lives next door. He comes once a week, maybe twice some weeks."

"How does this Jeremy get on with Mr Nagle and Mrs Martin? Do you know his surname?"

"James."

"James? I thought you said it was Jeremy," Cleary said.

"His name is Jeremy James. In that order, Inspector."

"And —"

"And he doesn't get on particularly well with Nagle. He and Mum are friendly to each other."

"And how about you? Do you get on well with Jeremy James?"

She smiled at him. "We're friends. Not lovers."

Cleary said: "Well, finally, do you think any of those people – who live or work here – would have wanted to hurt your Dad?"

Nola looked disturbed but quickly gathered her composure.

"Nagle and he didn't get on very well. Dad didn't like him. I think he suspected…" She paused. "I think he is… I think Dad was suspicious of him."

"Suspicious of Mr Nagle and your mother or —"

"There was nothing in it. Mum wouldn't… She wasn't that friendly with Nagle. In Dad's dark world he often had dark thoughts."

"Were you on good terms with your father?" Cleary said. "I'm sorry to have to ask at this terrible time, Ms Martin, but I have to ask."

"Do you?" She laughed but didn't answer. She stood. Peter looked at Cleary who nodded. "I'll take that as a yes, then," Cleary said. "Thanks for your time, Ms Martin.

Cleary was about to speak again when the door burst open, and Nagle came in. His face was red.

"When are you going to talk to me? You keep me waiting out here. You are treating me as if I am not even worth talking to. But I —"

"No, Mr Nagle. We are about to talk to you. You are as important to our investigation as anybody."

"What investigation? This is a bloody waste of time. The man hanged himself. Why don't you just accept that?"

Nola walked around Nagle and stopped at the open door and looked back. She said: "Is it okay if I go now? You can easily find me later if you need me. I won't be leaving the house." Cleary nodded and she left the room.

Cleary said: "Now Mr Nagle if you will calm down a little. And take a seat, please. What can you tell us about this household?"

Nagle flopped down in the armchair. "Well, what are you wanting to ask me? Some significant clue that you're trying to track down? Or is it just —"

"We would like to know about your relationship with the dead man. Were you on friendly terms with Mr Martin?"

"We got on all right— okay I guess. We were not great mates. I just work here."

Cleary said: "Did Mr Martin employ you?"

"No, Mrs Martin did. I don't think George thought a chauffeur was needed." He laughed. "There's no way he could have driven around, could he?"

"So, you mostly associated with his wife?" Peter said.

"She's my boss. That's all. I have a job and Margot… Mrs Martin is my boss. What does this all have to do with anything?"

"Did you and Mr Martin ever get into arguments about anything to do with this house or the car or your role in the household?"

Nagle punched down on the armrest. He looked around the room before settling his gaze back on Cleary.

"We might have had an argument here or there. They were nothing. Just a few… Umm, we did exchange words at times." He paused. "We never got into any physical stuff, fisticuffs, if that is what you're alluding to."

Peter was a bit surprised that the chauffeur was using such a word as alluding. He was annoyed at his prejudice.

"So, you drive Mrs Martin around town? I suppose you at times drove Mr Martin some places, also?"

Nagle said he drove both of them and occasionally Nola. He drove them to a variety of places: shopping, doctors and sometimes to visit friends. He said Mrs Martin could drive but is not comfortable doing so.

"That must be a big help to the family," Cleary said.

"I do a good job. I'm always on call. During normal hours and sometimes at night. I think I'm very important to them." He paused. "Despite what they might say about me."

"Do you think they might have said derogatory things about you, Mr Nagle?"

"Who knows? I can't please all of them, all of the time. Who can do that with any group of people? I know that I satisfy their needs as far as transport goes."

Peter wondered what other needs any of those three people might have needed from Nagle. He made a note in his book.

"I understand Mrs Martin found her husband's body hanging in the office," Cleary said. "Were you with her, Mr Nagle, at that time?"

"I ran in when I heard her scream. She screamed very loudly. She was crying when I ran in. Isn't that what one would expect when a woman sees her husband dangling from a rope in his own office? It was a cruel thing that George did."

"Did anybody else come in then?" Peter asked.

"Nola came in soon after me. I thought she was about to faint and helped her to the office chair. She became hysterical."

Nagle then explained how he called the police, comforted the women and offered them water.

"How did you feel about what you saw?"

Nagle seemed at a loss for a moment. He looked from one detective to the other. He began to speak and then stopped. Peter wondered if he was weighing his words before replying. At last, he spoke.

"I was shocked, too, of course. Who wouldn't be? Not every day one finds a dead body in the house he lives in. I thought that the best thing I could do was to help Margot... Mrs Martin, and Nola, through the initial shock. I think I did a good job there."

Cleary said: "Do you know of anyone who would want to harm Mr Martin? Did he have any enemies?"

"No." He shook his head. Then he said: "I didn't come across anybody who spoke badly of him. Except for the occasional reader who may have been pissed off about the way his last novel ended. I am not sure what they meant. I'm not a big reader, you see. I never read any of the big sellers. Inspector, as I said before, this is just wasting my time and the cops', too, I might add. There is nothing to be gained from sitting here for over an hour or whatever, answering questions involving a man who committed suicide. Ridiculous."

"We won't take much more of your valuable time, Mr Nagle," Cleary said.

Cleary looked at Peter, who said: "What sort of things did you disagree about?"

"Well, I don't know, some things— politics, football, sports, you know... maybe. I took his wife out more often than I took him. He didn't like being a passenger. He insisted on sitting in the front. Chauffeurs aren't used to that, you see. I think... I think he might have been a bit jealous of —"

"Of you and Mrs Martin?" Peter said.

"I thought that sometimes. Maybe even when I drove Nola out. He was a weird bird."

Cleary said: "Do you know of anyone who might have wanted to harm Mr Martin?"

Nagle shook his head. "As I told you a few minutes ago, not aware of anyone. But I wasn't with him all the time. As I said, I think maybe some of his readers might have, after his last book."

"Why do you think that?" Peter asked. "What reason would his readers have had to dislike him?"

"Not everyone likes the same books, do they? The last book he wrote didn't do well, did it? I don't know what they found wrong with it."

Peter wasn't sure either, but he was sure that authors didn't get killed because their books were unpopular.

"So, there's nothing suspicious about Mr Martin's death, in your view?" Cleary said. "No inkling of anything? Was his jealousy affecting other people? Did it make you angry?"

"Hang on, there. I wouldn't kill anyone for such a silly reason as jealousy on the part of someone else." He paused. "That is... I wouldn't kill anyone whatever. For... any reason that I could think of right now."

"Do you think Mr Martin was respected in the community?"

"I'm not the person you should ask about that –" Nagel interrupted himself. "There is something that I... perhaps..." He paused as if considering whether to say what was on his mind or not. Cleary nodded at him. Thus encouraged, he continued.

"I don't know whether this is important or if it means anything at all, but it may be helpful as you are convinced or at least thinking that Mr Martin's death was not a suicide. There were a couple of times when I had driven Mrs Martin to the shops to her hairdresser or supermarket. Sometimes she would leave George, that is, Mr Martin, outside sitting on a bench."

He stopped and looked at Cleary. The detectives waited for him to continue without saying anything.

"He didn't like to go into the shops anymore. I think he used to love doing that, enjoy looking around, especially in the newsagent's, and there is a photo shop there that sells cameras et cetera, and he liked to sit in the café with coffee and cake occasionally. But when his blindness got worse, he didn't want to, as he put it, 'stumble around' in shops."

Cleary said: "So, Mr Martin often sat outside by himself? Is that what you're trying to say?"

Nagle looked annoyed. He took a deep breath. "Yes, of course that's what I mean. Anyway, I saw him more than once sitting near a small girl, just a young girl, I think maybe four or five years old. Talking to her."

Peter said: "You think that he was doing something wrong?"

"Well… well don't you think, I mean these days… an old man seeming to be getting onto a young girl, a girl of that age, well I'm not saying he was doing anything wrong; he was sitting there in public view of course."

"What are you trying to say, Mr Nagle?" Cleary said.

"It didn't seem right. Him attracting young girls to his side while he was sitting alone. I mean, what do they call that on social media… you know, grooming."

Peter was torn between laughing and swearing. The man was preposterous.

"I don't see how George Martin could have been doing any such thing, in a public place, separated, perhaps, by several metres from a young girl. Was it the same girl or different girls? How many times did you see this?"

"I'm sure it was the same girl each time. And I, well, I only saw him talking to her –"

"Or her talking to him," Peter interrupted.

"Yes, course, both talking to each other, I suppose, and then anyway Mrs Martin didn't seem very happy about it. She would come out of the shops and tell George to 'come on and let's get outta here.'"

Cleary looked at Nagle for a minute or so, then said: "I don't want to dissuade you from giving us any information you may have that could help us in our investigation, Mr Nagle. However, I doubt that there could be anything untoward in George Martin's behaviour with a little girl he may have met a couple of times while waiting outside the shops. We will file that away in our minds.

Cleary changed the subject. "Where did you work before you worked at the garage?"

Nagle hesitated and looked uncomfortable with the question. The detectives looked at him without speaking, giving him time to come up with the answer.

"I worked at a private high school."

"What did you do there?"

"I was a Manual Arts teacher."

Cleary waited for him to add something more. When he didn't, Cleary said: "That was quite a career change. What led to that?"

Peter got the impression that his boss knew the answer to that question. As before, Nagle hesitated, looking around the room as if seeking an escape route.

"I had little choice. I… was asked to leave…"

Cleary said: "Can you explain that in more detail, Mr Nagle?"

Nagle snapped: "This is outrageous. Nothing to do with your so-called case."

"Let us decide that."

"Something to do with a student… a couple of students. Parents…"

The sentence ended in mumbling, so Cleary asked him to repeat what he had said.

"All right. All right. I have a bad temper you see and –"

Cleary interrupted him and told him that was enough, and he could go for now.

Nagle stood and looked at Cleary. "You don't have to tell anyone here about this, do you?"

Cleary stood. "No. There's no reason for that to go any further. You have been very helpful. Thank you for your time."

Peter stood as Nagle pushed past him. The door closed with a bang.

Cleary said: "Guess that only leaves the gardener James Jeremy or the other way round… Jeremy James, that's it. See if Constable

Brandon can locate the man. I will have a word with him, but I don't expect to get much out of that. We must be painstaking in this possibly cut-and-dried case."

Peter walked to the door and went out. A few minutes later he returned with the news that the gardener was not around today but would be back tomorrow.

"Okay Peter, we'll talk to him tomorrow after we check with Gaston. See if Forensics can shed any more light on this."

"You know," he said, "there are times when I wished I had taken up something other than detective work. I wonder what life is like for a gardener?"

Peter turned towards the door but Cleary asked him to sit down again.

"You know, Peter, I mentioned things that were missing from the office, but there's something else missing here," Cleary said. Peter, puzzled, hoped Cleary would tell him what that was, rather than ask him.

Cleary said: "There is a noticeable absence of grief in this place."

"Yes," Peter said. "Except, perhaps for Nola Martin." He wished he had kept that to himself but was pleased he hadn't when Cleary responded.

"You may be right there. You can tell she's been crying a lot. Look at her eyes. But I guess that can be faked. I think she may be the only one in the house distressed by George Martin's death."

Now emboldened, Peter said: "What did you make of Mrs Martin's answers? Do you think she is telling the truth?"

"She has a lot of sadness – and bitterness – in her. This has affected her view of life. The husband going blind led to collateral damage. She had valid reason to find it hard to adapt."

"She didn't appear to be grieving her husband's death," Peter said. "I mean... she was talking more about how everything affected her."

"That didn't seem a prominent thought in her mind. But underneath, I could see that she is struggling to deal with sudden death." He paused and looked straight at Peter. "But I'm not assuming it was sudden to her. If it was suicide it may or may not have been unexpected to her, but if she, or someone she knows, killed her husband, it would probably not be so sudden.

"Today's tragedy would have added to her existing sadness. Grief upon grief. We must still consider her a suspect, of course."

"What about Mr Nagle?" Peter said.

"Yes," Cleary said, "We will continue our enquiries into Mr Nagle's background. It does seem he came here quite suddenly."

Peter said: "Who do you think is the most likely suspect? I mean, that is, if it's not suicide." He looked down at his notebook and up again at Cleary. "Have you changed your mind on that, Inspector –"

"I didn't have anything in my mind to be changed, Sergeant. It appears to be a suicide. But it also could be set up to appear that way. And as I mentioned there are one or two things that make me suspicious."

"Do you mean the missing mug? I don't know how something that isn't there, can be a clue."

"You will come to see that. But the most important item that is not there is the voice recorder. We have been told George Martin always had it hanging around his neck and that he recorded everything that was said near him. That would mean it would have –"

Peter broke in breathlessly. "It would have recorded the final moments of his life if anyone was there or perhaps a suicide note."

"You're right."

Peter said: "So we must find that recorder."

Cleary smiled thinly at his junior. "That might be difficult if the killer or killers, if they exist, would have seen the importance of that recorder themselves and taken it, never to be seen again."

Before they drove away, Cleary said he wanted to have a look around the outside of the house. It was an imposing site: an old two-story building with large windows on both floors and wisteria going up the brickwork on the left side. Out the back they found a single car garage. It was open and empty.

"Looks as if someone is out on the road," Peter said.

"Lucky them." The Inspector sighed. They found a shed that contained the lawnmower and other gardening tools. It was not locked. There were bags of fertiliser and lawn food and a can of weed killer, that, judging by the tangle of weeds in the lawn out the front and along one side, was ineffective. There was a large, paved area near the back of the house. Two wrought iron chairs and a table stood near the back door. Cleary shook his head and nodded towards the car.

*You must stay drunk on writing so
reality cannot destroy you*
-Ray Bradbury, *Zen in the Art of Writing*

CHAPTER

3

That night after dinner, Peter apologised to Jan and said he needed to be excused from dishwashing duties because he had some important investigative work to do.

"Ooh, that sounds impressive," Jan said. "Do you have to go out?"

Peter said: "Umm, no, I have to read a book."

His wife looked disappointed. "I'll leave you to your 'investigation', then." She turned. "If you get stuck, we've got a few Agatha Christies on the bookshelf."

Peter looked up and saw, as he expected, Jan was smiling.

"Well, I guess if the dead man in here doesn't give me any clue to the solution, I may well have to turn to one of those."

Jan stepped back into the room. "That could be tricky."

Peter said: "Tricky? Why tricky?"

"You know how Poirot gets all the suspects together in a room and goes through them one by one by one, finally announcing who the killer is."

"This is a serious business, Jan," Peter said.

"I'm sure it is. Even Poirot wouldn't be able to help you in this case."

Peter was not paying full attention to her. He was looking down at the manuscript pages in his hand, but when he realised Jan was looking at him as if waiting for a response, he said: "That's nonsense."

Keeping a straight face, Jan said: "You can hardly have a dead man lined up among the suspects."

Peter waved the manuscript at her. "Go away. Haven't you got some serious TV to watch?"

Jan took a step back into the doorway. "It may be more on the funny side I think." She nodded towards the manuscript. "Like this business you're going to go through here tonight. It seems funny business to me, investigating a crime by reading what a dead man had to say before he knew he was going to become a dead man."

Peter sat down and opened the manuscript. He looked up at his wife. "I shouldn't have told you anything about this. It's police business and I was out of line. I shouldn't have revealed what this case is about."

Jan hesitated a moment then said: "That doesn't matter, Peter. I know you're a detective. A new one, but I'm sure you're going to become a great one. It's obvious who you are talking about because Katoomba is not a big place and when a famous novelist dies under suspicious circumstances –"

"I haven't said anything about suspicious circumstances," Peter said.

"You didn't have to, darling. That also is a talking point around the place. Many of the bank customers talk about it. The staff certainly does."

Peter let out an exasperated sigh. "Alright. I better get into this now, see what I can find out. If anything. Enjoy your TV."

Jan quickly stepped across and kissed her husband on the cheek. "I'll say good night, but I expect I'll be speaking to you before either of us are asleep."

He sat at the table and opened the manuscript of the book that was never to be finished, written by a man who had probably killed himself.

Peter re-read the cover page of the manuscript: Whispers in the Darkness: A Collection of Short Stories by George Martin.

He smiled at the subtitle daring him to turn the page if he liked being terrified.

Peter didn't enjoy being terrified or even mildly frightened, however he turned the page and began to read. He stopped in bewilderment after reading the first paragraph. He went back over it. That's odd, he thought, this isn't punctuated, so how will I know who is saying what? His eyes moved down the page. Damn. It's worse than I thought. It was all like that. This was going to be slow going. It appeared to have been hastily transcribed by Nola from a recorder. The digital recorder they were searching for, without success so far. Recordings of conversations and the man himself would be like this unless edited. "Oh my God," he moaned.

He took a deep breath and stoically applied himself to the night's reading.

> how did you go George
>
> as if you care
>
> get your eyedrops refilled a lot of good theyll do they wont give your sight back
>
> its only anti inflammatory now as you know Margot the day is long gone when any eye drops could save my sight from glaucoma

another dumb assistant at the pharmacy mum

yeah where do they train these people must teach them that a white cane being held by a person means he cant understand english.

you controlled yourself well dad

I stood right in front of the little twerp yet he turned to Nola about a metre away and asked if I knew how to use my own medication

I told him that if he asked the man himself he might be surprised to find he could not only understand spoken words but can clearly answer you in plain english sentences

good on you Nola Im blind not deaf or even stupid

I wouldnt be too confident about the not even stupid part just get used to all that stuff you should know that by now

what I should be used to by now is my wife's complete lack of sympathy for my plight I am used to it only time will tell how that will affect us

I supported you at first George but you wont accept facts you cant see a damn thing and yet you think you can write another book

I have to give it a go I believe I can do this with help from others

you expect a lot from us George mumbling into that recorder poking it in our faces and generally being a

33

nuisance you cant write this way your career is over why wont you accept the obvious

if I don't write I am no longer a writer writing stories is a part of me cant you understand that

all your talking into that thing wont make a book George you need Nola to transcribe it into the computer

its no problem mum

I have to prove to myself that I havent lost it

you dont have to ask yourself ask me you have lost it give it up

I will give up on life before I give up on writing my stories its sad that my publisher has more faith in my ability than my wife does Ill bust a boiler if necessary to meet Toms deadline hes giving me a chance

hang on mr Martin

what is it this time

your left shoelace is undone

damn I thought Id done that up properly

youll have a bad accident George if you're not more careful

Im a mature man been around a long time I dont need my chauffeur nor my wife to tell me about tying my shoelaces up properly many decades since I passed that milestone of relying on my mum to do that well mr Martin if we dont warn you you could have a bad accident like falling down the stairs

leave him Mark its Georges problem you warned him thats enough lucky you spotted it but he wont take any notice of me either

Im still here you know you dont have to talk about me in the third person.

maybe you do need help in tying them up George

I have to train my fingers to do more now they have to pay attention to what theyre doing like that with everything now its the same for all of you walking into a room with the lights off in the night you have to feel your way around but anyway I do thank you mr Nagel for your sharp eyes also I should thank you for using your observation to let me know that the trailing lace may have been spotted by others who couldnt be bothered telling me about it

good one George paranoid as usual someones trying to trip you up for god's sake George try to live in the real world

Im not paranoid I know what's going on in this house.

mums right you need to settle down I know how hard it must be adapting to a dark black environment but in time youll cope much better than you are now were here to help you

Im sure you are Nola but Im not so sure about others

hey I told you about your bloody shoelace

you work for mum and dad mr Nagle please dont swear at the person who is paying your wages

alright Im off

you certainly are

do you have to be like this all the time George were sitting here having a nice cuppa mr Nagel let you know about a dangerous situation created by you not tying your shoelaces properly and this is what happened Im going into the lounge room to finish reading my magazine

right you do that Ill be more careful going upstairs now

and if youre all done arguing Ill finish my tea and biscuit in peace and quiet

    Peter folded the current page of the manuscript back and laid it on the table. He was struggling to cope with the lack of punctuation and grammar. Jan was laughing at a TV comedy. He went to the kitchen to make a coffee without disturbing her.
    Something in what he had just read troubled the orderly arrangement of facts in his mind.
    The dysfunctional Martin household could drive any slightly off-balance person to suicide… or murder.
    He returned to the manuscript.

I dont know why Nagle is living in my house or where Margot picked him up from hes not a chauffeurs bootlace or more appropriately chauffeurs chamois Im sure he wants me dead being blind isnt good enough or is that bad enough for him if I could see his face his eyes I might see the insistent warnings tumbling around in my mind should be heeded but what can I do sometimes I dont even know when hes in the same room I stand in the doorway looking in I whisper a speculative hello but nobody answers I imagine him sitting on the big green sofa beside Margot not saying a word holding their breath staring at me smiling

I have happy memories of this room

hello dear very quiet are you in there sitting quietly ignoring me I can hear movement if not breathing dont answer if youre not in there a lovely room isnt it I think we especially liked being in here in the winter with the big open fire blazing crackling light flickering around a darkened room I remember maybe you dont want to talk about that now especially loved when I could see those days and nights I could see through the big window looking out into the mist around us fog at times and wed stand there close to each other do you remember that phrase dear close to each other not just physical wed stand there side by side my arm around you and look out into the darkened valley and feel the warmth on our backs and sometimes we kissed and sometimes we I can tell by your silence you dont want to remember any sometimes anymore I can hear the movement and Im sad that you dont answer me it says my memories belong only to me seems your mind is empty of anything to do with me except the present which so annoys you

George who are you talking to talking romantically to your cat for goodness sake

I thought that was you in there

I was walking along the hall and then your cat came out your stupid cat fido you were so romantic to a damn cat are you going to stand there in the doorway for long George

I want to go in and sit and read you can stand there as long as you like of course its your house but I would appreciate it if you would not talk to me while Im trying to read and if I fall asleep please don't wake me up Ill wake in good time

I wont bother you anymore Margot you may wake in good time we no longer have good times together

    After another half an hour of reading, Peter reluctantly closed the manuscript, his mind swirling with possibilities. He joined Jan on the lounge to watch TV. When they went to bed half an hour later, he had no idea what they had watched.

We can always find a cause for suspicion if we look for it
-Adolfo Bioy Casares, The Invention of Morel

CHAPTER

4

Peter picked up his briefcase, checked that it was secure, and turned to Jan who was standing near the kitchen table with a folded tablecloth in her hand.

"I better go. I have to pick up Inspector Cleary on the way."

"Peter," Jan began, "there's something I want to run past you."

Peter put the briefcase down on the table. "Is something wrong? Or can it wait till I come home tonight?"

"It won't take long. And you don't have as much time at night now it appears... with your homework investigation."

"Righto. Let's have it."

She pulled out a chair and sat.

"This looks serious. Should I sit down also?"

Jan laughed. "Oh, Mum and Dad have asked if it would be all right for them to visit us for a little while in the New Year. No set date but sometime maybe the middle of the month. They would like to be here for my birthday."

Peter put his hand on the briefcase but didn't move. "I, I don't see any problems here. As you know, I may be still involved in this investigation. I hope it's all wrapped up before Christmas but maybe it won't be. But they're coming to see you, not me."

"That's great, Peter." She paused. "Do you think your parents would like to come too?"

Peter shook his head vigorously. "No, the world is in a bad enough state as it is without us initiating World War Three in our own home."

"Don't be so silly. They would get on all right. I think they would if we all worked hard at it."

"It'd be a first, wouldn't it? I think we had better leave the clash of in-laws for a future date. Anyway, we don't have enough bedrooms to put them up. I mean. We have enough really. There is a bedroom for your parents but the other room –"

"The nursery, is that what you now call the other room?"

Peter put the briefcase down on the table again. "Yes, the nursery. It's got other stuff in it. It hasn't got a double bed or even a single bed. I don't think Mum and Dad would want to sleep in the cot. Anyway, they would break it."

Jan stood up suddenly and pushed the tablecloth onto one of the cupboard shelves. "You might as well go to work then. You're not taking this seriously."

Peter picked up his briefcase and walked over to Jan. Standing behind her, he put his arm around her waist. She turned her head and they kissed briefly.

"I take any interaction between us and your Mum and Dad and my Mum and Dad very seriously. But facts are facts. We don't have a second bedroom for a second lot of guests. As long as we have the nursery… the spare room made up as a nursery –"

Jan pulled away from him and turned to face him. "Nursery will remain a nursery. It's too soon to give up and pack it all in. Is that what you're hinting at?"

Peter moved to kiss her but she turned her face away. He swung around and walked towards the door.

"You better go and try to find the killer... who may already be dead."

"Jan. Don't talk about this case like that, please. And do not mention it to anyone outside this house."

"Oh I see, in other words, not to anyone other than you, Detective Sergeant Peter York. You can count on it. I won't betray your confidences. You better go and I've gotta go soon, too."

Peter went out the side door into the garage. He was angry and tried to start the car when it was in gear. He cursed and moved the gear lever before starting it. He put into reverse. It started to move. He jammed the brakes on and swore. "Bloody hell. Better open the door. Jan would be even less happy if I knocked the garage door down." He reversed into the street, turned and drove off.

He had cooled down somewhat by the time he picked up his boss and he told Cleary what he had gleaned from his previous night's reading. At first, the Inspector didn't seem to be concentrating.

"Are you paying full attention to the traffic, Peter? You are spewing out a lot of conjecture - 'maybe,' 'if' and 'perhaps' – few facts. Ahh, watch out."

"Saw him. The thing is, Sir, that —" Peter looked at his boss, who waved his hands towards the windscreen. Peter refocused on the road ahead. "It's an unrevised draft. I can't tell yet what his mood had been. Depressed, excited, crazy or sane."

"He sold a lot of books, I know," Cleary said.

"Not so many in recent years. His last one was a relative failure."

"That must've hurt the man. Affected his morale," Cleary said.

"Seems he decided to turn to short stories. Poor bugger will never know if that would have worked."

"Perhaps he already knew it wasn't going to work."

"Anyway, I'll have another look into it tonight."

Peter parked the car and the detectives went into Dr Gaston's office.

Dr Paul Gaston, a bespectacled, grey-haired man in his fifties, had a weary air about him. Understandable, Peter thought, in someone who had worked for decades in this gruesome job.

Gaston took his glasses off and scratched the side of his nose with one of the wings. He jiggled them by the wings as he spoke.

"We have found traces of a drug in George Martin's body. I would say that he, or someone else, wanted him to be sedated when he was hanged. Maybe he, or someone else, wanted to ease the pain."

"Or make sure he didn't fight against what they were doing," Cleary said.

Peter began: "He couldn't have hanged himself while he was drugged, could he? He wouldn't have thought he could do that. He was …"

He stopped speaking when he realised the other two were grinning.

Cleary said: "Can you tell me, Paul, whether the drug was in his system very long before his death?"

"Not with any certainty."

"That's an interesting development. Something else to think about."

Cleary paused when he saw that Dr Gaston was about to add something.

"That's not all, Mitchell, George Martin had terminal cancer. Prostate cancer."

The detectives were obviously shocked by this.

Cleary said: "How long did he have? Can you estimate that?"

"Not a lot of time but certainly longer than he gave himself – or somebody else did."

Getting back in their car, Cleary said: "A few surprises there, Sergeant. Let's go and see what our gardener friend has for us."

The detectives drove to the Jameses' house which was next door to the Martins'. Cleary told Peter that it was better to interview the man in his 'native environment' than in the foreignness of the Martin home.

Jeremy James was a tall man, and in his thirties, Peter estimated. He had sandy hair, cut short at the back, that somehow fell over his forehead. But he admitted he was hardly an expert on hairstyles of young people. Not that he was old at twenty-eight, he told himself, wondering why he was even thinking such a thing.

"Have you come to see me about Mr Martin's death? I don't know how I can help you."

They stood in Jeremy's garden, near tomatoes that were tied back on stakes. They were flourishing, Peter thought, plump and red ripe.

"They are fine looking tomatoes you have there, Mr Je… James," The Inspector said. Peter smiled as his boss almost misspoke. "Do you grow all your own vegetables?"

The young gardener pulled himself up straighter, until he was a bit taller than the tomato stakes he was standing among. He looked at the two detectives then turned back to the vines and pulled two fine examples of Roma tomatoes off the vines and handed them to Cleary.

"Yes, I do. It's a bit like a hobby, but it's also my job. It feeds me and Mum and anyone else I can share them with."

For a minute or two the three men glanced around the garden taking in a variety of vegetables in a small plot. Peter wasn't that knowledgeable about vegetables, but it looked like a fine crop to him.

"I understand you do some work each week for the Martins. As you said, there was a tragic death there yesterday."

Jeremy looked at him earnestly before saying: "I think all deaths are tragic, sir."

"Yes, yes, of course, no question about that." He paused a moment. "What do you actually do next door?"

"I look after the lawn and their small vegetable area. It isn't as big as I have here. It's an easy job. I also keep the weeds under control – try to - and do some cutting back of shrubs and prune trees in the backyard."

"How did you get on with Mr George Martin?" Peter asked.

"Fine, fine, we got on all right. Most of the time. Except for…" He looked up at the house and back at the detectives.

"So, there was an exception to your good relationship, then?" Cleary said. Jeremy nodded. "What was that about?"

"It was just, just a tiny thing."

Jeremy studied the tomatoes again, without looking at the detectives. Peter thought that he regretted saying too much.

"How small a thing was it?" Peter said.

"It was Nola. Me and Nola. He didn't like us seeing each other." He picked another tomato and dropped it into the basket. He turned around as if anxious to get away.

Cleary said: "Did the late Mr Martin forbid you and Nola to meet? Did he think you were getting too serious, each of you?"

Jeremy looked uncomfortable and glanced around the garden again.

"He was all right. There was nothing in it. Nothing between the two of us. And nothing between Mr Martin and me."

"Do you know of anyone who might have wanted to harm Mr Martin?" Cleary said.

"I think he was generally very well liked. He kept to himself much of the time because he would, he was writing a book. He didn't come out to the garden when I was working. Didn't interfere with me and give advice to me about what I should be doing." He looked at Cleary and said: "Will this take much longer? You see,

I have to get away to another gardening job on the other side of town. I am already a bit late."

Cleary nodded. "Just about done. How about Mr Nagle? Did you have any differences of opinion with him?"

"I hardly ever saw him. I think he and Nola had problems. I don't know what was behind that. But Nola was often angry about some confrontation that the two of them had."

"And how about Mrs Martin," Peter said, "how did she fit into that household? Did she try to keep the peace? Did you have much to do with her in your job there?"

Jeremy was obviously tired of all the questions and just wanted to get onto his next job. "She was okay. We never clashed. I don't know of anything else that went on in that house." He started to walk away from the detectives. Cleary called out after him, thanking him for his time.

As they walked back to the car, Cleary looked at the two tomatoes. one in each hand, selected the smaller one and gave it to Peter.

"Let's go and give Mrs Martin the news from Dr Gaston."

> Murder is always a mistake. One should never do anything that one cannot talk about after dinner.
> -*Oscar Wilde*

CHAPTER 5

As soon as Mrs Martin opened the front door to the detectives, she said: "How much longer will I have to put up with all of these people tramping around my home, turning everything inside out and upside down? All for nothing. You are obsessed, Inspector. You don't seem to appreciate how grief-stricken I am. I have lost my husband."

Cleary apologised for the disruption, said it was necessary and assured her that the search team would be finished soon.

"Finding the recorder is important. It may make everything clear." She glared at him, shook her head and walked ahead of them into the lounge room.

Once seated, Cleary began directly. "Did Mr Martin take any sleeping medication of any sort – tablets?"

Margot sat back, apparently surprised at such a question. "We all sleep very well thank you, Inspector. As far as I know, no one here takes- or took- such things." She ostentatiously looked at her watch and clicked her tongue.

"Do you have an appointment for shopping, Mrs Martin? Perhaps at the hairdresser?" Cleary said.

She shook her head. "No, Inspector, it's just that I have only a certain amount of time to do what I must do today. And I am also annoyed that I have to answer so many questions for what should not require answers."

Cleary said: "That is where we differ, Mrs Martin, I believe there are questions still to be answered. A man who was a famous writer would surely want to write down, or record, why he was doing what he was planning to do. Commit suicide."

"Who can tell what my husband was thinking? He didn't communicate very much with me. Not in the past few years, anyway." She paused and looked at each of the detectives in turn. "We weren't on good terms. Recently, if you must know. We lived our own lives. Slept in separate rooms."

Peter said: "What did he think of that arrangement?"

She seemed to be thinking for a while. "He got used to it."

"It must have been difficult for you, Mrs Martin, coping with a man who was blind. We understand that from what you told us yesterday."

She nodded. "We got used to that, also."

Cleary asked her how long her husband had been blind.

"He has been losing his sight progressively over the past few years, and it was a sort of transition period. He could see bits and pieces around the house and that helped a lot when he lost all of his sight." She paused. "I think he has been completely, if I may use that term, blind for about eight months. And, you are right, it has been difficult. I had a lot of trouble taking up the slack around the house. And he wasn't the best... patient."

"He would have had trouble adapting to his new circumstances, I would think," Peter said.

She looked at him without answering, then turned back to look at Cleary, who said:

"How do you think he was handling his life in utter darkness? Did he ever wish that his sight could come back —"

She laughed. "He wished for a lot of things. None of them attainable, all of them requiring miracles."

Cleary nodded.

"Of course, Inspector, he would want his sight back. He was a writer. And he had to make many adjustments to be able to continue doing that."

Peter said: "Such as using dictation on the computer and that voice recorder that he carried with him?"

"Yes, those damn abominations. Never felt safe talking to him. He said he was only getting ideas, as I told you, for new stories, but he seemed to be addicted to it."

Peter thought that in this house, maybe it was more a security blanket.

"There is a lot of extraneous material in the printed manuscript that Sergeant York has been reading, Mrs Martin, to see if there are any hints to your late husband's state of mind.

She flapped her skirt above her knees and back down again. Shifted her feet on the floor. "You don't have to read all that guff to know what he was thinking. He told us often enough. Let me tell you, Inspector – and you too, Sergeant – George Martin was sick of his life. He saw his race had been run. His last book wasn't successful, and he thought as a last desperate measure to keep his fame, he would turn to short stories. I don't think he expected that to be successful."

"Mrs Martin," Cleary began, "did you know —"

"Please, I can't sit here too much longer. I must get out."

Cleary held up his hand. "Just a little bit longer, please. Did you know that Mr Martin had a terminal condition? Cancer?"

She fell back in the chair. Her face betrayed that this was indeed news to her.

"What? How can you know that? What sort of terminal and –"

"An advanced state of prostate cancer. The autopsy showed that, as well as the large amount of sleeping drug in his system. We believe he didn't have much more time to live."

She was flustered and tried to start sentences several times. "But… But… That means he… Why?"

"Indeed, Mrs Martin, you may ask why a man who knew he was going to die anyway would go to the trouble of killing himself. But then again, maybe he wanted to save himself from a painful and miserable death. If he did hang himself, it may have been because he thought it would be over much quicker."

Peter left the room and returned with a glass of water which he handed to Mrs Martin. She nodded her thanks and sat, sipping quietly.

"We have also checked with Mr Martin's ophthalmologist and confirmed that he was indeed blind without any hope of his sight returning."

"Why did you do that? I never doubted that."

Margot stood and brushed apparently non-existent fluff off her clothes. Maybe she was just pushing out any creases she saw. Cleary motioned to her to sit down again.

"I don't see any reason why you are keeping me here with all this stuff."

"We thought you may be interested in the autopsy report." She sat again and Cleary continued.

"Not much longer, Mrs Martin. Did you or your husband employ Mr Nagle?"

She looked surprised. 'I did.'

"Has he been working here very long?"

"Six months or so. He was a mechanic at the garage where our car is serviced. We discussed the terms and I gave him the job. He has done it very well."

"Had he been a chauffeur with anyone else before you employed him?"

"I don't know. That wasn't important to me. I just wanted someone who was a competent driver who could take me places I needed to go. It was obvious that my husband could no longer do that. And I don't drive any more. And once again, Inspector, you have me puzzled. What on earth has any of this to do with my husband hanging himself? Please put any more questions in writing and when I return from the shops you can give me that list and I will reply to them tomorrow. Is that a good idea?"

Cleary didn't reply. Peter knew he didn't think it was a good idea.

Both detectives stood. Margot looked at them and decided it was all right to leave. She nodded at each of them as she went out, shutting the door more loudly than usual.

Cleary sighed and was about to say something to Peter, when the door opened and Nola came in.

"My turn again," she said, and without waiting for an answer, she sat where her mother had been sitting. She smiled at the two detectives who returned to their seats.

Her smile vanished at Cleary's first words. She was stunned at the news of her father's terminal cancer. She said she didn't know anything about that. Her father kept his medical conditions – if any – to himself. The cancer and the sleeping drug were news to her, she said. Nola brushed tears from her eyes with a tissue and crumpled it in her hand. Cleary gave her a few minutes and then said: "I can see that was a shock to you, Miss Martin." He changed the subject. "We talked with Jeremy James this morning. He said that––"

"Why did you talk to him? He doesn't live here."

Cleary ignored her question. "Jeremy said your father was against you and him having a relationship. Did he actually forbid you seeing each other?"

Peter thought the question caught her by surprise.

"I'm an adult, Inspector, my father wouldn't, couldn't, forbid me from doing anything of that sort."

Peter said: "What sort of thing are you referring to, Miss Martin? Friendship or--"

"I told you we were just friends. How can my relationships have any bearing on my father's suicide?"

Cleary reminded her that they had not yet ruled out other causes of her father's death. "We need to find out if anyone held a grudge against your father."

"I certainly didn't if you're implying that. And Jeremy doesn't hate anybody. I can't speak for anyone else."

Cleary told her that would be all for now and she left the room.

Cleary rang George Martin's GP, Dr Craig Mallory, and made an appointment for them to see him the next morning at nine forty-five.

"After that, Peter, I have to return to the station to deal with paperwork. While I'm there, I'd like you to go around the neighbourhood and ask questions to check if anyone had seen anything unusual on the night or day that Martin died."

He couldn't give Peter anything definite about what he should look for. He just hoped that something would turn up out of nowhere, Peter thought. Still, he didn't mind doing that. He enjoyed talking to people.

They say a person needs just three things to
be truly happy in this world: someone to love,
something to do, and something to hope for.
-*Tom Bodett*

CHAPTER

6

After dinner that night, Peter sat down at the end of the dining table with the manuscript in front of him and a cup of coffee and two biscuits on a small plate beside his left elbow. Despite tiredness, he was looking forward to delving further into the mind of an author who may or may not have killed himself.

    Im sorry I cant stop now

    what are you talking about who are you

    not talking to you old man its this girl bothering me cant you hear her

    I can hear someone sobbing

Im late for something important no I cant help you your mummy will come

I dont know where mummy is she lost me cant you –

your mummy will find you shes looking for you now Im sure that shell come any minute wait here near this man

can you help her I am –

I said I cant

youre just sitting there with nothing to do

Im blind if you cant see that then maybe you are also please that sobbing wont help you

nobody will help me thats why I'm crying Ive lost mummy I was waiting outside the toilets for her and I walked away a little bit and turned another corner I think I mustve gone the wrong way because that was inside the shops and and I

we will get on better if you can stop crying I dont like hearing crying

I dont like crying

sit down for a minute Ill try to help you whats your name

Its its... I dont know if its safe I shouldnt talk to somebody I dont know a man with a big stick why do you have a big stick at the shops it doesn't matter Im blind I need the stick to help me find where Im going I wont hurt you

Im right here not far from you on the end of the seat why dont you look at me

I told you I cant see I am blind.

dont your eyes work

no they havent worked for a few years now not properly now tell me your name and Ill get some help

you wont hit me with that stick will you

course not Im not a bad man what is your name

Emma its Emma e-m-m-a cant write that down can you

I dont need to write it down I just need to say it hey Siri find centre management at Katoomba Plaza yes that one hello centre management my name is George martin and I am sitting out in the area not far from the side entrance I believe there are some trees here Im telling you this for a reason if you can wait a minute there is a little girl lost here she is crying she has lost her mother no I dont know who her mother is can you put an announcement out over the pa saying Emma is waiting for her do you know what the name of the spot is green zone okay yes do that please Emma her name is Emma shes a little girl and she is crying because she has lost her mum thank you

we have a message for one of our customers in the centre would Emmas mother contact centre management your daughter is lost thats me thats talking about me Im Emma

yes and your mummy will hear that and she will come we just have to wait she might be close to us now or she might be a long way away

oh goody that was a good idea

thank you so much I was so worried so worried I was crying too darling

this man helped me mummy

you are so good just didn't know where I could look anymore my name is Marcia Johnson

Im George Martin.

I am very grateful thank you for taking the time to help my little girl

I was glad to help her she is a nice polite little girl and after her crying stopped she was well in control of herself and patiently waited for you to come

may I ask are you blind

yes I am

his eyes are broken they dont work he has to use that big stick to see where he is or where he is going but it doesnt help him see me or you

I know darling it is even more wonderful that you kindly helped Emma some people wouldnt bother even those who can see youre probably right

we can go home now I have had about enough of this place thank you mr Martin

you were a long time

I stopped to have coffee with mr Nagle you don't have a problem with that do you

I like having coffee too

heres Mark now can we go

I know we can

just being polite

thank you Margot I am ready

sometimes, like now, the wind blows so hard along the ridge that this old house seems to quake in fear boards and beams groaning through the big window in the living room I imagine winds long fingers probing into the leaves and limbs of nearby trees shaking ruffling as if searching for small birds trembling inside the foliage spitting autumn rain against the window spattering dead and dying gold orange brown yellow and black leaves against the pane turning the lovely view down over the valley and ranges into an incomplete jigsaw puzzle marred by the holes of missing pieces once I loved this house I thought it was wonderful when we bought it before Nola was born perched on a hill and we could look down over the valley across the mountains two storeys spacious rooms big windows let in lots of light which Margot later covered up with heavy drapes to keep the cold out she said then I hadn't noticed the cold but in recent years I have the blue mountains can be a cold dreary place in winter but I love the atmosphere two levels lots of room to move around in and enjoy the company of family and friends we dont get much company these days but I still love my mansion in the mountains but now I am depressed in this house which is dark to me the views have gone from my sight only the cold remains in my bones I know whats going on I wish I didn't know I wish I didn't hear what I cant see they think I cant hear they know I cant see but Im sure they believe I may hear more than they want me to hear that makes them nervous I reckon all of them sometimes when I walk down the long hall towards our lounge room quietly I seem to hear voices there as I get closer the sounds become whispers I go to the doorway and stand looking in as if I could see them

I always say hello what are you two doing here I wait and there is no answer I say hello again silence I stand turning my head slowly from side to side as if I could actually see around the room I imagine them sitting there quietly holding their breath I wonder how long they can hold it before they collapse on the floor turning blue but whats the use of me waiting maybe there isnt anyone in there when I suspect there is all I can do is walk away usually I think its Margot and Nagle bloody Nagle in my house quiet tete a tete with my wife and thats not all the other night I came out of my bedroom and went along to Margots bedroom I thought I could hear unusual sounds in there I stood there for a little while not sure if I was imagining things I decided I didnt want a confrontation so I walked back to my room and I opened my door again I heard another door open and close turned my head towards the end of the corridor past Margots room I called out who is that bloody...

Nagle answered its just me mr Martin did I startle you

I asked him what he was doing up here on the first floor he said I came up to go to the toilet

why would you come all this way there is one next to your bedroom

it seems to be blocked Ill have a go at fixing it tomorrow morning if I cant get it right Ill call the plumber will that be all right mr Martin if I call old Jessop

what could I say cant have him coming up here every time he wants to go to the toilet if that was true I didnt believe it I checked next morning pressed the flush button but what did that prove he said hed already fixed it my wife isnt the only one whos developing a relationship our daughter is also Im sure Nola is a week or so ago when I went to the lounge room door and said hello et cetera Nola answered and I asked her what she was doing because I thought I heard her talking to someone there was silence for a while and I again wondered how long she or anyone else there might be able to hold their breath then she said its just me dad sounds like more than just you silence again Im here too mr Martin a man's voice said I knew the voice it was Jeremy our gardener this wasnt his usual domain he had spoken as if he had just realised that he was in the room I asked why he was there

Nola answered its such a hot day dad that I asked him to come into the shade for a little rest and a drink thats all right with you isnt it it was so nice

of her mr Martin I could hear him move as if he was
getting out of the chair yes yes thats all right Nola
I really couldn't say no to that young man and have
him stand out there in the hot sun doing the job he
is paid to do of course I could say that but I left it
and walked away another time when I heard giggling
in the kitchen and asked the question at the door
they both answered and said its me its me another
rest on a hot day another drink to cool his fevered
brow or whatever fine keep on with it but don't forget
to finish the lawn on the footpath they giggled as I
walked away I keep hearing voices in different rooms
I should say I keep thinking I hear voices in different
rooms if nobody answers then maybe there is nobody
there but I am only blind not deaf long life meaning I
wasnt born yesterday I feel alienated in what was once
my lovely mansion seems to be a house of mystery
now only my stories keep me going I spend most days
in my office thinking up stories dictating stories one
day to be revised by Nola if she ever gets around to
it revising deleting crap improving grammar its a
lonely life I live with my characters they dont say
much to me just like when I speak into the rooms Im
sure there are people there but they seldom talk back
no I am wrong I shouldnt say that there are times
when they do answer but I always get the feeling that
they are mocking me are they smiling at each other
maybe winking I might talk to Stephen about this if
my brother ever comes to visit me again it seems a
long time since he was here we get on all right phone
calls are not the same as talking face to face would
be so good to have a normal loud conversation with
somebody in the same room even if I cant see the face
I better get back to work the more I think about it
about this house and its dark secrets the more morbid
I become I don't know why I talk of mysteries here
in one way nothing out of the ordinary is going on

or else my fears are actually true will I ever know I may never know I may die before all is revealed that may well be a day of rejoicing in my house I believe Nagle plans to kill me it becomes more certain each day I feel it in his actions and hear it in his talk he thinks he owns the place and it seems being blind isnt enough for him he wants me dead who would listen to a blind man who spends his time making up stories but sometimes like when he was so precious that day we were driving goodness knows where and he decided he had to have the classical music station on hell no I got that wrong he wanted country music on thats right I wanted classical music anyway he got annoyed because I turned it over he said what are you doing asking me what I was doing with my own radio in my own car I dont want to listen to that trash I said well I want to listen to Marty Robbins he said so there we were two grown men in the front seat of my car switching stations back and forth it was too much but Margot thinks he is the bees knees she would quickly change her mind if she ever heard Nagle carrying on like that like a small kid having a tantrum big kid in a big car that I own outrageous shouting at me the way he did she might not be so cosy with him if she heard that sort of thing not so cosy in the lounge room where they whisper away together stopping when they hear me coming down the hallway and all that over country music for god's sake whats happening to my life it used to be so simple I must go to sleep

NIGHT RIDER
A SHORT STORY BY GEORGE MARTIN

George Putnam was in the middle of nowhere when his car radio went dead, abruptly ending a beautiful rendition of the Blue Danube Waltz. He was cruising along a country road just before midnight, heading for Starke Mountain, when the music died.

Maybe a road bump had jolted it off, George thought, poking at the radio with a fat finger. Nothing. He lightly banged it with the side of his closed fist. No good.

He turned the on/off knob and the radio came to life. It had been turned off. By itself. "How can…" George dismissed the minor mechanical aberration and sat back, relaxing as the Danube swirled around him.

He'd been in a cheerful mood since leaving the Golden Oil service station, half an hour earlier. He'd had a burger and chips, and a good hot coffee. It was the last stop before home. Even the sight of an almost flattened car wreck dumped near the side fence hadn't spoilt his mood. Another poor sod who had lost control of his vehicle. George often saw the results of what he considered to be careless driving.

Now, he just had to get up and over the mountain. No problem. He'd done it many times. He'd phoned Alma to let her know he was just a couple of hours from home.

Home. He was looking forward to that after his week away in the country, calling on his company's clients, checking their stock, taking new orders. He'd done well. His book was very satisfactory, filled with orders for tablecloths, sheets and other Manchester.

He enjoyed driving at night. He believed it was the best time to travel, with fewer vehicles around and it was safer because headlights always warned when something was around the bend.

Then, the music suddenly stopped, again.

"Shit!" George said.

He banged the radio without result, then tried the knob. It was off again.

"What's wrong with this piece of junk," he shouted. He turned the knob and the classical music station returned.

George sighed, flexed his shoulders and settled back into his seat. On these long country trips, he liked to listen to the classics. He had left the scattered lights of Mapleville behind and was driving through gently sloping country towards the mountain. He sucked on a couple of mint lollies — he liked to have two at a time —enjoying the sonic beauty of Beethoven's Missa Solemnis. It was up-tempo, like him. The car's interior was a warm and cosy cocoon in the surrounding wintry darkness. Two tiny padded bears swung on a cord, bouncing just below the rear-vision mirror. George found them distracting but Alma had given them to him and thought they looked cute.

"Two cuddly bears, dancing away to remind you of us," she'd said.

So he'd left them there. He was used to them now. And near the end of a long trip away, he found they worked — made him hanker for a big cuddle with Alma.

It was about ten o'clock and the full moon shone on trees and fences and farmhouses and shadowy animals near barns. George didn't notice much of the darkly passing scenery. He was a careful driver, so he kept his eyes focused on the road ahead and the occasional vehicles whizzing towards and past him.

Alma always waited up for his return, keeping a late meal warm for his arrival. She always …

Suddenly, the orchestra stopped and there was some country singer.… Maybe Dolly Parton. George couldn't tell for sure. He avoided such stuff. But he knew it wasn't classical music. Although the announcer had probably called it a "classic".

"What the hell…" He touched the on/off knob, but, of course, it hadn't switched off this time. It had changed stations! That was impossible. But it had happened. He fiddled with the tuner until it was back on his station. Good. He'd have to get it seen to next week.

Then somebody … perhaps Willy Nelson … was singing about being on the road again.

Perplexed, George looked down and moved the tuner again. How could it jiggle around?

A blaring horn shocked George back to the road. He'd wandered across the centre line and a huge semi-trailer was heading for him. It was too big to safely change direction abruptly, not this close.

Desperately, George swung the wheel left and the big truck screamed past in a streak of lights and colours and rocking metal. He saw a blur of a driver's contorted face and waving fist. He was glad he couldn't hear what the driver shouted.

George was shaking, but his hands gripped the wheel tightly. And in the background that damned country music. He bashed the radio with his hand.

"Bugger, what the hell's wrong with the bloody thing?" He reached down, feeling with his hand, eyes focused on the road, and turned it off.

He thought he heard something. Not from the radio. It was off. Sounded like a snigger. Then the radio clicked on again. Another snigger? Or the wind?

George looked across the car and saw his reflection flickering in the window. It smiled at him. Except George wasn't smiling. George's mouth was set grimly after the near miss with the semi. The reflection waved at him. Then held up a hand, with thumb and forefinger touching, and twisted them back and forwards. As if turning a knob.

George knew he needed a rest. He was tired; he must be hallucinating. He slowed right down and drove off to the side. There was safe room for that. He looked at his reflection that wasn't his reflection. The shadowy form grinned and mock-wiped his — its — brow. Phew!

George turned off the engine, jumped out of the car as if it was on fire, and ran to a low fence of horizontal logs, near a few grey trees. He sat, puffing, on a log; he didn't run much. He was built for comfort not speed, as Alma sometimes told him. He cupped his face in his hands. They were trembling and he wished he hadn't given up smoking two years ago. A smoke would be good. He took three mints from his pocket and sucked hard. He stared at his car for a long while, oblivious of the cold. Occasionally, cars whizzed past, as normal. But it wasn't normal, George knew that. What the hell's going on, he asked himself. He couldn't think. Am I crazy? Did someone put something into my coffee at the Golden Oil? Am I having a brain stroke — he had no idea what that meant.

Slowly, he calmed down and began to think more logically. The car was just sitting there. It wasn't as if something mechanical had broken down. The engine ran, brakes worked, steering (when he paid attention). There was no sign of anything else around — or in — it. All quiet, as it should be. George was the only sign of life at that spot. He called Alma on his mobile phone.

"George, what's wrong?" she cried out before he could speak. "Where are you? Is anything..."

"Wait on, Alma. It's OK. All A-OK. Just been delayed a bit."

'Oh. You gave me such a scare, there, George."

"Don't worry. All OK. Might be half an hour or so late. That's all. Don't wait up if you're tired."*

"Of course, I'll wait up. Take care, George."

He hung up and faced his car again. It was just his car. The cold was seeping into his bones and no doubt it had cleared his mind, too. Another car flashed by. A woman's face looked at him from the back window. The driver didn't. George wasn't surprised nobody had stopped to see if he was all right. Nobody cared these days. Or were too scared to stop on a dark, isolated mountain road for a stranger. He knew he wouldn't have stopped either. Never know who might be around.

He got up and walked slowly back to the car. The engine started before he reached the door. Or so it seemed, but George thought he'd probably not turned it off in his panic to get away from it. That was it.

"No more of that, George," he said aloud.

Soon he was back on the road and climbing up the long stretch to the top of the mountain. He just wanted to get the journey over and done with. He turned the radio on. More Strauss. That's good, he thought. Everything was as it should be. He sucked two more mints and smiled at his self-caused "nightmare" and began humming along. He flicked the bears to make them dance wildly. He was close to the top of Starke Mountain. Then just a leisurely half-hour downhill drive and fifteen minutes through suburban streets and he'd be home.

He jumped when the radio went off. He reached towards it then pulled his hand back.

"No, bugger it. I don't need music. Be home soon." He hummed to himself. Someone else hummed, too. Very faintly, but George felt it was "On the Road Again". He wiped sweat from his forehead. Drops stung his eyes. He turned the heater down.

The radio came on again. Bloody country music. George looked at the passenger side window. Only his reflection. He thought. He ignored the radio. Even when the volume increased. Soon some lovelorn fool was filling the car with his loud lament.

George banged the radio, stinging his knuckles. He turned it off. For several minutes it stayed off. George sighed and wiped the sweat away again. The car was so hot, He looked at the heater. It was full on!

"Leave me alone," he shouted. He turned the heater down. The radio snapped back on. Loud country whining again.

Still no shadowy figure in the window. That was a good sign. He gasped when he saw a thin face grinning at him in the rear vision mirror.

"Who are you?" he screamed. He half turned and saw nothing. A loud car horn spun him to the front. A car was heading for him because he was once again on the wrong side. Desperately, George spun the wheel over again. A big green car went by, weaving erratically as its driver took avoidance action.

George yelled: "Do you want to get us killed?" Us? He knew he was the only live being in his car.

The heater was back on high. The radio was blaring. George saw a face staring at him through the windscreen, as insubstantial as a reflection in the glass. Then a disgusting odour filled the car. Rotten. Decayed. George almost vomited, from the heat and the noise and, most of all, the stink.

Shadowy lines, like smoke, wisped around George. He turned his face this way, then that, trying to see what devilish creature was causing this hell. Nothing substantial; just a face grinning in front of him through the windscreen. Then it was gone. He thought of stopping again. Rest. Clear his mind. Call the NRMA.

He felt something sitting on him... Something with no weight. Not real. But he sensed it was there. Suddenly the steering wheel was turning by itself, towards the cliff face.

George tried to wrest control back from his ghostly passenger. Yes, it must be a ghost, he thought, pushing with all his strength to no avail.

"No, let it go!"

George heard a snigger again. Just before his car smashed into the rock face.

***

The police sergeant watched the driver's body being slid into the back of the ambulance. A phone lying on the side of the road was ringing. The sergeant went over but it stopped before he picked it up. He looked at it for a moment and put it in his trouser pocket.

He spoke to a constable who had finished writing in his notebook and was putting it in his shirt pocket.

"That's four this past year on this stretch of highway, Bob. Six if you count two on the Mapleville end."

"Hard to see any cause either. It's not a dangerous bit of road. It's not raining. No fog. Nothing out of the ordinary."

"Like before, we'll wait for the reports on body and car." The sergeant shook his head. "Damned if I know. Never seems to be any cause. Not mechanical, or road conditions. Seems like it's always driver failure.

"Anyway, for now, better get this traffic flowing again."

George's car was being towed away. Police started removing the barriers and easing banked-up vehicles through.

Marilyn Bates sat in the passenger seat watching the skinny figure of her husband Barry walk back to the car. He opened the door and slid into the driver's seat.

"Thank goodness we can go at last," she said as Barry turned the key and their car began to slowly move forward. "How many killed?"

"Just one. Driver on his own."

"That's the trouble. Drivers alone late at night. So easy to fall asleep. And look what happens. Holds us all up."

Barry said drily: "Wasn't too pleasant for that poor bugger, either." He wished he was driving alone. He turned the radio on and they drove up the mountain road towards Mapleville, listening to an opinionated talk show.

Then the radio went off.

"Why did you do that, Marilyn?"

"I thought you did. I'd rather us talk than listen to that right-wing rubbish, but I didn't touch the radio."

Barry turned it back on. Then he scowled when his favourite commentator was replaced by classical music.

"Bloody hell, woman!" he exclaimed. "Why can't you let me drive with my news show on? It's educational and informative."

Barry tuned back to his station.

"And biased," Marilyn shot back. She looked at her husband and past him, amused by the trick the night was playing with his reflection. She smiled back, past his real-life scowl.

Suddenly, she screamed and slapped Barry's shoulder.

"Are you crazy?" Barry yelled. "Why did you hit me?"

"Don't go squeezing my thigh, you pervert."

"Don't be stupid. I'm not that desperate."

Marilyn knew that all right. The radio talk changed to classical music and Marilyn felt pudgy fingers creep along her knee and gently squeeze her thigh.

Something sniggered and she smelt mint...

THE END

To survive, you must tell stories
-Umberto Eco, The Island of the Day Before

CHAPTER 7

Unlike many of Doctor Mallory's real patients, the detectives didn't have to wait long. It was a large room, with bookshelves, cupboards, a big desk, a green metal filing cabinet, and across one wall, an examination table. There was a small fan heater behind the doctor's chair, blowing onto his legs, or so Peter assumed.

"Thank you for giving us this time, Doctor."

"I'm not sure how I can help you, Inspector."

"I understand you were George Martin's GP. Is that right?" Peter thought he knew this already. Doctor Mallory looked at him for a while without speaking. Cleary said: "Had you known Mr Martin for very long?"

Dr Mallory was a round sort of fellow, with a round sort of face. He was about mid-fifties with big bushy eyebrows that did not yet show the grey flicking through his hair. He wore round-framed glasses that looked too small for his eyes. He was leaning forward on the desk holding a pen that made Peter wonder if he was going to be asking the questions.

"I have known… George for about twenty-odd years or more." He paused, looked around the room and studied the calendar on the wall behind him as if that would give him the date when he first met Martin. "Yes, I think it was probably twenty-two years." He nodded to himself.

"How was Mr Martin's mood the last time you saw him?"

"He was always reasonably happy. I saw him about three weeks before his death. He was a bit downcast, of course, at the lack of success of his last book. But, having said that, he seemed full of the challenge of writing in a different genre."

Cleary nodded. "Short stories."

"Yes, yes, it seemed to me that he was looking forward to what he could produce in this new format."

"You knew, of course, Dr Mallory, that George had cancer?"

"He was dying of prostate cancer. Some would say dying with it rather than because of it. But to me that was going to be the cause of his death. It just seemed so unnecessary that he should decide to get a head start on nature. To hang himself."

"Do you know if any other members of his household knew of this? It seems that nobody else did, or that's what they are telling us."

He waited as the doctor doodled on a scrap of paper for no apparent reason. The doctor looked up and said: "I don't think George told Margot or Nola," he paused, "or that Nagle bloke."

Cleary switched subjects.

"Did Mr Martin have a sleeping problem? Trouble getting to sleep at night?"

The doctor looked surprised. "Seems a bit late to be worrying about George's sleeping habits. But to answer your question, George was not bothered by any problem to do with sleeping. He never complained to me of insomnia. And, as far as I can tell, he didn't suffer from sleep apnoea. Why do you ask?"

"Our forensic man found that Martin had a large dose of a sleeping drug in his system. Apparently, the day he died."

"If George was planning to hang himself, it seems odd that he would want to put himself to sleep before he did so." Doctor Mallory once again looked around briefly and scribbled on another piece of paper before screwing it up with the first piece and throwing them at the rubbish bin on the other side of the room. Both missed.

"Perhaps to ease shock, the pain?" Cleary said.

"Well, well, he would also risk falling asleep before he achieved what he was aiming to do. I know that sleeping tablets don't act instantly and it would take a while before he started to feel drowsy and couldn't do anything much, but there was still a risk that he might wake up in the morning and realise, with a shock perhaps, that he was still alive."

Doctor Mallory looked at Cleary with a face that had a glimpse of a smile.

"Can you tell me anything, Doctor, about the Martins' relationship? Were they a happy couple? I know I'm asking you difficult questions, but I have a difficult job to do."

The doctor considered for a moment, picked up the pen again, scribbled one line and then dropped it as if fed up with this whole business.

"You tell me, Inspector. Do you suspect that there is something other than suicide, here? Are there suspicious circumstances… such as an overdose of sleeping tablets which I didn't prescribe?" He raised both hands and slapped them on the desk.

"I'm asking this because it does seem odd that you are asking questions that may hinge on people acting in ways they shouldn't." He took a long time getting that sentence out, pausing between each word, as if it was painful to expel it.

Cleary said they were keeping options open.

"Well, I can tell you that George was very unhappy about his marital situation. He had loved Margot for a long time, but in recent years they had grown apart. This grew into a chasm after he became blind. As his vision decreased, Margot withdrew further from him. George felt that looking after his needs when he couldn't see what he was doing or even what he was eating, became a burden for his wife whom George had once described as the love of his life."

"Do you know anything about this fellow Nagle, the chauffeur?"

Dr Mallory shook his head so hard that his spectacles almost fell off his nose. He simultaneously paused the swing of his head and straightened the spectacles.

"I have my doubts about Mr Nagle. Let's leave it at that. I don't know where he came from or why exactly Margot brought him into the house. It's a bit strange that he was given that job."

"But surely they needed someone to drive. Now that Mr Martin couldn't drive anymore. And I don't think that Mrs Martin is keen on driving."

Doctor Mallory scribbled on another piece of paper, studied it for a moment and looked up. Peter wondered if he constantly scribbled like this when consulting.

"I apologise. You're right. I have no right to say that. Of course, they did need someone to drive the car." He looked at his watch.

The detectives stood and turned towards the door.

"Thank you for your time, Doctor Mallory," Cleary said. "I appreciate your frankness. You have been helpful."

Cleary dropped Peter off near the Martin home and drove back to the station. Peter began going stoically from door to door in the neighbourhood without much success at first. People seemed reluctant to come to the door. It was as if they knew that the caller was a detective wanting to talk to them. Many doors didn't open at his ring or knock. But he persevered and later in the morning his luck changed.

He was about to walk away from an older house diagonally across from the Martin's home when he heard someone coming at last. The door was opened more than the crack that many other people had given him. He had begun to think that people were afraid that suicide was contagious and they didn't want to be infected. In this case, the door was opened wide, and a large, totally bald man stood there. He had not shaved for a day or two, but his face was friendly.

"Yes," he said, "you have some questions for me? I think you might be the police."

Peter detected a slight slur in the man's voice.

"Yes, I just want to ask you a couple of questions, Sir. You know about the tragedy that occurred recently in the street?"

The man seemed very pleased to be asked about this. He stepped out of the doorway and onto the verandah. Peter had to back away to make room for him. He was a big man in a khaki shirt and ill-fitting denim jeans.

"What sort of questions do you have? Do I call you Sir or Constable or —"

Peter said: "You can call me Detective." The man smiled as if impressed by that.

"Did you notice anything unusual, untoward, in the few days before or after the recent death of Mr Martin?"

The man scratched the side of his nose, as if thinking, but it was obvious to Peter that he already knew what he was going to say.

"Well, not much from day to day. A very sleepy street this is. Or it was until the sudden death here. Terrible. A tragedy. I feel so sorry for Mrs Martin and their daughter."

"But did you see or hear anything unusual?"

"There was something I think, the other night before Mr Martin… before he died. I got home late. I was late because I…" he paused and apparently decided he didn't have to give a reason why he was home late. "And I was out here where I am now. To have a smoke. Before I went to bed. And I saw a figure, someone walking very fast along the street over there and then turning in at the gate, he walked around the side of the house. I thought that was unusual."

"Did you recognise that person? Was it a man or woman?"

He scratched the other side of his nose for a moment. "I don't think it was anybody I know. Maybe a bit familiar. I'm pretty sure it was a man or at least someone in trousers. Seemed to know where he was headed and hurried there quite quickly. Looked like he was expected."

Peter asked him what time this was.

"It would have been just after midnight. Odd, don't you think?"

Peter didn't answer.

"And have you seen that person since?"

"No. Certain of that. I'm sure he's not there now though. I see quite a lot from here. And I'm out on this verandah quite a bit because I smoke, well, a lot. Be the death of me, Alma tells me. Good job too, I think sometimes." He paused for a while looking out at the street.

"So, you didn't see this man leave?" Peter said.

"No." He spoke as if he had already answered that question. "I was out here late the night after that as well and I never saw hide nor hair of anyone else." He paused, rubbed the tip of his nose and added: "But I sometimes doze out here."

Peter thanked him, took down his name, and said: "You have been helpful, Mr Cawthorne."

"Excuse me, Sergeant, sorry Detective, I'm a bit puzzled by this interview."

Peter looked at him.

"Why?"

"It's a bit odd for a Detective to be going around asking questions about what we all thought was a plain and simple suicide."

Peter didn't know what a plain and simple suicide was. He nodded at the man and thanked him again. Nobody else in the remaining houses had seen any suspicious person late at night, or at any other time. Peter waited in the street at a pre-arranged corner until Inspector Cleary picked him up.

> Your mind is working at its best
> when you're being paranoid.
> You explore every avenue and possibility of your
> situation at high speed with total clarity.
> *-Banksy*

CHAPTER 8

Peter had helped Jan with the washing up. She had washed and he had wiped the dishes, putting them away one by one. They had chatted about some friends and what they might do at the weekend, and she had mentioned a Western on TV that Peter might like. He had hugged her and kissed her on the forehead. She sighed.

"I suppose you are going to spend your night with that dead man again. To communicate with a voice from beyond the grave."

Peter looked at her and saw there was no glimmer of humour.

"I am sorry, Jan, but I must do this."

"Do your colleagues spend their nights reading ancient manuscripts?"

Peter thought 'ancient' was a bit much. "We can't interview the victim in this case. So, in one sense, I am getting information from a man who may have died in suspicious circumstances."

Jan threw the tea towel on the sink. "Suspicious circumstances? If you had been investigating this by yourself, without the help of the great detective, Inspector Cleary, there would not be any suspicious circumstances. You know, Peter, that people are doing away with themselves all the time."

Peter stopped himself from saying each one only does it once. Wisely, he held his tongue.

"But you go ahead and do your duty as a good detective. I will sit in there again enjoying whatever comes up on TV."

She turned away and walked into the lounge room.

Depressed now, Peter pulled out the manuscript from the cupboard drawer. He took it into the dining room and sat, as usual, at the end nearest the kitchen doorway. He opened the manuscript at his book-marked place. He realised then, that he had not made coffee. He sighed and went to the kitchen. Returning with a coffee and a biscuit, he settled down to read.

> hey little fellow did the nasty noise frighten you it woke me too it wont hurt us all outside the house it's only thunder and probably lightning settle back on the bed cosy and warm Fido that big one even scared me let me cover your ears little man calm now Ill put this cover over you Is that better loud enough to wake others in the house even that nasty Nagle who we don't like
>
> scarier for you fido youre seeing the flashing light Ill put my hands over your eyes no you don't like that sorry Im going to see whos up I'll put the light on for you and pull the blind down creak creak door creaks boards creak under me and around me when I touch

the walls as if mimicking the creakiness of my bones at each step

the timbers and pieces of this house creaking under my steps matching up with the creaking in my knees in my bones in my legs we have gone altogether old house havent we now you sound like I feel shaking and trembling and creaking always creaking hard to sneak anywhere in this house it might be more peaceful if I were deaf not blind if I wish that maybe I would end up being both

tiles shaking and theres another noise at the end of the hall not creaking more like the rhythmic beating of this old house's heart no no not that theres somebody in the spare room more than one voices groans squeaking is that Margot not her room who the hell is squeaking and groaning in the spare room I will find out by god I will find out thunder shaking the place

I must be careful that I whisper now as I go along I should lie in bed ignore everything but I cant

I cant tell if the hall light is on it doesn't matter to me but it might matter to others

for gods sake is nothing sacred we each have a bedroom once Margot and I had the same bedroom enough of that

me a blind man creeping along the hall in the middle of the night cant count on life continuing as it once was cant count on everything being idyllic things change because people change thats a woman I hear should leave them to it but I cant she is my wife after all

hey whats happened

I happened I have caught you I bet Nagle is there too

ad its me why did you turn the light on turn it off I am naked dad

Nola what why

turn the bloody light off didn't you hear me

no I wont touch the bloody light Nola remember Im blind I cant see you I cant see what youre wearing or not wearing I cant see what you are doing or not doing I cant see where you are in this room but I can guess with a very good chance of being correct

why did you turn it on then

force of habit whos with you

Im sorry mr Martin

youre not bloody sorry you cant tell me that but you can tell me who the hell you are

he cant see you he is all right you dont have to poke me

where did I put my

on the end of the bed on the end of the bed are you blind

okay okay don't harass me

is that you Jeremy

you dont have to answer that

I know its you getting into my daughter in my own home you are employed as a gardener not as a fornicator

bloody hell get out of the old testament dad

I love Nola mr Martin thats why

you don't have to be sorry Jeremy you dont have to apologise Jeremy you don't have to explain why we were in here fucking you can act like a man who loves fucking whether you love me or you dont love me is none of my dads business

I know I dont have to do anything say anything I mean I dont have to

one thing you wont have to do in future Mr James is our gardening you are no longer our gardener I will get somebody who is more responsible someone who doesnt go behind my back

with your attitude your old-fashioned morality we had to do it this way and I loved it I have always loved it do you hear that old testament man this is not the first time

your ears have not been sharp enough I will live where I can be happy with a man I love Jeremy can you see my robe twisted up in the blankets here darling

darling whats this darling rubbish you two kids how can you know anything about love

where have you been in the past decade dad dad I am
twenty-nine nearly thirty some kid eh

what is all this racket even worse than the thunder
what the hell is going on in here

aww mum see what youve done now dad

Nola you are half dressed Jeremy why is was your
shirt open and oh my god your zipper

Jeremy and I have been in here enjoying ourselves our
lips our bodies and not bothering anyone else in this
house but then my father had to burst in on us naked
and all no bloody privacy here

but your dad cant see what does it matter but I can see
whats been going on

you must have had some idea about Jeremy and me

I I sort of did mr Nagle gave me a hint but I guess I
didnt take it very seriously after all hes just a gardener

Margot what is happening I heard all this noise and

Nagle you saying you heard this noise above the storm
in your room downstairs are you sure

dont be so stupid George this house is normally quiet
at night and any noise travels a long way especially
your snoring

Im sorry about this mrs Martin we didn't mean
to disturb anybody we thought we didnt need to
announce it make a big fuss

that didnt work out well did it

none of your bloody business Nagle are you in your pyjamas Nola is he in his pyjamas

Im not in the fashion police dad

well talk about it tomorrow Jeremy you can't go out in the storm you sleep here ill go back to my room

are you decent Nola dressed

I am dressed but whether I am decent or not is a matter for someone else

Im going back to bed I suggest both of you men do the same good night George good night mr Nagle

so I wait here alone once more in the dark whispers from Nagle is he goes to Margots door a brief whisper from Margot what are they saying how the hell can I ever know that

there is no comfort in this bed any more probably never was if I was honest but it is worse now I cant see anything in the room with or without the lights but I know there are no people in here only the ghosts of memories memories of happier times when everything was out in the open and can never be out in the open anymore so not a lot to live for not for my reputation that has dwindled in recent years not in my new venture I doubt that my short stories will set the world on fire I dont have much to offer anyone anymore I cant help Margot with anything I cant drive them anywhere and after tonight Nola may not ever talk to me again what a way to go

That night, for a change, Peter re-read the previous pages. This was something new. Something to tell his boss about. He had picked up in this piece of the manuscript that Nola had lied to them.

She had said Jeremy James was only a friend. "Not a lover," she had claimed, while looking him in the eye. Why would she do that? Why would the daughter of a man who may have hanged himself tell a lie? That should not matter. Had that night's drama started a rift between father and daughter?

"I've had enough of TV for the night, Peter," Jan said walking up behind him and bending over to kiss his forehead. "I'll leave you to your important work."

She went to the bedroom. Peter picked up his coffee and drank some more. It was cold. Of course.

He and Cleary would have to interview Nola Martin again and Jeremy James, too. What was going on with that pair? George Martin's little recorder had recorded the incident which would seem to have led to Nola moving out of the family home to live with Jeremy. Now she was back.

As he thought further over that fracas caused by George bursting in on the two naked lovers, Peter felt lonely.

He couldn't understand Nola's attraction to Jeremy who spent much of his day hanging around with tomato vines, digging up potatoes, attending to strawberries and goodness knows what else. For Jeremy, she was a luscious catch. He blinked away the image of Nola - whom he had only seen fully dressed - standing naked on the bed. Not proper for a cop investigating a possible murder.

He stuck his slim bookmark into the spot and closed the manuscript and put it away for the night. He left the not-quite-finished cup of cold coffee on the table, knowing he should have taken it to the kitchen and rinsed it out. But not tonight. He turned the light off and went into the bedroom where Jan was quietly sleeping. He had always found that a pleasant sound. It

83

wasn't really snoring, just sleeping noises. She only had a sheet over her and it was pulled partly down to waist level, revealing the pink nightie he had bought for her birthday.

He hadn't expected her to be awake but was still disappointed. He climbed in beside her and put his arm across her waist.

Jan said sleepily, "Is that you, Peter?"

He waited a breath and then said: "Who is ziss Peter, you are about asking."

"Oh, just someone I sleep around with."

"What! Ziss is not good. Ziss not good at all, ziss –"

Peter's words were shut off by Jan's lips closing over his. They reached out and pulled each other closer. A frenzy of lips and tongues, hands and legs soon proved to Peter that to the contrary, 'ziss' was very good indeed.

They lay back smiling at the ceiling. Peter rolled over, looked at the clock on his bedside cabinet and groaned.

"Look at the time."

"Just goes to show that what they say is true: Time flies when you're having fun."

"I didn't mean to disturb your sleep but I'm sure glad I did."

"I had to do something to silence that appalling comic accent."

Peter laughed and closed his eyes.

"Before you nod off, I've been meaning to ask you something about George Martin's books. You've read a couple of his books, haven't you?"

Without opening his eyes, Peter said: "Three or four perhaps. They were OK. Not my favourite genre but they were certainly popular and to some extent, still are."

"Set in the bushranger era, aren't they?"

"I would only say sort of."

"Doesn't sound like you're very clear in what they are about," Jan said.

"They are actually set in the future when Australia is governed by a dictator. Democracy is gone; dictatorship is in. And the books follow the exploits of a band of bushrangers in the rainforests of north Queensland fighting against the dictator's troops. Going further back in another country's history, they're a bit like Robin Hood and his band of merry men."

"Like they were, say, Ned Kelly's merry band?"

Peter imagined the twinkle in her eye.

"A bit like that. But they are darker than those tales. This group of outlaws had to fight very hard to make even a small dent in the dictatorship's authority." He paused. "I think I would put George Martin's books into the thriller category with a touch of fantasy. They're fast-moving with lots of ups and downs for the heroes and heroines with some main characters not always surviving every book."

"I see. I'm sure they are thrilling to read but I think I'll stick with my favourite genres. Thrillers are a bit too thrilling for my little heart."

"You'd better not read any of his short stories. They are even darker— quite horrific at times."

He rolled over and kissed her. She laughed, "Talk about thrilling." She kissed him back.

Peter was struck by a sudden thought. There was, he realised, something in the pattern of George Martin's writings that could indicate a major change of mood. His novels, although often starkly graphic and occasionally telling of tragic events, were, nevertheless, entertaining stories that usually ended on an upbeat note with the good guys winning. Not so his new approach to writing short stories. The ones Peter had read so far were dark, often horrifying, chilling, terrifying. Those adjectives were ones that he had thought as he read one short story after another. And while they were gripping, hard-to-put-down-stories, the good guys hardly ever won against the forces of darkness.

Yes, he thought, that was something he will tell Inspector Cleary about. George Martin's mood had turned from hopefulness to hopelessness.

He realised Jan was gazing at him. He clicked his mind back into the conversational tone.

"Sorry, darling, I was just thinking of something that may be important. Something that…"

"Something more important than our conversation?" she said. She was smiling.

"No, it's not important for us. For you and me. It may not even figure in our investigation."

He tried to get to sleep but his mind was now focused on tomorrow when he would talk to Cleary about the two things that he had realised tonight. But, in honesty, he thought Cleary would probably not be impressed by what he had read about Nola. After all, it was only a young woman lying about who she had sex with.

"You know, Jan…" he stopped. She was asleep.

Soon he was also.

> Always tell the truth, that way you don't
> have to remember what you said
> -Mark Twain

CHAPTER 9

At 10.30 the next morning, both detectives were seated in Nola's office at the Council Chambers. She had not wanted to meet with them. She said she was "very busy" and tried to have it put off but Cleary had insisted. They were sitting across a big brown desk, facing each other. Cleary said: "I appreciate you taking the time to talk to us this morning, Ms Martin."

She shifted some white pages and a brown envelope together on her desk before looking up and answering him. "I really do not have a lot of time, Inspector."

Peter said: "We don't have much time, either. Frankly I'm surprised that you're back at work so soon after your father's death."

"Are you an expert on grief, Sergeant? Work is a distraction. And I don't want to sit around at home. Is that alright with you?"

He looked across at his superior and saw that Cleary was obviously annoyed at him.

Cleary said: "There are only a couple of questions we have to ask. It has come to our attention, Ms Martin, that some information you told us during our initial interviews may not be correct."

Nola didn't seem disconcerted by this. She looked directly at Cleary and said: "I don't know what you are referring to."

Peter was eager to interrupt again but a look from Cleary cautioned him to keep quiet.

"We spoke to you about your relationship with Mr Jeremy James." She nodded. "You said, and I think I'm correct in quoting, that you and Mr James were 'friends not lovers'."

Nola looked down at her hands and ran fingers over the nails of one.

"Oh, I am being rude, detectives, I should have offered you coffee. Or tea. Would you like some now? And a biscuit or two, perhaps?" She smiled at them, but it was forced, Peter thought.

Cleary was not to be distracted. He raised his right hand, palm facing her.

"No. We're fine, thank you, Ms Martin. We would prefer to get to the point."

For fully a minute the two detectives gazed at Nola who shifted her eyes from one to the other and back again. It was obvious to Peter that she was working out how to respond.

"Who told you otherwise? Has someone been spreading lies about me and Jeremy?" She was calmer now. She smiled at Cleary.

Cleary said: "For a start, you have lied to us." She looked aghast. "It was your father who revealed the truth about your relationship."

"That's very cruel, Inspector. My father is dead, so we all know he is not telling anyone anything."

Peter couldn't help himself. "He has. He has recorded it, Ms Martin. Do you remember him bursting into your bedroom – sorry, I think it was the spare room, he said – one night. We are not sure –"

Cleary took over again: "We are not sure of the date, but it is apparent from what was recorded in your father's manuscript that this event happened. Can you clearly and without any prevarication, tell us what happened on a night when you were in a bedroom with Jeremy James and your father burst in?"

Her face paled and she began stammering, but very quickly gained control of herself. "Yes, you are right. That did happen. I had forgotten about that." She laughed a little bit. "That shows how insignificant that night was, doesn't it? It was of such little importance to me. I had sex with our gardener. That is it. We are friends but are not lovers in the normal sense."

Peter thought, buggered if I know what the normal sense is.

"I'm surprised that you left this in the manuscript you have been editing." Cleary said.

She looked at him for a moment, then said: "Why? It is not a criminal offence yet, is it?" She waited briefly for an answer and when none came, she said: "I slipped up. I edited it in the original transcription on the computer but forgot that Dad had an earlier printed version in his office drawer. A big mistake, hey?"

Peter wondered what other contradictions there might be between the two versions.

"For the sake of having a true record, Ms Martin," Cleary continued, "Will you tell us whether you had sex with James on more than one occasion? And did you move in with him?"

"So," she said, now fully in control of herself, "in answer to your question, and in answer to any similar question you may want to ask me, we had sex more than once. We enjoy it." She looked at each of them again for a few seconds. "You are both adult men, so I am sure you know how good it can be and why healthy young people like to do it as often as possible. It is the Christian thing to do."

Cleary raised an eyebrow. "Christian?"

"Yes." She smiled again. "You know, the Bible tells us to 'Love thy neighbour.'" She paused. "And no. I did not move in with Jeremy. I thought better of it. I knew Dad needed me around. And I wish I had done more of the most important thing he asked me to do: to revise and edit that blasted manuscript. I have been concentrating on the short stories because the publisher had given him a deadline. I'm going to edit the remaining stories and send them together with the dozen or so he had already written.

"I've neglected, to some extent, the other… what I call 'ramblings' and will get back to them later. Look at what embarrassment it has caused me. I am very busy with my job and I couldn't give as much time to the manuscript as Dad wanted."

"And your mother couldn't do that?" Peter said.

"No, their relationship had moved into a very sour zone." She paused.

"Or Mr Nagle, for that matter?"

Nola gave him an odd look and didn't bother answering.

"And as to another question you might ask: Dad and I made up after that terrible night. At the end, we were great mates."

Abruptly, Cleary asked: "How did you all get on with Stephen Martin?"

"I think we were good together. We didn't see Uncle Stephen a lot. As you may know, he doesn't live in the Blue Mountains, he lives in Bathurst. He has a pharmacy there."

"Did he visit your father very often?"

She shook her head. "Not very often. They were on friendly terms. He's coming up soon."

Peter made another note in his book. "Good. We need to talk to him. Do you know when he'll be coming?"

She didn't directly answer Peter. After a few moments' consideration, she said: "I'll let you know in the next twenty-four hours."

The detectives stood and thanked her for her time. She smiled and said: "Anytime, gentlemen." They left.

DATE WITH HORROR
A SHORT STORY BY GEORGE MARTIN

James Lawson was having a good time. There weren't many things he liked better than eating and drinking and dancing in dimly lit nightclubs. He loved the laughter and the music, and he loved the women who sometimes went home with him. James had always adhered to his father's advice: don't pick up women you don't know when you're in a bar or nightclub. Or more specifically, he had said: don't take strange women home, James.

Usually this was no trouble. Usually there was no problem with this. James had a lot of friends from school and work. They were, like him, in their early twenties, and they liked having a good time as much as he did. There were some beautiful young women among those people. So, usually James felt the lucky one to be taking one of those friends home for the night.

But occasionally, he saw someone outside his circle of friends who attracted his attention, and he wished he had the nerve to make a play for her.

One night, James saw a woman whose beauty was so striking that he pushed his father's advice to the back of his mind and approached the woman.

She was standing at the bar alone, drinking. He went up to her, smiled and said hello. He expected to be rebuffed. She was about the same height as James, had long blonde hair, and her face, when she turned to look him, was extraordinarily beautiful. Her blue eyes seemed to shine and shimmer in synchronisation with her smile. Skin was perfect. But despite the eyes that looked so deeply at him, it was the lips that so impressed James.

Although her mouth in some way seemed large to James, when he looked directly at her red lips they didn't seem any bigger than anyone else's. Perhaps they were wider - went further across the face under that perfectly shaped smallish nose.

She was dressed in a loose light green shirt and casual trousers, also a shade of green.

"Hello," she said, smiling even wider. Her teeth were lovely and white.

After that opening exchange, James was momentarily lost for words. He wasn't going to say anything like, "Do you come here often?"

He said: "I am sorry to be so... well... so upfront, but when I looked across and saw you, I couldn't believe how beautiful you are. I... I –"

She laughed and James thought it was a wonderful sound. Those wet lips opening and closing, teeth glistening. Her eyes staring only at him.

James said: "Can I buy you a drink? Or are you hungry... Or..."

"Or would I like to dance? Was that what you were going to ask next?" She put her drink down on the bar. And moved towards him. "Yes, I do dance. And I would like to dance with you."

James almost fell over the barstool next to her in his rush to hold her. They moved out onto the dance floor.

"Also, in case you were going to ask, I don't come here often. I guess I don't go anywhere often."

"I do sometimes come here... But no, not often."

"What is your name?" He told her. "James, I think that suits you. You want to know my name?"

"Yes, please. What is your name? I was about to ask, actually."

She laughed again. "My name is Angela. Do you like it?"

James said he did, shaking his head up and down. Yes, he did, he said, several times. They danced and she pulled James closer to her. Very close. And James liked the feeling. He couldn't help looking around to see if his any of his friends had noticed. He hoped they had. He had never danced with such a soft but vibrant body. She moved with a litheness that he had never felt before.

Later, James bought her a drink and one for himself, and they sat at a small table. She drank and he drank. They talked, but on the way back to his place James couldn't remember what they had talked about. His memory didn't go beyond her blue eyes peering into his and laughing, smiling, wet red lips. White teeth.

They went up in the lift to his apartment. She admired the view, which James had never thought was worth commenting on. Except for the corner of a nearby park, it was mostly other buildings, much as you would see in any small city.

James was embarrassed to see that he hadn't made his bed that morning. He rushed over, started straightening sheets and cover. He didn't do it very well. Triangular section of sheet dangled down towards the floor.

She said: "Oh, don't worry about that, James, it doesn't have to be neat. I am sure it won't be neat when we have finished."

When we have finished? James found himself greatly aroused. Though she had been so forthright with him before. That meant the time was approaching when they would start…

"You have a nice place here, James," Angela said. James didn't know if he did or not. He didn't care. He went over and put his arms around Angela and the feel of her body against his sent arousal to a level he had never experienced. This couldn't last.

She gently pushed him aside and moved towards the double bed. She unbuttoned her blouse and shook it off, letting it fall to the floor, James gasped. She reached behind her and undid her bra. She let it fall as well. James was staggered at the beauty of her breasts—large, round and… Dad, if only you could see me now. He chuckled to himself. He loved this strange woman. He wanted to run a hand up onto each one of those firm breasts. And… then she let her pants drop. She wore no knickers. She was barefoot now.

James was struggling in his haste to undo his shirt buttons. She came up and pressed against him and in a moment, his shirt was off. She then reached down to his trousers under the belt and unzipped, pushed them down and pushed his underpants down.

He sat down on his bed, urgently undoing laces, shoes, throwing them across the room and the socks under the bed. She was on him. They kissed and hugged and caressed until James could barely contain himself. She rolled down lying on her back. He arose over her. Her skin was so, so soft and smooth. He pushed in. His mind was filled with the ecstasy. At this moment he couldn't believe his luck. Her face was smiling up at him, her mouth, larger than ever, welcomed him. His lips sank down until they were touching hers, he was surprised at how small his mouth was against hers. She hissed but her lips were still welcoming him. They seemed wider than his head. Her skin felt suddenly rough and scaly, something was very wrong. He struggled and tried to pull away. He was horrified by what was happening. Was this a nightmare?

She had a tight hold around his back, her hands were rough and grating across his back like sandpaper, his legs flailed up and down, but he couldn't move away.

"Don't go away, now, James. Just when I was beginning to enjoy myself. Yum," she said. James wanted to scream.

His head was being pulled down into an enforced kiss. Then in terror, he saw that mouth, those lovely red lips, expanding and expanding until they were big enough to take his head and he was sucked in. Despite his struggle he was sucked in even further. And then the sucking in became sucking out of his life. He was quickly drained. Tossed aside, he fell to the floor - white. Staring lifelessly. A scaly, long-nailed foot pushed him under the bed to lie with a pair of black socks.

THE END

To be blind is not miserable; not to be able
to bear blindness, that is miserable
-John Milton

CHAPTER
10

Peter sat at the table and opened the manuscript. He heard Jan turn the TV on in the next room, then sighed and began reading.

    can you wait for me here George

    Ill only be in the shops for a little while I think youll be all right here

    how long will you be this is not a good place to stand too many people walking around bumping past me

    George you make such a fuss come over here with me this bench will do you just sit and rest you like doing that

I am not dumb Margot so dont treat me as if I have no mental capacity this will do I hope you wont be away too long though

Ill be as long as it takes

all right but you dont have to sigh so much just be quick

I might need the toilet

Mark will be here soon and so will I

I dont care about what Nagles doing I bet hes off with another girlfriend and shes gone already never lets me finish a sentence I wish

why are you talking to yourself mr Martin

is that you Emma

yes and you brought your big stick to the shops again

remember Emma this white stick helps me to see where Im going without bumping into people or things why are you giggling is that funny

it is a bit

does anyone fall over your stick when youre trying to miss them

sometimes not very often

does it hurt not being able to see

it doesnt hurt are you here with your mummy or daddy do they know where you are

we can keep talking

Im not very good at talking to little people

is your mouth broken too is that why you are not good at talking see my mum is just over there

no my mouth works fine only my eyes are broken

why are your shoes different colours are you going to a special party or something

what do you mean about my shoes they are just normal shoes I wear them lots of times especially when I go out

it just looks funny one shoe is brown and one is black do you have big long ones like a clown

you have a nice laugh like a giggle that has grown up I didnt know my shoes dont match all colours feel the same people have to tell me these things but sometimes they cant be bothered

Emma where are you I see you now

thats my mummy I have to go now

Emma honey you shouldnt be bothering him Im sorry mr Martin

Ive enjoyed our conversation shes sweet I just wish I could see her goodbye Emma goodbye

his eyes still don't work he cant see us at all isnt that sad

yes it is

mr Martin I remembered something I remembered if you go to the doctor the doctor will fix your eyes mummy went to the doctor about her sore foot and the doctor fixed that and now she can walk properly again if the doctor fixed your eyes you would be able to see me and how pretty my dress is

dont run away from mummy like that you might get hurt

I wanted to tell him something

she is just trying to help me with some advice

Im sorry

mummy I think your doctor might be able to fix his eyes and then he would be able to see us like the doctor who fixed your foot now you can walk again

I dont think he needs us to give him advice

Im grateful for any help anyone offers me

I would like him to be able to see me to see my lovely dress it is pretty isnt it mummy

yes yes now we must get back to the car I have to get home sorry again dont worry about it I get a lot worse advice than that

if you use that stick that helps you see where youre going and you touch me with it could you see me could you see my smile

dont be so silly come on

I wish it would work like that I would love to see your smile go with mummy now

sadly I wont ever see her smile I cant even see the sun shine

who are you talking to George

get up now George I am back Mark is at the car so we will go

Margot you didnt tell me I was wearing odd shoes

I didnt have the time to check we were in a rush to get out today

I have been walking around among all these people at the shops with one brown and one black shoe and it took a little girl to tell me that

my own wife let me go out in public looking like a clown

you are like a clown sometimes George now come on

When Peter had sat down earlier that night, manuscript open before him on the dining room table, well-equipped for a long session with biscuits, cake and a big mug of coffee, he had intended to go even deeper. Read more. Keep at it until the early hours of the morning. Discover something important about this mystery.

He had apologised in advance to Jan who had given a stoic smile. They had kissed with a token touch of the lips.

Now the coffee was drained, biscuits and cake eaten and Jan in bed, and he didn't feel certain of offering anything new to his boss. He expected Cleary would ask him to stop reading any further.

Peter thought that would be premature. He had seen things in what he had read so far that made him believe George Martin was a very sad man who had a lot more than blindness to deal with. But he was also a man who someone in that toxic household - or beyond - might have wanted to kill.

He had glanced ahead a little and was excited at what it might bring. There was a reference to suicide, and possibly even murder, in what lay ahead tonight, but he was too tired to continue. He looked at his watch, sighed, and put the manuscript away.

Suspicious we are, we men who walk the earth
-*Robert Fagles, The Odyssey*

CHAPTER 11

The next morning Peter could see by the expression on Nagle's face that he was unhappy at being asked to come in for further 'interrogation', as he described it. The chauffer dropped himself down into the single armchair, then shuffled his feet around as if trying to get a good foothold on the floor. He crossed his arms, then uncrossed them and finally sat back with his arms on the armrests, palms flat down, and faced the detectives.

"Thank you for your time, once again, Mr Nagle," Cleary said. "Hopefully, this will be the last time we need to talk."

"I don't see any reason why we had to even begin talking," Nagle said.

Cleary ignored that remark. "We would like to know what your relationship was with Mr George Martin. "We know he was not your employer. We know that Mrs Martin was your employer. How did that work for you?"

"I don't get what you're trying to do here. What is any of this to do with George hanging himself? Surely there isn't any need to delve into personal relationships."

Peter knew there were very likely several reasons why this was necessary, but he didn't interrupt his boss.

"Mr Nagle, was there any reason why you would wish to harm Mr Martin? Did the two of you –"

Nagle seemed about to explode. "Wish to harm him? What the hell are you talking about? I didn't give a stuff about him." He paused, thinking about what he had just said. "I mean, I didn't have any reason to dislike him - or hate him. I think someone would have to hate him to kill him."

"Yes, we think that. I know you and Mr Martin had disagreements, but how deep did they go? If you didn't have any wish to harm Mr Martin, do you know what his feelings were towards you?"

Nagle sat back and thought a minute. "He may have. He seemed to be, well, jealous, jealous of –-"

"Who would he have been jealous of and what would have caused that jealousy?"

"I think he resented me being friends with his wife. But that was all we were. Not... not even friends. It was a happy boss and worker relationship between me and Margot... I mean, Mrs Martin."

"Nothing more?"

Nagle folded his arms then unfolded them again. "Nothing more." He directed his next remark to Peter.

"Make sure you put that in your book, sonny. Write there was no intimate relationship between me and Mrs Martin. Got that?" Peter wrote 'not lovers'.

Cleary said: "Do you think Mr Martin was happy?"

"How the hell would I know? He was not as happy as he once might've been. I suppose there could be many reasons for that."

"Do you mean he was saddened by the lack of success of his last book? Or something else?"

"From what Margot… Mrs Martin, said, I think that did upset him. He had to change his approach. I don't understand these writing things, but I think he was changing what sort of story he was going to write. That could have upset him." He looked around the room and said: "I dunno."

"You may not be able to answer this, Mr Nagle, but did you observe any mistreatment of Mr Martin? By anybody?"

Nagle opened his mouth to speak, but closed it and rubbed his forehead. He looked at Cleary and then Peter and back at Cleary before answering.

"I suppose there were some things that happened. Things I thought were a bit unfair."

"Can you give some examples, such as?"

"Mrs Martin was often…" He paused. "This won't go any further, will it, Inspector?"

Cleary shook his head. "Of course not." He, too, paused. "Unless we hear something that would be needed in court. But I don't think it is likely."

"She was very impatient with poor old George. She couldn't cope with his blindness, see, and would often snap at him for simple things such as dropping food off a spoon onto his clothes. Spilling coffee from an overfilled cup. You know how the baristas do it these days, filling the cup to the brim. Well, George sometimes had trouble lifting such a cup to his mouth because he couldn't see if it was level on the way up. Little things like that."

"He had trouble eating and drinking tidily?" Peter asked.

"Yes. And with his clothes. Mrs Martin was impatient. She couldn't be bothered helping George with his shoes, for example. Matching them, you know. I think once she deliberately let him go to the shops with a tear down the back of his shirt. She just couldn't be bothered pointing out things to him.

"I almost felt sorry for him on those occasions. I knew he was trying his best. If you can't see, you just can't see, can you?" He looked at the detectives for a sign of agreement. Cleary nodded. Peter was too busy writing to look up.

Cleary stretched a leg out in front of him and bent it back towards the chair.

"It doesn't seem to have been a very happy relationship."

Nagle scoffed. "That's putting it lightly. I don't think happiness was part of their relationship. Not recently. I think at one time they were very much in love. I think that ended before George went blind. But then, I don't know. I'm just the bloody chauffeur."

Cleary changed tack. "What do you know of Mr Stephen Martin?"

Nagle seemed surprised. But he also relaxed, as if this line of questioning wasn't going to be a threat to him.

"I only met him once. As you no doubt know, Stephen Martin doesn't live here. He has a pharmacy in Bathurst. And he lives there, of course. He visits here on occasions."

"Did he and his brother have a good relationship? Are you in any position to be aware of that?"

"I don't think I am, really, because I didn't see them together often. However, having said that, I do know George looked forward to seeing his brother. He sometimes spoke to me of how much he valued the times they spent together. He said he needed reassurance from Stephen from time to time, and Stephen provided that. He told me once that Stephen was his best friend. Even further, he said he loved Stephen."

"Do you know that someone, possibly a man, was here late on the night Mr Martin died? Do you know of a visit here by Stephen Martin or anyone else that night?"

"I don't know anything about that. Do you mean this person was Stephen?"

"We don't know that."

"I was probably asleep. I don't stay up very late, you see."

"Even if you weren't awake and didn't see anyone here, did you hear about a visitor who came that night?"

"Nobody mentioned any such thing to me."

"Did Mrs Martin get on very well with Stephen?" Cleary asked.

"I don't think they saw each other very much. Well, not while I was around anyway." Pause. "I have no reason to think that she disliked him He is a jovial character who's well-liked and well-respected beyond his own family.

"Mr Nagle, do you know if Stephen Martin is married?"

He thought for a while. "I think he was once. I think his wife left him. I am sorry Inspector, I can't help you there. I'm a relative newcomer here. I haven't been around for very long. In this family, in this home."

"I understand that, Mr Nagle. You have been quite helpful. I appreciate your frankness. You have no need to worry that anything unnecessary will go further than this room."

Nagle relaxed back into the chair and pushed his hands together.

"I am glad to have been of help. I can't see what I said could have altered anything that should have been obvious to you from the start. George Martin hanged himself. I don't think any of these time-wasting interviews can really help you in any way. But I appreciate you thanking me for my time. Can I go now?"

He rose slowly and when Cleary nodded, walked quickly to the door and out.

"What do you think, sir?"

"What he told us was very helpful. Useful."

"You think he was telling the truth all the way through?"

"I got the impression that he was being as truthful as he felt he could be. I think in some areas to do with Mrs Martin and perhaps their relationship, it was a bit fuzzier. Not necessarily lying, but not telling all the truth."

Peter said: "How do you think we're going then, sir? Are we reaching a conclusion in this case?"

"I am still not sure, Peter, I think the most likely scenario is that George Martin did hang himself, unassisted by anyone else. I suspect there is more to come here."

Peter wondered if what he had read last night could change the Inspector's view. "So, you think we are not at that point yet? I may have read… will I continue reading the manuscript?"

Cleary stood and looked around the room before answering. "Yes, better keep at it until you reach the end. Something may jump out at you."

Peter thought one or two things may have done that already.

Later that night, Peter continued his reading.

> concentrate I must concentrate not keep getting distracted by Nagle or Margot I know she thinks Im being silly wasting my time writing but thats the nastiest thing shes said shes the one wasting her time I wont be killing myself any time soon

THE SUICIDAL KILLER
A SHORT STORY BY GEORGE MARTIN

For some time now I have wanted to kill myself. Trouble is I keep meeting people who have less reason to live than I do. So, I kill them instead.

> mmm thats a start a decent first paragraph maybe it started when I thought of the title the suicidal killer I keep wandering off it doesn't matter what it began with its only important how it ends I pride myself on good endings you should know that Nola

I won't take too much of your time right now, going into all the reasons why I needed to kill myself. It isn't a secret. I will tell you later but suffice to know that I was fed up. There didn't seem to be any way out of my predicament. Any way to escape the misery I was feeling. I thought it would be easy, probably not painless, but pain wouldn't last very long. I don't mean to make suicide seem a good way out. It's a stupid thing to do.

Anyway, I thought the train was the best and easiest option at that time, so I headed for the local railway station. I went in peak hour, when I knew there would be a lot of people jostling around. I stood at the end of the platform where I knew the engine would be. I watched several trains come in at that platform: number two away from the city. I placed myself where, when I launched off the platform, me and the engine would collide quickly.

I checked my watch. The next train was seven or eight minutes away. I hoped it would be on time because I didn't want to talk myself out of it. But then, somebody else talked me out of it in my case, and into it in their case.

Not that what I was contemplating would be suicide. No. More like murder, I guess. Well, to be factual, it would be murder.

Two women were standing near me waiting for a train also. I thought they were in their mid-thirties if I was any judge. And I'm probably not. One was pretty, blonde, good figure. Her friend had short brown hair and a pretty face that was stained by tears. She was mumbling something I couldn't hear.

I shuffled closer, pushing past a couple of other people who shifted slightly to let me through.

"It was too much, Betty," the brunette said. "It was the sequence of it all. Repeatedly breaking my faith in him. How many times, I thought, would he continue to break my heart?"

The blonde put her arm over the friend's shoulder and pulled her slightly towards her. I shuffled a little bit closer to the brunette who was only about a metre or less from the platform edge. I still hadn't decided what I would do, but I was truly saddened to see this lovely- looking young woman in such a sad state.

"I think if you could just steel yourself to walk away from it, Harriet, you would get over it in time. Once you are out of his influence things would become clearer to you. You don't have to put up with this sort of crap."

I didn't agree with her. I knew that grief of this sort didn't go away very quickly. Mine hasn't. Every day is misery every time I wake up.

"I have tried to do that, Betty, but it hasn't worked so far. He keeps promising me that he will change, but all he does is change women, and all the time I'm the one he doesn't change and comes home to, breaking my heart over and over again. Now he says it's all over. He said that last night."

Betty looked around at the people standing nearby and lowered her voice a little. "There are plenty of fish in the sea, Harriet. It's just this time that is painful. I know how I would feel if Charlie was doing this to me." She paused. "I am sure he isn't doing that now."

But Harriet couldn't be consoled. In fact, she howled even louder, causing some discomfort to those around her who were obviously not wanting to hear this sort of thing while waiting for the train to go home. People began to edge a little further away from her. But not me. I moved closer. I couldn't let this tragic thing continue. I know how much I want to end my life and Harriet sounded like her life was as bad, probably worse, I don't know. I looked along the platform and saw the train was coming before I could decide exactly what I would do.

You must remember that this was my first time at either killing myself or anybody. Her crying was so dismal, so sad. She was so wet that even the top of her blouse was dripping.

The train was suddenly upon us, and I pushed somebody aside and shoved hard with my shoulder. I felt and heard rather than saw the body fly off the edge of the platform into the path of the train.

Betty screamed. Everyone screamed. I think I did too, but I knew I had done Harriet a good turn.

There was shock on her face as she went over the edge and into the path of the train. I'm sure my face registered even more shock because the terrified face looking up at us all as she fell was not Harriet's. It was Betty's.

And then she was gone except for blood on the line and part of the body projecting from under the train front. Harriet was on her knees screaming. What a pity I had made a mistake. Now I would have to make amends by trying again. This was very important because Harriet would be more despairing than ever. I'll have to make it up to her, by killing her. They were pushing forward, and I was trying to get away.

I was shaken up, as you would expect; it's not every day you kill somebody. Not even when it's for the best motives. As I went through the turnstile, I could hear the shouts and I could hear

Harriet screaming: "She was my best friend. My very best friend. I didn't expect her to jump. Hearing about my worries must have caused her to do that." And then she screamed in hysteria, her words indistinguishable, and I walked away.

A week or so later I faced up to the fact that I couldn't live with myself any longer. What my wife had done and what my best friend had done and what his friends had done all accumulated to absolute misery in me. How could I ever find someone else like Jenny? She was the absolute love of my life. She had been for two years. We were going to get married...now...

Last night I went down to the riverbank. To a nice quiet spot where not many people would be. There was a bridge over it at that point. I walked onto it and looked down into the water swirling around the rocks. The water was deepest there. I couldn't swim, so once I made the jump that would be the end of it for me. I would end up somewhere downstream, I supposed. People would wonder why I had done it. Maybe Jenny would come forward and say... No, she wouldn't say I loved him dearly. I thought he knew that. She wouldn't say that because she doesn't love me anymore. That is quite plain. What could be plainer than her saying I do not love you anymore! I don't want to know you anymore. I love someone else. I am going to move in with him...get out of my life. What could be plainer than that? I didn't have any other women friends. A few at work look down their noses at me. When I mentioned my sadness to one of them, it was all she could do to stop from laughing. I didn't understand that.

Suddenly, I realised I wasn't alone on the bridge. There was an older man standing, like me, looking into the depths of the water. I had never seen him before, even though I had been to that bridge many times with the same intention to end my life. Always I had been cowardly and walked away. Not today, I determined, not today. The man was tearing up pieces of paper. I moved closer and saw that they were photographs. Faces of people. I asked him what he was doing.

"I'm trying to get rid of the horrible life I live. It is all wrapped up in these photos of my family. I want to get rid of them all. Just as they have got rid of me."

"How can you say your family has given up on you? Or whatever it was you said? Just what has your family done?"

He looked at me for several moments before replying. His hands kept tearing photos into little pieces and dropping them into the water. As he tore them up, he was mumbling something or other. At last he spoke: "My wife and my two sons and three daughters: that was my family. Now none of them want anything more to do with me. They have kicked me out of their lives. And I love them so much still."

"How can such a thing happen, all those people? What did you do?" I moved closer to him.

He ignored my presence and kept tearing his photos up, but after a while he turned to me again and said: "I gamble too much. I lost our family home. Lost everything. My wife has had to go back to work just to earn enough money to live. They all blame me."

So they should, I thought, but didn't say.

I asked: "What are your plans now?" I was feeling a bit excited by now. This man was a lot sadder than I was. This meant that perhaps I wouldn't end my life tonight. He was only a slight figure, maybe in his sixties. He didn't look too happy. Understandably. I walked over to him till I was only half a metre away. He looked at me oddly, as if wondering about what the hell I was doing.

"When this bag of photos is empty, I walk away. Go over to that bench near the tree and sleep there tonight." He looked me straight in the eyes. "I don't have anywhere to live you see. I think it will be a painful night. I believe I will cry again. I know now that tears won't make any difference to my heartless family."

I stood near him for several minutes as he tore the remaining two photos and dropped them into the water. Lots of pieces of paper floating on the water now, some white, some showing up the other way, showing colour. At last he tipped the bag over and nothing came out. He bowed his head onto the railing, and I heard him sobbing. This was no good, I thought. Call me a softie but I couldn't resist helping him. I had to put the man out of his misery. No time for me to be selfish. I could do me another time. I am a strong man and quick when I need to be. I took a step towards him and grabbed the seat of his trousers and his shoulder and tipped him over the bridge. He looked up at me in horror, not gratitude, as he fell into the water. I realised I hadn't asked him if he could swim, so I watched with heart in mouth. I didn't want to be charged with attempted murder. But then he disappeared under the rushing water, and I went over to the other side of the bridge and looked down as he floated past. It wasn't long before he sank, then I didn't see him anymore. I walked out of the park onto the riverbank and stopped at a little convenience store to buy some cold meat for dinner. I was happy that I had helped another human soul. Given peace to somebody who was in great distress.

That was the beginning for me. I was so busy helping others week by week that I never actually got around to doing myself in. There were reports in the paper about the deaths and the police were suspicious that they weren't the suicides they had appeared to be at first. What if there had been a witness in some cases? I did get a bit worried.

One day I read in the paper that a Detective Inspector Smythe was on the case. I tracked down the station he worked at and followed him out one night at the end of his shift. He walked along the street and went into the pub, ordered at the bar, and took his glass of whatever it was - beer I think - to the table. I sat nearby and I watched him. He was alone and didn't give the appearance of waiting for anybody else. He ordered another beer and sat cradling it in his hands. He looked downcast. My hopes were raised by his demeanour. Maybe he was in bad straits, or in misery. Maybe I could help him, before he got onto me.

I picked up my beer and went over to his table and asked if it was okay to sit near him.

He looked at me suspiciously for a while, then nodded. I sat and drank silently for a few minutes. He drank quietly to himself. Then he said: "It's a tough life sometimes, isn't it, mate?"

This surprised me. This was the detective looking to me. Me who was helping people end their sad lives. I nodded and took another sip of beer.

"Doesn't it depress you, mate, all these deaths of our citizens? Being killed everywhere. At first, we all thought they were killing themselves. We put it down to suicide, but then there seemed to be too many of them."

"Yes," I agreed, "there does appear to be a spate of them. Why do you think they are not suicidal people?"

"It was my boss who first thought of this. The bugger put the job onto me. He said that too many people were dying mysteriously. So I now have to deal with it." He sighed. "As if I don't have enough on my mind without all this extra stuff. Enough misery of my own." He sipped some more beer before looking me in the eye. "Those people aren't the only ones who want to end it all."

"No, no," I agreed quickly. "You are right. I know there are a lot of very sad people around. Perhaps you are one of them." I certainly hoped so.

"I am a bit down at the moment," he said. "It's hard to take seriously in cases of this sort. You see," he looked down at his beer, of which I think he had been drinking too much. He was speaking too frankly for a Detective Inspector to a stranger in the pub. "I'm sick and tired of my life, so what can I do about it, mate?"

"Well, well," I volunteered, "maybe you could look at ways to end it all."

"Not as simple as that, mate. Good of you to be so helpful. But I don't see a way out of it all. My job now is to concentrate on catching this bastard."

"How do you know it is just one person?" I asked.

"I know a fair bit about it all," he said.

He drained his beer and stood. "Well, mate, time for me to go home to my lonely flat. I have worked enough hours today."

I waited until he had gone out the door and then rushed after him. I followed him along the street. My heart was pumping, my hopes were high. This man might be an ideal person for me to help out. Because it would help me also to get him off my back. What a delicious irony. He seemed a nice enough chap, but he was also very, very, very sad, I told myself.

It was a bit of luck that he didn't get into a car and drive away. He turned the corner and I followed him. In ten minutes, he reached his house. I almost caught up with him but made sure he didn't sense me coming.

He unlocked the door of his little home and disappeared inside.

Now what, I thought. What was a good way to do this so that it would appear he had taken his own life? This was a problem.

Maybe a fire would be a good thing? A fire that would appear to have been lit by the man himself. Did he smoke? He hadn't in the pub, but then you are not allowed to do that anymore anyway. Maybe he was dying for a smoke. I could hear him moving around inside. I waited nearby in the dark for what would have been an hour or so. The weather was fine, so I wasn't cold. But I was also quite warmed up by the thought of doing another good service for mankind.

Then with a bit of luck I saw him come around the side of his house with one of those big wheelie bins. It seemed quite light. I didn't think a man living alone would generate too much rubbish. There would be plenty of room inside the bin. Without thinking too much, and before he could take any action to prevent me running at him, I was on him grappling and trying to lift him over headfirst into the bin. But he was stronger than I expected, and we wrestled and wrestled. I thought I had him heading into the bin, but he kicked me, and I yelled and jumped away and he grabbed hold of me and tipped me into the bin headfirst. He slammed the lid down. I was stuck upside down, in the darkness panting for some time. I felt the bin moving, my feet popped the lid slightly open. The detective must've bent down and peered in. I heard him speak then.

"Well that just about wraps up another case for me, mate. Thanks for falling into my trap. I'm just waiting for the lads en route to arrive from headquarters and they'll take you away like the rubbish you are. We've been onto you for a week or two but haven't been able to catch you in the act.

"Now you will end up in prison, in a little cell of your own where you won't be able to get up to any mischief.

"Don't worry about my sadness, mate, I am okay."

I felt betrayed. He was happy as Larry. What a way to treat me. Me who was trying to help him.

"You say you are not living a miserable life?"

He laughed. "No, no don't you worry about that. My wife and the kids are standing on the doorstep clapping me. Another successful case. I'm the apple of their eyes you see." Then the bin was lifted roughly, jolted across the footpath, and dumped into the back of goodness knows what. Would that be the end of it for me? You never know with human beings, do you? Sometimes there's just no gratitude in people.

THE END

Murder is such a charged word. You know how some people fixate and won't let things go? They're called cops.
-Tim Dorsey

CHAPTER
12

The next morning, Cleary had made an appointment to see Stephen Martin. It was not to be until 11am, so he and Peter went first to talk again with the gardener, Jeremy James. This time, Jeremy wasn't in the garden, he was sitting at his dining room table with what looked like a catalogue of plants. He didn't get up but gestured towards chairs around the table. The detectives sat on either side of the long table.

Cleary spoke first. "Interesting reading?" He nodded at the colourful catalogue.

"I find it not only interesting, but informative and helpful to me in my job." He closed the catalogue. "Why do you want to see me again?"

"It is just routine, Mr James. Detective Sergeant York and I just have a few more questions to help clarify the picture."

"I didn't think I was in the picture."

Cleary ignored the comment. "You see, Mr James, we have been given conflicting statements about the relationship between you and Ms Nola Martin. We spoke to her yesterday, as you may already know, but we need to ask you again about your relationship."

Jeremy put both hands on the table and appeared to be about to stand up, but he relaxed and sat back. He looked directly at Cleary.

"We didn't think it was any big deal. We are friends."

Peter said: "A bit more than the usual friendship, I believe."

"Well… well, things happen. We are… attracted to each other." And he looked directly at Cleary. "I don't understand why my sex life has anything to do with your investigation of a suicide." He looked down at the catalogue and idly turned the pages. Then he looked up. "What's the point of all this?"

"We need to know of any antagonism or other strong emotions surrounding the people in the Martin household," Cleary said.

"But I don't belong to that household."

"George Martin recorded that during the night when he discovered you and Ms Martin together in bed – as I understand it – that Ms Martin was very angry with her father. And she told him that she was moving in with you. We didn't read anything that indicated you agreed with it."

"I suppose I did," Jeremy said. What young fellow wouldn't have agreed with it, Peter thought, but didn't say.

"Did this change of residence happen?"

Jeremy said: "Just two nights. But then Nola was stricken with guilt about deserting her father at a time of need."

"Because he was blind?" Peter said.

"Yes."

"Subsequent to that fracas, did you, Mr James, get into any further dispute or row with Mr Martin?"

"No."

"I understand Mr Martin said you were not going to be doing any gardening at his home anymore. That you had lost your job with him."

"He never followed that through. He welcomed me back two days later. And since then, our relationship had been friendly enough."

"And how would you rate your relationship with Ms Martin now?"

"It is going along quite nicely, thank you, Inspector."

"Did Mr Martin's wife or Mr Nagle show any more aggression towards Mr Martin because of that evening?"

Jeremy paused, his finger on one of the items towards the bottom of the left-hand page of the catalogue and looked up. "I don't think there was any animosity between any of them. But then I wasn't there all the time, was I? Nola certainly didn't come and tell me that anything there was causing her anguish."

Peter thought they probably never had much time left to talk about other matters.

They all stood up, with a squealing of chairs across the tiled floor.

"Thank you for your time, Mr James," Cleary said. "We appreciate it is a difficult time for you. You may be pleased to know that we will soon finalise this matter."

"You mean you will tell everyone that it was indeed a suicide?"

Cleary shook his head. "I can't tell you that yet. We shall see within a day or two. Thank you again."

Stephen Martin met the two detectives at the front door of his brother's house and welcomed them. He was a big man, taller and more thickset than his late brother. He had sandy hair and a tanned face; he wore a khaki shirt with the sleeves rolled up, and blue jeans. He looked the part of a countryman, but he was, in fact, a pharmacist who had a shop in Bathurst. As they walked down the hall, Stephen talked about the weather and country life and then as they entered the lounge room, Cleary said: "Are you staying here for a while?"

Stephen grinned. "Yes, there are plenty of bedrooms. I might be here for a couple of days. In and out. I hope I can help you in some way, detectives," he went on, "but I fail to see how I can, because I was not here at the time and, to tell you the truth, I am emotionally shattered.

"I loved George. We were very close as brothers, but not close in distance." He sat in an armchair with Cleary and Peter opposite him on the long lounge.

"I won't waste your time, Mr Martin," Cleary said, "I know you're a busy man with a business in another town. But I do appreciate you giving us this time."

Steve Martin didn't reply. He sat there with his hands clasped, leaning forward, arms between his knees. He waited for Cleary to speak again.

"You say you were nowhere near here on the day your brother died."

"No, I wasn't."

"Mr Martin, a neighbour has told us that on the night your brother died he saw someone of your build walking quickly along the street. It was about midnight. That person went around the side of the house. Would that have been you?"

Martin seemed surprised by this line of questioning. "Well... well, it could have been me. I certainly came here late one night." Pause. "Yes, I think you are right. It might have been the night George died."

Cleary said, "Surely you would remember if it was the night your brother died?"

"His death was such a shock to me. I have my days all mixed up." He paused again. "My staff laughed the other day when I went in on my day off. Would you believe that the boss doesn't even know what days he works?" He chuckled. The detectives didn't smile.

"So, you were here within hours of Mr George Martin's death?" Cleary said, "You must have left in the early hours of the morning. Do you know what time you left this house?"

"Well, I had to get back to open the shop… I guess it must have been around 1am. Yes, yes."

"George was still alive then?" Peter said.

"I'm sure he was, he was asleep in bed."

He clasped his hands and relaxed back into the chair. The detectives glanced at each other, then Cleary said, "Why did you come for such a quick visit?"

"I sometimes do. Or have done. From time to time, I have to see business associates in Sydney's CBD." He looked at Cleary. "I can give you their names if you would like."

"Do you come by car? When you visit here that is."

"Of course."

"The person who reported seeing someone coming to this house on the night your brother died, said that person was walking hurriedly along the street. There did not appear to be a car in the picture."

Martin didn't answer immediately. He looked uncomfortable. Eventually, he said: "I had parked in the side street near a vacant allotment. You can check that allotment out for yourselves later if you wish. I have a car that makes a loud noise when it starts up, I don't like to disturb the neighbours in the early hours of the morning. I parked where there is no house." He smiled at Cleary.

"Very neighbourly of you," Peter said. He wrote something in his notebook.

Martin smiled. "I try to be."

Cleary said: "Now, Mr Martin, I know you are a pharmacist. Were you aware that your brother may have been taking sleeping drugs recently?"

Martin looked surprised. "I didn't know that. He certainly didn't need any help getting to sleep. He often told me how he quickly went off each night."

"It seems, according to our forensic guy, that your brother took a lot of sleeping tablets before he hanged himself - or was hanged by someone else."

"Oh my God. That doesn't make any sense, does it, Inspector?" He looked from one detective to the other, then back focusing on Cleary. "George never asked me for drugs of any sort. Have you checked with his GP? Dr Mallory?"

Cleary nodded. "We have. He says the same as you. He hasn't prescribed sleeping tablets at any time for your brother."

"We'll look further into that. Make a note of that, Sergeant. Another thing, Mr Martin, did you know that your brother had a terminal condition?"

He sat back in the chair and Peter thought he had been surprised by the question. However, after pausing for a few seconds he spoke confidently.

"Yes. Sadly, I did know that. I don't think anyone else in the house knew. George told me some months ago and asked me to keep it quiet."

There was something in the man's way of speaking that made Peter wonder if he was telling the truth.

"So you knew he had… sorry, what exactly was it? I'm not good at these medical things at times. Peter, you must have it recorded in your notebook –"

Peter took his time turning the pages. They both waited for Stephen Martin to offer the answer. He didn't.

"How did he describe it to you, Mr Martin?"

He paused. "Umm, he wasn't clear about that… I think he was too upset to talk clearly about it. Yes. Terrible, just terrible. Poor George. You know, I don't know why he would have killed himself if he knew he was dying."

"That is part of the mystery, isn't it, Mr Martin? I don't think that anyone who knew in advance that George was going to die would have murdered him."

"My brother looked after his health very well, Inspector. At the slightest thing he would see the doctor. His attitude was the same as if you hear a noise in your car, you don't let it develop until it's a great big expense or something damaging to the engine or other part of the car. You know he used to rail against waiting around in the doctors' rooms." He chuckled. "He hated that, you know."

Peter said: "Most people hate that."

Martin looked at his watch. He looked up at Cleary and asked if they would be much longer. Cleary said they were about done but might need to talk to him at another time.

"So, you are still suspicious about the cause of George's death?"

Cleary nodded.

"But, surely, Inspector, if a man hangs himself. That should be obvious that it was suicide. How could –"

"I believe we will have the answer to that within a day or two. In the meantime, we have your address in Bathurst and, if necessary, we can contact you there. I don't think Peter would mind a ride into the country. Would you Peter?"

"I would enjoy it, sir."

Peter was glad that they finished earlier than expected, because he wanted to get home and try to finish the manuscript. He knew Inspector Cleary was getting impatient with the lack of progress despite his belief that there were clear clues in the manuscript. But he also wanted to get in an hour or two before dinner so he would not be up so late. He knew that Jan had not been feeling the best over the last couple of days and was showing annoyance at the hours he spent every night with that 'damned book'. So, he grabbed a coffee and some biscuits and sat down and began reading.

> its so good to be in a quiet home for a change
>
> hey what the hell hello is there somebody up there

who did that trying to kill me threw that bloody bucket at me

what is it dad I heard you call out why are you so agitated

you're halfway down the stairs with a bucket at your feet

I didn't think anyone was home what are you doing upstairs

well I am home and was trying to sleep while youre kicking the bucket

not funny Nola somebody just tried to knock me down with a bloody bucket a heavy bucket I heard it rattling down the stairs banged into my legs and if I hadnt been holding on I would have been knocked over and lying at the bottom of the stairs dead or worse crippled for life

dad theres nobody else up here as far as I know

I guess that makes you the number one suspect

so you reckon you're on my bucket list not a very efficient way to kill you throwing a bucket down the stairs and hoping it hits you

well how else can you explain it buckets dont fall down stairs all by themselves

believe me dad there's nobody else up here perhaps fido knocked it and it overbalanced

a cats not strong enough to push a metal bucket over

well dad I just don't know Ill come down and have a look at your legs pull your trousers up so I can look at your shins

I can feel the blood lucky if theyre not broken

Ill come down Ill clean it up and take you to the doctor

thats all well and good Nola but who's got it in for me

youre so paranoid

you would be too if people were throwing buckets at you no need to scoff Im the one with the injury

there how does that feel

thank you I'm glad you are here

Ill help you to the car and well see a doctor

well probably have to wait a bit you know how it is give you something more to be grumpy about

I know but at least sitting around there gives me ideas for stories like the one I got last time I was hanging around in the doctors waiting room with all those other poor buggers on uncomfortable chairs for hours they must think finding out if we had a fatal disease or not wasn't that bloody urgent

WAITING FOR GOOD
A SHORT STORY BY GEORGE MARTIN

At first, the man in the pale blue suit was resigned to his fate. It wasn't a new situation to him. But, as the minutes passed and the wall clock ticked on, he became irritated, annoyed, bored.

And, oddly, he felt a tingle of unease.

It was just the waiting. Affected his mind. Always did. He knew he was an impatient man. But he was also a busy man. He could arrange his daily work to a smooth-running schedule. Why couldn't this place, also?

The receptionist — or was she the nurse? —was out of the room. Not that it mattered. Despite her crisp white uniform and shiny white shoes and professional smile that went on and off like a red, pink and white neon sign, she didn't do anything to reduce waiting times.

The man in the pale blue suit felt the uneasiness again. He wondered why. He'd waited like this many times before. In many waiting rooms. Right name for them, he thought. Just a bloody nuisance, he told himself. Nothing to fear — unless they found something fatal.

His eyes flicked around the room. Several others were waiting like him.

Usual waiting room bunch — an elderly couple with heads close to each other, a middle-aged woman knitting, a mother with a child on her lap and the woman in bright red who had come in just before him. Young, pretty, blonde, with blue eyes that were sweeping the room also.

Wonder what her problem was. Looked healthy enough. Whatever it was, she was still waiting. Like him. Although she, too, had briefly seen the doctor.

She smiled at him. He just frowned. Her eyes seemed agitated, and he looked away.

He felt there were more people in the room, but he couldn't turn to see any wider than his eyes moved. Odd. Must be the injections.

At least it was a quiet place. The others were waiting more stoically than he was, he thought. No impatient mutterings. But then, none from him so far either.

Just low murmurs of conversation. Usual stuff. Even the kid was behaving himself — or herself, he wasn't sure which.

They must be seeing different doctors, he thought. Hell, bugger them. It only mattered that he was wasting so much time here, sitting in this uncomfortable chair among a mob of strangers.

He wondered how long had passed since he first walked in. He tried to look at his watch and was surprised he couldn't. Couldn't lift his left arm, couldn't bend his head down. He moved his eyes down towards his wrist, but his sleeve covered the watch.

He could see the edge of the red clock on the wall facing him. He couldn't see what time it was.

He knew it had been a long time. Longer than a doctor's appointment should take.

To be fair, he had already seen the doctor — a specialist in abdominal problems. Briefly. Then a couple of injections and wheeled back here. To wait some more.

God knows if he'd needed to go this far. Most likely nothing wrong. But he had always believed in checking any malfunction in his bodily systems. Always best to catch these things early.

So far none had turned out to be anything serious.

God, how many hours had he wasted just waiting for bloody arrogant doctors to see him. In all those years none had ever apologised for keeping him waiting. Not one. Ever.

The woman in red was still smiling. She was a lot more patient than he was. Patient. There's the word. Must be why they call us that. We have to be bloody patient to go through this stuff.

The specialist had been friendly enough when he got in, not long after he'd arrived. So soon, in fact, he'd thought it was his lucky day. First, the young woman had gone in, then just ten minutes later, it had been his turn.

"Come in, Mr Ballard, take a seat," the doctor had said, indicating a chair in front of his desk.

"Now, what's the trouble? I see you've just come in without a GP's referral…"

"I just like to manage my own health. See who I expect is best able to help me. I don't need to waste time with middlemen."

The specialist frowned.

"Hmm. I see. You'll not get any medical refund, you realise…"

"I don't care about that," the man in the pale blue suit broke in.

"Well, you're not the only one these days. I get a few like you."

"Let's get on with it, can we," he had interrupted. "I've wasted too much time already."

The man in the pale blue suit remembered how little interested the specialist had seemed when he explained about his stomach problems. No doubt he'd heard it many times from many patients.

"Hmm, what does your wife think about this?"

"I never said I was married…"

"Partner, then…"

"Whether I have partners, wives or nothing isn't important, right, and I don't care for your bloody probing into my private life."

Remembering how he had put the little, trumped up, so-called specialist in his place, the man in the pale blue suit smiled, inside, without moving his mouth.

The doctor was short, balding, metal-rimmed glasses magnifying piggy eyes. Very unattractive. Unlikely anyone loved him either, which made the man in the pale blue suit wish he could smile. But the receptionist seemed to adore him, fluttering in and out of his office with big smiles and small talk.

After poking and prodding him for a few minutes, the doctor had said he'd have to give him an injection, "Or two", and then examine him a "bit more intimately, without pain".

No pain sounded good to the man.

The man had asked what it was, and the doctor had told him not to worry. They'd soon get rid of that. "What's that?" he'd asked.

"Don't worry anymore, Mr Ballard." And then came the needles.

The receptionist helped the doctor. Probably a nurse, he thought. They'd sat him in a wheelchair first. After a few minutes he had lost feeling in his limbs and he got drowsy. He vaguely recalled being wheeled into the waiting room.

Through a white curtain, it seemed to the man's foggy mind. Through a small changing room.

The nurse/receptionist's voice droned in his consciousness: "You just wait here first, Mr Ballard. I understand you don't like to wait." And then it sounded like she giggled.

He thought he heard a voice, doctor's or nurse/receptionist's saying: "And how are you going, Miss Robbins? Comfortable?" Probably talking to the woman in red. No answer from anyone.

The man in the pale blue suit was getting more and more inpatient. This was ridiculous. Then he saw a movement and voices. He swivelled his eyes and saw the doctor's nurse wheeling the young woman out.

At last, he thought. Surely, I'll be next. The others can wait their turns, whenever that was.

His vision was blurred now but he could feel some eyes on him. Probably hoping like he was that they would be next. Bugger them. Every patient for himself. Let them wait.

He really, really, wanted to see what time it was. He knew time was passing because the clock was ticking. Odd, he thought. He was sure there hadn't been a clock in the wall before. He had had a good look around back then. No clock.

He realised the seating was different, too. This was a different waiting room. Oh well, whatever, wherever, he just wanted to get out.

After a screamingly long wait, during which he became more drowsy and more fearful, he sensed movement and heard voices. They were wheeling the woman in red back in.

At last. Please. Let me be next. Surely, it's me next.

He was. And he felt a tear run down his immobile face as they wheeled him towards the doctor's office. Thank God. He saw the young woman's face as he was wheeled past. Her red lips were smiling. A happy soul, he thought. So that must have worked out all right, he thought.

Then, fleetingly, he caught her eyes. There was terror in them.

Soon, he was being given another injection and he lost consciousness. His queries about what was happening were lost in nothingness.

The man in the pale blue suit woke again. He was back in the waiting room. His view was slightly different this time and he thought he was sitting in one of the room's armchairs, not the wheelchair.

He could see the woman in red across from him. Her bright red lips were still smiling but her eyes were filled with horror.

He heard voices to his left and moved his eyes to see the specialist and the nurse/receptionist sitting together on a two-person sofa. There was a small coffee table in front of them and they were eating and drinking.

Afternoon tea. The nurse/receptionist raised a delicate little white cup to her lips and drank with a slurp. She giggled and the specialist pushed a piece of cake towards her mouth. She seemed to suck it in with delight. The doctor sipped tea.

"Well, that was a good day's work, Miss Carter, hmm?"

"Indeed it was, Geoffrey. Just look at our group now. Coming along nicely."

"Only need a couple more to get the balance right."

"Yes, Geoffrey. You have done well. Today's couple just right: male, female, young, older, and the lovely bright red dress such a good contrast with the pale blue suit."

"Hmm, lucky there. Quite nice."

The man in the pale blue suit realised he was having a nightmare and would soon wake up. He saw that they were staring at him. The doctor spoke.

"Ah, Mr Ballard, how are you feeling? I'm happy to tell you that your stomach troubles are over…"

"All your troubles are over," the nurse giggled.

"Oh, don't be cruel to the man, dear. He's still getting adjusted to his new…"

"Role," she broke in, "as a waiting room patient. Don't you love our wonderful little tableau, Mr Ballard?"

"Hmm, you and Miss Robbins will have to wait a little bit longer. You can enjoy each other's company for a while before the last of your life leaves."

"You can look around a little, and see what a comfy place we've created here," the nurse/receptionist said.

"Geoffrey and I relax in here every afternoon. So good to sit and enjoy a waiting room without complaining patients, isn't it, Geoffrey?"

"Indeed, it is, Miss Carter. No pressure. No abuse. Just a quiet recording of patients being…"

"Patient," she giggled and took another sip.

The doctor got up and walked close to the man in the pale blue suit. He bent down and peered into the man's eyes.

"And don't worry — too much. Time will pass and you will no longer know where you are. Or anything.

"Just takes a few weeks for my special sort-of taxidermy method to take effect. Be patient, can't hurry these things."

The man in the pale blue suit looked away from the magnified piggy eyes.

He looked at the knitting woman whose work had not lengthened in the past several hours, at the mother with a perfectly behaved, non-fidgeting toddler, at Miss Robbins and saw her shoes were on the wrong feet — and then at the elderly couple, who looked back with their dead grey eyes.

"More tea, Geoffrey?"

"Why not, dear? We've got the time."

"It's a nice tableau…but I think we could do with something more. Maybe somebody in uniform."

She said: "Yes, perhaps a sailor or a policeman. Maybe one of those who come from time to time enquiring about missing people."

The big piggy eyes pushed closer to the man in the pale blue suit. "Or a nurse," he whispered.

One of the eyes winked at the man in the pale blue suit.

THE END

It is better to live in a corner of the housetop than in a house shared with a quarrelsome wife
-*Proverbs 21:9*

CHAPTER 13

Peter was weary when he sat down to continue reading the manuscript. He knew that Jan was annoyed at the time he was spending on this night after night. Tired or not, he intended to read as much as possible tonight. He hoped it would come to an end soon.

> gods sake George can't you even cope with getting a piece of meat into your mouth
>
> be patient mum
>
> I have tried to be patient Nola but just watching my husband struggling to do a very basic thing eating his food at the dinner table well it makes me sick

are you going to stick your bib in now Nagle

I just want to say we should all concentrate on our own plates

Margot thats where the action is for you enjoy what you cooked its delicious

you are right Mark it shouldnt be a problem because a plate isnt a very big area

I wish George would cut completely through the meat before he lifts the fork to his mouth

well that was another fun family meal fun for the others perhaps for me it was a taste of humiliation bites of embarrassment belittling drips and drops throughout I used to enjoy eating out sitting around a table in a restaurant with family and friends I never do that now

I dont want to be part of the entertainment in any of those places I hadn't realised how hard it is to eat when you cant see what is on your plate it should be easy.

its a bugger when I dont know gravy has spilled off the side of the plate onto my shirt and trousers

now dinner isnt pleasant even in the safety of my own home entertaining only Margot and Nola and Nagle how often the conversation stopped and I knew their eyes were fixed on me struggling to cut right through a piece of steak sometimes Nola offered to help me

but that only made me feel like a toddler in a highchair again I should wear a bib I know that I just cant tell when I have stains of sauce or gravy or ice cream or anything on my shirt but everyone around the table can see it

you can lead a blind man to his plate but you cant help him eat

I try to work out some strategies to deal with my food every day Nola sometimes helps by telling me where the various items of food are on the plate potatoes at nine o'clock, sausages at six o'clock, beans at twelve oclock but I still must be more careful about cutting things right through before I lift the fork the conversation stops at such moments I know they are all focusing on the end of my fork even Nola

sometimes I bravely carry on as if Im quite happy to have a big piece of meat or a big piece of other food on my fork and shove it all in my mouth and chomp into and eventually swallow other times I put it back on my plate and saw and saw until it is cut right through I lift it to my mouth and smile around the faces

Margot said tonight I swear youre just pretending to do it this way George otherwise there wouldnt be any of this pantomime night after night

he is not pretending mum its quite easy to tell that he cant see its one of the side effects of blindness Nola sharply reminded Margot

this would be an even more lonely place for me if it wasnt for my lovely daughter

it should be obvious to everyone that I am blind completely everywhere I look is like looking at a blackboard not even the lights above the table help

I have to reach out when there is a teacup in front of me feeling gingerly with my fingers until I find the handle and then lift it carefully trying very hard to keep it level so I dont spill it over the edge it is often a triumph when the hot liquid reaches my mouth

I wish I was pretending I could sneak looks at what is going on around me they wouldnt realise that I could see the thought makes me chuckle but now back to my writing

LOVE IS BLIND
A SHORT STORY BY GEORGE MARTIN

Brenda was very pleased with herself when she found a reason for losing her sight so suddenly. She was quite pleased that she had discovered how to be completely blind, so suddenly. She knew that being blind was going to be wonderful. She had enjoyed telling Ralph about this. She was not surprised when her husband didn't show a lot of sadness that his wife of fifteen years was going to be blind. Unable to see anything she was doing.

But the thing that made Brenda most happy about her impending complete blindness was that it was not going to happen. She was going to be able to see as well as ever. And she would be able to watch Ralph and see what he was getting up to, day by day, night by night.

Brenda had thought of this ploy a couple of months earlier. She had planned it meticulously. Worked out the details. She knew it would be difficult to carry on the same way in everything she was doing. She knew she would have to stop driving the car. Ralph would have to take her some places. To the shops, to appointments with eye specialists who she never actually saw once she was in the offices. She would sit for a while outside the offices and then go out again and call Ralph to come and pick her up.

She read a lot about blindness. Tried to memorise the things that she shouldn't do. She couldn't cook some of the things she normally did. She had to pretend to Ralph that this was a very difficult task, and sometimes meals wouldn't taste as well as they used to. She would sometimes spill things, deliberately knock things over. And all the time she was laughing inside.

Ralph had asked her at the beginning what was causing it. "But this is extraordinary, darling," he had said. "It is not often, surely, that sight goes so suddenly."

"The doctor is looking into it very carefully. She says it is rare. But it seems the retinas in both my eyes are detaching. All those little nerve cells sit in a little blanket over blood vessels that provide oxygen to the ganglion retinal nerves or whatever. She said something like that anyway."

Ralph looked at her. He didn't realise that she could tell that he was looking at her.

"Is there anything they can do? Any medicine, drops, surgery?" She wasn't sure that he was hopeful of anything helping her. She could see his brain ticking over with the idea that he would be able to carry on his long-lasting affair with Shirley in plain sight.

"I may have left it too late, Ralph. I think I'm doomed to permanent blindness."

She knew her husband, her unfaithful husband, was facing his own doom. The whole charade planned so that she could murder him.

She found it fun when she walked into the bedroom one day and found the two of them in the bed. She was supposed to be away for the rest of the day but had crept back for just this reason. She opened the door, and she heard a gasp. She could see them both there on the bed naked. His mistress had her hand over her mouth. Brenda gave an innocent smile and said: "Are you in here Ralph? I can't see you, so I don't know if you're here or not. Just say something. Or make a movement. Just something so I know you're here. I thought you were going to be at work while I was away.

"It's just that I thought I heard some noises as I walked into the hallway."

Brenda was enjoying this. She could see all their embarrassment. She almost laughed out loud when she saw Ralph trying to cover up the body of a woman lying alongside him. He had rolled over and Brenda could see that he wouldn't be doing anything more with her for a little while.

Ralph was spluttering. Trying to find some words. At first, he'd been shocked at being discovered in this position. Gradually he had relaxed as was apparent and realised that his wife could not see anything in the room.

"I... I... didn't feel well at the office and eventually... eventually Bob came over and suggested I take the rest of the day off. I was so grateful for that. Just not feeling well. So that's —"

"So that's why you're lying here in bed, is it?" Brenda asked.

"Yes, yes, that's... that's exactly right." He rolled over onto his side with his back to the woman hiding under the sheet. Brenda thought he was trying to signal to her that she didn't need to hide because his wife couldn't see. Yes, Brenda was loving this whole entertaining tableau. "But...but...but, darling, but why are you here? I thought you would be at the shops until at least closing time. You always are." Then he thought again and paused. "Of course, I know you can't see, now, but I thought Liz was taking you there."

Brenda smiled. "I'm not well myself. Must be something going around, hey, Ralph?"

Ralph rolled across to the edge of the bed and sat with his feet on the carpet. He reached back behind him pulled the sheet back and patted her shoulder, signalling it was alright. That they couldn't be seen. She rolled over the other way and sat on the edge of the bed, her bare legs going down onto the sheet onto the floor. Ralph stood up.

"Well, darling, I am feeling a bit better now. I stripped down a little bit and I got into bed. I know you don't like me getting under the sheets with my clothes on.

"You are so right, Ralph. Much better to take your dirty clothes off before you get into the bed."

She saw him move across to the room to the chair and get dressed again.

"I just had time have to pull my outer garments off. I'm not fully naked, you know." He chuckled as if he had made a funny comment.

There was a sudden hiccup and Ralph tried to cover it up by hiccupping deliberately himself. But Brenda knew it was coming from his Shirley who had put a hand over her mouth trying to keep it in. She hiccupped again.

"You have bad hiccups there, Ralph, are you okay?"

He said he was and went to the bathroom and got a glass of water.

He came out and said "I'll just have this water here. That should stop them. Sorry, dear."

He handed the cup to the woman sitting on the edge of the bed. She threw her head back and took a big draft of water. She handed the glass back to Ralph. She stood up and Brenda could see why Ralph had found it hard to end his relationship with this woman. Wow, what a body, and long dark hair going down her back, yes, she was a beauty. But soon she would be in mourning. Mourning for the end of the relationship. For the end of Ralph. And, perhaps, she had a sudden thought, perhaps she would not be around anymore either.

Now there was an idea. Why not get rid of both of them? She would think about altering her basic plan.

Brenda walked towards where Shirley was sitting, tapping along with her long white cane. She stood there facing Shirley and looked up at Ralph who had turned pale. "I suppose you have left the bed clothes all a mess, have you Ralph?"

She lifted the cane and poked around the sheets alongside Shirley who seemed paralysed. "Yes, what a mess." She lifted the cane and poked Shirley in the stomach. A squeal like a mouse came between the fingers that covered Shirley's mouth.

"Did you hear that, Ralph?"

"I think it was a bed spring."

"Couldn't be that you're not on the bed, are you?"

Shirley rolled backwards and then half crawled towards the edge of the bed.

"Yes, I'm sitting down on the bed now." Brenda could see he was still standing, and Shirley had pushed past him and was quickly dressing. She rushed around the bed and out the door. Brenda smiled at the sound of click.

"Odd sounds in this room today, Ralph. Squeaking bed and the door clicking closed by itself. Are you still in here?"

He went to the door, opened it, looked out. He closed it firmly. "I think it's alright. Maybe you didn't close it properly when you came in and it clicked shut then."

Brenda didn't think her husband saw his mistress again. It seemed Shirley had been spooked by the poltergeist in the room.

And so it was for many months, with Brenda saying how her sight was not showing any improvement, and her doctor saying there was no hope of getting her sight back. She could see that Ralph was not very concerned about this at all. Brenda thought he intended to find someone to replace Shirley.

The time came when Brenda got bored with carrying on this game. It was a game to her, but it had a deadly consequence at the end. She didn't love Ralph anymore. She hated him.

One night while Ralph was asleep, she went to the garage and removed the spark plugs from the engine. She knew all about these things. She wasn't a dumb blonde.

So, the next morning Ralph couldn't drive to work. He had to walk down to the end of the road and catch a bus. During the day, Brenda replaced the spark plugs. She drove the car out of the garage and drove around the suburb.

She knew the bus timetable and she had checked with Ralph to make sure he was coming on the five thirty bus. He was.

The street was a long one with no trees and there were hardly any people around.

Brenda sat in the car a block from the bus stop and waited. The bus was on time, and Brenda saw her husband get out and walk up the street towards her. He was the only one to get off as she had expected. It wasn't a busy route. She revved the car up and drove it down the road, accelerating until it was going a hundred kilometres an hour. It was going a bit more than that by the time it hit Ralph and sent him flying over the fence into the front yard of a house. She accelerated away, then drove to the nearby railway station, where she parked and mingled with the commuters coming from the station.

She felt safe in her blue overalls and a black wig. No one would recognise her. She walked quickly to a phone box and rang the police. She reported the car had been stolen. And walking very quickly home, in the block before their house, she removed the wig and went inside.

The police came to the house later to report the dreadful news that her husband had been mowed down, not their words, by a hit-and-run driver. Brenda cried. One of the cops offered her his hanky to wipe her eyes.

"Poor Ralph. To go like that. I loved him so much. And I will miss him, dreadfully, and..."

She tried not to be too melodramatic. It was hard to sound as if she was grieving greatly. But she did her best.

One of the cops said: "When did you last see your husband?"

"I... I guess it was about two months ago."

They were startled by this news. And asked where she had been. Or where he had been.

She told them she was blind. A sudden loss of sight caused detached retinas, she believed.

The other cop said: "It seems, Mrs Wilson, that your husband may have been run down by his own car."

Brenda shrieked. "Hold on. It was stolen. I reported it to you guys a while ago. How could that be?"

The cops looked at each other. The first one said: "It is a very sad event. A sad coincidence." He paused. "A tragic, yes, a tragic coincidence, Mrs Wilson."

"But don't you worry yourself about that aspect," the other cop said, "we will get the one who did it."

They asked if she needed someone to comfort her. To be with her tonight. She said she had a friend, Liz, who she was sure would come and stay with her for a while tonight.

"That's good. And we will check on you later if you like. And we will let you know if we catch the one who did it."

"Thank you, officer, you are so kind. I'm sure I will be alright. We had been married for a long time. And so, I will miss him greatly."

"I'm sure you will. We normally would ask you to come and identify him, but…" He paused and looked into the room before continuing, "You obviously can't do that, Mrs Wilson, can you?"

Brenda tried not to laugh. "No, of course not, I can't. You know, I am pleased that I won't have to do that gruesome task. His parents could but they are overseas at the moment."

The cop said: "Do you have a good clear photo. A recent photo that we might take and help with our ID?" Brenda turned around and walked over to the cabinet in the lounge room. She picked up a big photo, hesitated, put it down. She reached for a smaller one in a silver frame. "This one is clearer, I think." Then she gasped.

"That's very interesting, now, Mrs Wilson, that was very clever of you." The other cop nodded.

"We will have to talk further with you Mrs Wilson. And with your eye specialist. Can you give us his or her name, please?"

THE END

What is Christmas? It is tenderness for the past,
courage for the present, hope for the future
-*Agnes M. Pahro*

CHAPTER
14

Peter looked at his watch again. After midnight. He sighed and picked up his third cup of coffee. He stretched his arms and moved his head around to ease the stiffness in his neck. Then he turned to the next page in the manuscript.

> hohoho there'll be none of that happy christmas stuff around this house not this year probably not ever again long ago when Nola was little we had happy family christmases even providing gifts from santa claus after we had discussed it Margot and me we thought it would be all right to go along with the myth of santa claus big mistake
>
> Nola cried because she said the gifts santa had given her were not as good as the ones her own mummy

and daddy gave her I thought thats as it should be I didn't want some mythical man getting credit for all the money we spent on gifts from him so I insisted we give the best gifts the ones she would love I wanted them to come from us so the piddling little ones that she saw on Christmas morning in the big bag were a shock to our little girl she knew what friends of hers were expecting and in due time received

from then on after the whole myth thing was explained and the magic was broken for Nola christmases became consistently boring mundane family affairs for just the three of us

about ten years ago when I first put the lights up around the house I thought we had created a bright new christmas tradition I know sitting up on the top of this hill as our house does that our display was the envy of the neighbourhood each year I would get up on the ladder string lights around test them out and voilà what a lovely sight people would come along our street driving slowly or walking just to see what we had

and then this year it all went awry Margot was trying to dictate what we should have Nola was making other suggestions to contradict her mums ideas and Nagle bloody Nagle he thought he should run the show scrambling up and down the ladder like an overweight chimpanzee and he knew more about electrical wiring and reckoned he knew more than I did my light displays were fine before he came along and even Jeremy from next door butted in this year he is only around this house to do the gardening and now he seems to bob up in and out of our house and there he was out in our front yard pointing and shaking his head trying to tell us what to do about our light display

I was determined to do it the way I had always done it Jeremy and Nola got the ladder and extended it to the roof but when I started to climb up all hell broke loose you would think I had committed a crime

Nola shouted no dad you cant see what youre doing

Margot screamed at me dont be an old fool George you cant do that how can you go up the ladder when you are blind and when you get to the top if you ever do how will you know what youre doing

she was right of course but pride wouldnt let me stop pride wouldnt let me take notice of that amount of common sense I started to put my first foot on the ladder and then grab hold with my arms and put my other foot on the next rung it felt all right the ladder was holding I was getting a bit higher and a bit higher not as fast as previous years but I knew how to be cautious

Nagle shouted Mr Martin you will be stuck if you keep going up there like that you wont be able to feel your way right to the top

as if he knew

I am perfectly capable of climbing a ladder thank you I said

I didnt feel it

mr Martin Jeremy shouted you dont have cables and lights with you you wont have them up there to string along the roof

Margot and Nagle started laughing not the ho ho ho of santa claus something nastier than that

Nola called out and I could tell she was worried for me I paused halfway up I was a fool to attempt that I thought I could do what I had done the past ten years I thought I couldnt put a foot wrong what an idiot I can't believe I tried to do something for which eyes are so important but what the hell arent they needed for everything we do I did put a foot wrong my right foot slipped off the rung suddenly I had one leg dangling at the back of the ladder and the other at the front and I was only hanging on with one hand because it had slipped off

Nola screamed Margot laughed Nagle pointed and said look at the mess the old fool has got himself into

Jeremy ran to the foot of the ladder and started to climb up it was getting dark and I didn't think they would be able to see very well soon either after all the lights werent on yet Nagle ran over and pushed Jeremy aside

leave this to me sonny he said he then clambered up the ladder to me I don't know what he did or how he did it I just know that before I could know what was happening I was over his shoulders with legs dangling on one side and my arms waving about on the other

no wonder they all laughed I am being unfair Nola wasn't laughing she was crying as my head bumped around on the downward path I heard Jeremy comforting her

we reached the bottom and Nagle dropped me there I was half sitting half lying on my back not seeing what anyone else was doing but I knew I was a figure of fun to one or two of them

I went inside and got a cup of coffee for myself later they all came in thought it would cheer me to know that the lights were all on now all the lights for Christmas were up on our roof Jeremy said are you okay now mr Martin that was very brave of you to go up the ladder when you are blind

bloody stupid Margot said

Nola offered to get me another cup of coffee I accepted her offer because other people make better coffee than I can make I either have too much milk or not enough or it's too close to the top of the mug to be carried safely

life is often like this I must try to cheer myself up again

I get myself out of these depressions by writing another story thats what Ill do now.

THE MAN WHO PUT UP CHRISTMAS DARKS
A SHORT STORY BY GEORGE MARTIN

It's good to be outside again. In the sun. So bright. There's Mrs Bailey down there, waddling along. As always. Still large. Red and white polka dots popping in and out of the shade under the trees. Sun's stinging my eyes a bit. Only to be expected after being in the dark for so many months.

Mustn't complain. Who'd care? Who ever does, now? Not since those early years when my Beatrice wondered what had happened to me. She wailed and cried a lot. I saw some of it, down on the street. People hugging her and consoling her. An embrace here, a pat there, much wiping of tears. But life — or this — goes on, and on, and Beatrice eventually got on with her life. I missed her for a long time. But life goes…

Oh, there's Peter Mancombe. Wonder how his business is going this year. Seems jolly enough, talking with Bob Merrill. Both waving their hands around a bit. Oops, old Pete nearly hit Mrs Bailey then as she wobbled past. Don't think she noticed, though.

Bob seems to have gotten over the loss of Patty. Nice little girl who settled in after a while. As we do. Wonder if she's watching her dad.

The front door creaks open below me, and I hear Silas Tweep walking on the verandah again. The old man's got more stuff to put up, more of his unusual Christmas decorations.

Tonight, again, town folk will come into the street, gawking and "Ooh-ahhing" at the bright Christmas lights and ornaments on all the other houses. And on their lawns, Santas and reindeers and fat little elves and, oddly, a large illuminated green frog next door.

And, again, they'll shake their heads outside Mr Tweep's place. Some will laugh at his "decorations". Some will just hurry past. A few foolish ones will jeer and call out things like "You're spoiling the street, Tweep" and "Why don't you get proper Christmas lights, old man?" and "Hey, Scrooge, why do you hate Christmas?".

A favourite taunt each festive season is "They're not Christmas lights, they're Christmas darks". And the crowd laughs. And sometimes people chant "Christmas darks. Christmas darks". Dumb, really. Some kids shout out insults like "Dopey ol' Silas Tweep" and "Silas Tweep, what a creep".

That's what Patty said. Once.

And I, up here, cringe and shudder a bit, knowing there will be more Christmas "darks" next year.

Mr Tweep is on a stepladder hanging his black crepe paper from the verandah ceiling. I can't actually see him. But in years past I've heard passers-by make comments about what he gets up to. He strings twisted black lengths of paper and ribbon back and forth under the verandah roof. Later, he'll stretch some of it out and up the front of his house, connecting this black, unfestive web with our line of dark balls, which swing in the light breeze above the verandah roof.

He hums quietly as he works. A slow, dirge-like tune I've never recognised. Depressing. The hammer thuds as he drives in some more nails. A softer thud tells me he's missed the nail and hit his thumb, or finger. A loud curse startles the two men on the footpath. Bob says something and they separate and with vague waves go in different directions along the street.

The front door creaks again, then slams. Mr Tweep has gone inside.

I enjoy my short month in the sunshine. I'm glad we are here. If it were the northern hemisphere Christmas would be darker and much colder. Imagine being shut up in a box for much of the year and only coming out when it was very cold. Brrr. Doesn't bear thinking about.

I count my blessings. That's one. And…

Oh, there's Betty Jones with her son Jack. Look at him. Butter wouldn't melt in his mouth. Be different if he comes back with some of his school mates. Especially, that Clint West. They don't know how lucky they are… So far.

Betty is walking quickly, trying to hurry Jack along.

"Come on, Jack. This is no place to dawdle."

"Look, Mum, old Tweep the creep is putting up his Christmas darks."

"Hush, Jack. He just has a different idea of decorations than most folks. And don't talk so loud. He might hear you."

"Look at those balls up there. Pitch black. No light at all from them. They don't even shine black like red lights shine red and blue lights shine…"

"Come on, I've got to get to the bakers before it shuts."

Betty walks on but Jack stands, staring up.

"Mum, I reckon they're like little black holes. Clint reckons he's never seen anything so pitch black before."

She walks back and grabs his hand. Pulls him after her.

"That Clint's opinion isn't worth a damn. You should stay away from him. He just means trouble. Come on."

They go and I enjoy the silence. Do it while I can. Won't be much quiet around this street tonight. Young and old clamouring around the colourful lights along the street. Listening to the recorded carols coming from the Hickey place.

The whole thing is a change. Better than nothingness. Eleven months in my own company.

At first, for a while I had my watch. Somehow seemed important back then to know the time. And day and date. It wasn't luminous though, and the dial was hard to see. Then the battery died, and even though the time is right twice a day, I can't tell when that is. And one day a year, it's right about being the eighteenth of December, but I never know when that is, either. It's useless. Can't do what it was created to do.

Like me. I exist but I think my life force has died, too. I don't think I'm dead, but I'm not really alive either. I've thought about me a lot over the years and just can't figure it out. How can a big, strapping fellow like me be in here, so small? Seeing and hearing, but unable to communicate with anyone.

Is it magic? Is Mr Tweep a magician? An evil one, if he is. Or is it some incredible quirk of nature? Of science — quantum stuff? I'll never know.

Only Silas Tweep might know. Maybe he doesn't know either. Maybe he only knows enough to take advantage of whatever it is. Maybe... why bother thinking on and on.

Sometimes Mr Tweep talks to us through the year. Opens the cupboard in the basement and takes the boxes out. He runs his hands through his "collection" He chuckles in his dry way and his eyes shine. Sometimes he claps.

Then we get put back in the dark. And look forward to Christmas.

Sometimes, as the dark balls swing outside in the breeze, I catch sight of a few of them moving silently. Dull, black, ominous.

They are easily seen in the daylight, of course, but it's at night that they're most frightfully clear. The deep, unnatural blackness stands out against the night's familiar dark — as if the night has holes in it, reaching away into some unknowable void.

I think Patty's not far away. And Johnny Petrie is next to her, I think. He was here before me. I remember I was a kid when Johnny disappeared.

An hour or so has passed without me realising it. I can tell because the streetlights have come on and the road is wet from the drizzle. For most of the year, I hardly know whether I'm sleeping or awake. I just … am. Time passes, regardless. Day dreaming. More nightmare than dreams. What can you do if being awake is when the nightmares strike?

It's night now and a few early birds are strolling along the street. I can always hear them coming, chatting and laughing. Sometimes a mum sings to her small children. Sometimes a dad joins in.

Of course, there's the usual jokes and insults thrown at the old house. I don't know if Mr Tweep hears any of it. If he does, he never responds. Not by rushing out the door and shouting back, anyway.

He does respond, eventually, in his own way. I found that out.

Oh-oh. Here's trouble. There's a small group of boys coming. I can hear their loud, raucous comments about houses down the street.

Now they're here. Laughing up at Mr Tweep's decorations.

I'm sorry to see Jack Jones is with them. He seems a nice boy at times, a fine support for his mum, now his dad's dead. Pity that Clint is with them. He's a troublemaker. The other two, Ashley and Ian, are easily led, too.

Clint picks up a stone from the gutter and throws it at the house. I hear it hit the wall. Foolish boy. Jack shines a little penlight torch on the house.

"Nowhere near anything," Jack says. Ian and Ashley laugh.

"Poor shot, Clint," Ashley laughs.

"You can't do better," Clint shouts. He throws again and the stone hits a verandah post. The boys laugh. Clint bends down and looks for more stones.

"Hey, shine your torch down here," he tells Jack.

The beam skims around and stops. Clint picks up some stones and hands them to the other three.

"Let's see you do better."

The other three pause, looking at the stones plopped into their hands. They just stand there while a man and two small girls walk past. Jack turns his torch off.

"Go on," Clint says. "Have a go at the windows."

A car pulls up and the driver, Ted Blake, tells his son Ian, to get in. He seems glad to have a reason to leave. Then Ashley hands his stone to Jack and says he'd better go, too.

"Chicken lot," Clint jeers. "All right, Jack, it's just you and me. You first. Go for the left window."

Jack looks as if he'd rather go for home. I hope he does. But, all of a sudden he draws his arm back and throws a stone. It smashes through a stained-glass panel on the front door. Oh dear. The boys stand there looking shocked.

Mr Tweep comes out and walks down the front steps. I can see him now, A bit. There isn't much light. He holds up the stone that had gone through his door panel.

He's dressed, as always, in his old-fashioned black suit over a grey shirt and black tie. His hair is long and uncombed. He looks his age, or what I expect a hundred or so would look like.

"Does this belong to one of you?" he asks in his croaky voice. Jack and Clint seem transfixed. No people are around at the moment.

"Umm, it's..." Jack stammers.

"It's his, sir," Clint says in a wavering voice. Jack looks horrified at his friend's betrayal.

Mr Tweep opens his fingers and the stone falls to the ground. He steps backwards.

"Come and get it. Get it off my property."

Jack takes a step up the path. Pauses. Another step, his eyes fixed on Mr Tweep, who is standing at the base of the steps, long arms hanging loosely by his side.

"You, too, boy. I know you were both in this."

Clint seems unable to turn away. I know the feeling. He walks up alongside Jack. They walk slowly towards the stone, still staring at Mr Tweep.

It's raining lightly again but the boys don't seem to notice.

"Jack, where are you?" Betty Jones is hurrying along the street. She stops on the footpath outside the Johnson's across the road. Thank goodness.

I look down at the boys to see if Jack has heard his mum. Maybe he has, maybe he hasn't. Hard to know, because the boys are gone. The stone is still on the path, But Jack and Clint are not.

"Jack, we have to go home now."

Sorry Betty. Jack's got a new home now.

Once I would have been saddened by this. Once I might have cried. Once I had feelings. Once… but what use are thoughts of once? Now there is only now.

I hear a rustle nearby, and turning, I see I have two new neighbours. Two new black balls, "darks", shake beside me. They always shake at first before the new occupants get used to how things are now. It will take a day or two, then the balls will just hang there, moved only by the wind and rain.

Down in the street, Betty's getting more agitated. She's stopping passers-by and grabbing them, asking if they've seen her little boy. No one has, of course. One man talks to her for a few minutes and then makes a call on his mobile phone. Then he goes off.

Soon, Clint's parents drive up. The three talk, then separate and walk quickly along the street, covering both sides and both directions. They end up again outside Mr Tweep's place.

"They can't have just disappeared, Betty," Mark West says.

"Then where are they?" Beside me, the new balls shake wildly.

Now the other two boys are there with their parents. Everyone's talking at once.

Ashley says: "Jack and Clint were standing right over there," he points at Mr Tweep's house.

"Clint was throwing stones at old Tweep's pace," Ian says.

"Our Clint wouldn't do that," Brenda West objects. "Never."

Well, never again, that's for certain.

"I knew that place was dangerous," Betty says. "I'm getting the cops to search it."

A newcomer to the group, standing in the darkness of a tree, chimes in: "You do that, Betty, but I can tell you now they won't find anything."

"We must try, Beatrice," Betty says.

Beatrice. My Beatrice? That was? The woman steps closer to the group and I see it is her. Thirty years older, but I'd know her anywhere. Any time.

"I know, Betty," she says in that lovely voice of hers and I wish I still had feelings.

"They can't have disappeared," Mark West says again. I can see he's stressed because he doesn't know what to do. Nobody has realised, yet, that there's nothing anyone can do.

Ted Blake puts his hand on Betty's shoulder. She seems not to notice.

"The cops went through every place along here when Tom Johnson disappeared," he says.

"Yes, found nothing," Beatrice says. "Tom just vanished from the face of the earth."

Here I am, Beatrice.

"These things seem to happen around that old place. Gives me the creeps," Brenda says.

Ted puts his phone back in his shirt pocket.

"I've called the cops. Someone'll be here soon. Brenda was ringing everybody anyone could suggest. No use. Then they broke up to search some of the places they'd already looked.

The police came and, with apologies to Mr Tweep, asked his permission to look around inside. Of course, they were back outside in half an hour or so. Nothing. No sign of anybody. Mr Tweep was all politeness as he bid them goodbye.

Parents cried and hugged each other. Betty said she would never stop looking and would stay up all night. Brenda said she would, too. Mark said he had to get up early for a work meeting but would start again after lunch tomorrow.

Soon, I was alone again. Except for my fellow "decorations". The new ones had been shaking something terrible over the past hour. They'll settle down as feelings drain out of them over time.

Of course, Christmases will still be special when they come out to look at the world again, Christmas after Christmas. All quiet in the street now. But, in the distance I hear Betty calling Jack's name over and over. One of the balls shake again. He'll learn.

Then, suddenly — what a shock — I see a light to my side. I look and, I can't believe it, there's a light in one of the new balls. How can that be? Then it brightens even more and — I've never known anything like this — the ball grows and explodes. Just cracks open and disappears as if it had never been.

Jack is lying on the front lawn. Shaking his head, Feeling his arms and legs with twitching hands. Then he's standing, then walking on wobbly legs towards the footpath.

"Mum."

The front door opens, and Mr Tweep comes out.

"Boy!" he calls.

'Mum, where are you?" Jack cries out.

Then Betty's running up and hugging him and crying and wiping her tears and wiping his tears and cradling his head in her arms and kissing him.

"Oh Jack," I thought I'd lost you. Where have you been?"

"I... I... don't know, Mum. Somewhere dark. Up there, I think." He pointed to Mr Tweep's roof.

"How did you get up there?"

Jack didn't know. It was all a daze to him. It always will be, I'm sure. He had no idea where Clint was. Nobody ever would. Except us up here. And Mr Tweep.

"It doesn't matter, darling," Betty said through happy tears. They walked off, Jack so enveloped in her arms that he could hardly walk straight.

Below, I heard Mr Tweep curse. Then he walked onto the lawn and looked down at something. He cursed again and bent down. He stood up with Jack's little torch in his hand. He went over and smashed it against a veranda post.

I think some time has passed. It's raining heavily now, and the wind is buffeting us. I can just make out the broken pieces of Jack's torch in the gutter.

Light. Of course. Light. I wish I had a light of some sort. Torch. Matches. Ah well, life — or this — goes on. But when I think of Mr Silas Tweep standing in the rain cursing and throwing the torch away with a vicious movement of his old arm, I feel happy.

I didn't think I could do that.

THE END

> Blind people are just like seeing [sighted]
> people in the dark. The loss of sight does not
> impair the qualities of mind and heart.
> -Helen Keller

CHAPTER 15

The next morning, not too bright and too early for Peter, he sat in the Martin lounge room with Inspector Cleary. Nola sat facing them from the long lounge. Cleary asked: "Did Mr Nagle ever take your father to medical appointments?"

She shook her head. "Why is that of any importance now, Inspector?"

Cleary didn't answer that directly. "Is it likely that Mr Nagle would have learned about your father's cancer?"

"No. He didn't like travelling with him, to medical appointments or anywhere else. Especially after that ruckus in the car over the radio stations. Dad said that he would never travel with him alone again."

"What about taxis?"

"Hardly ever. He said he didn't want to sit there talking about nothing. And after the last time when he was badly treated by a cab driver, he said never again."

Peter thought the man had said, 'never again' quite a lot. He didn't blame him.

Cleary said: "Tell me what happened. Did the cabbie assault your dad?"

"No, not that. The driver didn't think that my father knew where he wanted to go. He obviously thought, as many people do when they are dealing with a blind person, that he is not only blind but dumb. Dad was quite clear about his destination and as the trip was taking longer and longer, he became anxious. He told the driver he was going the wrong way."

"The cabbie wouldn't have appreciated that," Cleary said.

"No, the driver snarled at him." Nola smiled. "He insisted that he knew where his passenger wanted to go. He had been driving a cab for many years, twenty-five, I think he said."

Cleary asked if her father had ended up where he wanted to go. She shook her head vigorously.

"No, in the end, the driver shouted at him and insisted that he had taken Dad to where he had wanted to go. He pulled over with a squeal of brakes, got out and walked around to the other side and pulled the door open. He told Dad to get out. So Dad was left standing on the footpath without knowing where he was. Imagine that, Inspector. Abandoned in an unknown place. Blind."

Peter said: "Dreadful. What did he do?"

"Dad rang me on his phone. But by then, of course, he had missed his appointment. The appointment he had made three months earlier, such was the demand for the specialist."

Nola was sobbing and looked at the detectives with wet eyes. In the silence, she stated the obvious— that it isn't easy being blind. "So now maybe Dad has got some peace." She wiped her eyes.

Peter nodded and said, "On the bright side, did that experience give your dad an idea for another short story?"

"He did tell me later, that it gave him a good idea."

She dabbed at her eyes again and smiled. "Appropriately, he called it Driven to Despair. You should read it."

"You have, I imagine," Cleary said.

"I have," she said. "In fact, I have, to some extent, revised most of the short stories in that manuscript you have been reading, Sergeant. You probably noticed that some of them are works in progress."

Peter said: "I've noticed, so far, that some are incomplete, but the finished stories are cleaner and make more sense than some of the other…" He paused. "Can I call them 'ramblings'?"

"Yes, I haven't touched the ramblings yet. I intend to turn to them a bit later after I have settled down. I'll do my best to get his work published."

Peter hoped that she would succeed.

Cleary stood quickly and said, "That will be all for now. Thank you for your time, Ms Martin."

DRIVEN TO DESPAIR
A SHORT STORY BY GEORGE MARTIN

The night was as miserable as any Jeremy could remember. So was he. Miserable. At 3 am he should be home in bed with Rosemary. Instead, he was shivering on a dark footpath, sheltering from the swirling, drenching rain under a narrow roof. He had surrendered his umbrella, after struggling against the wind which continually blew it inside out and threatened to pull him into the air like Mary Poppins. Two spars had broken, sticking through the black material like skinny, silver bones.

He had dropped it in the street bin and now hugged the darkened shopfront in a vain attempt to keep dry. Dryish.

He shouldn't be there. Wouldn't be if Jamieson hadn't collapsed and Davies hadn't got him to fill in on the late shift. Bugger. Not Jamieson's fault, but...

It was damn cold. Jeremy stamped his feet, sending sparkles of water into the air. He was glad to have the gloves Rosemary had given him. He turned at a scraping noise and saw the umbrella being blown out of the bin. It spun down the street. Good riddance to a false friend. A car splashed past: a glistening, blue blob in the ill-lit street, occupants just dark blurs through the steamed side windows.

"Where's that bloody cab?" Jeremy said aloud. Again. Nobody answered this time either. A cat cried from a nearby alley. Creepy. Like a tortured soul wanting rescue from... what? Nothing. Only wind and rain. Jeremy wasn't going down any fantasy-horror alleys tonight. Not even a bloody awful night like this would shake his pragmatic mindset.

He rang the cab company again, protecting his phone from the rain as best he could. Same answer. No answer. Nothing useful anyway. Short-staffed tonight. Storm. "Tell me about it," Jeremy mumbled. Wouldn't be long now. Not long. Same as ten minutes ago.

He pushed the phone deep into his inside jacket pocket, rubbed it around a bit in case it had water on it. He thought again of ringing Rosemary. No. She'd be sound asleep. Maybe text? No, might still wake her. And if it didn't there wasn't much point anyway.

Suddenly, a car turned the nearest corner, on Jeremy's side. Headlights hit him and he felt exposed, which was silly. There wasn't anybody else around. And he was waiting for a car. A cab.

He squinted into the light and was relieved to see it was a cab. At last. It was moving fast. Jeremy rushed to the kerb, eager to get in and start for home. It didn't seem to be slowing. Surely he can see me? Jeremy thought.

The cab skidded to an abrupt stop, front wheels veering towards the kerb, and then wobbling away. It splashed water from the gutter up Jeremy's trousers. "Great," he muttered.

The front passenger door swung open, and Jeremy bent down. The driver was leaning across, grinning out at him. He said nothing. Jeremy scrambled in and pulled the door shut.

"Are you wanting a cab, sir?" the driver asked, smiling at him.

"Been wanting one for a long time," he said. The driver nodded and leant back into his seat.

"Where would you like to go, sir?"

Jeremy stifled a sigh. He'd already given his destination to the operator. A few times.

"Kentville. James Street."

"Fine, sir. Kentville. Straight away."

The cab took off with a squeal. Jeremy was flung back into his seat, losing his grip on the belt as he tried to fasten it.

"Steady on, I haven't got my belt..." Click. "Okay. Right now."

The driver hadn't seemed to notice. He was leaning forward, staring through the windscreen, intent on driving. But still smiling.

Too fast in these conditions, Jeremy thought. But never mind, he'd relax and let the driver do the job he did every day. At least he was on his way home, sitting in a warm, dry cab. Well, warmish. Jeremy wondered if the heating was working properly. He could hear the fan. It didn't sound very strong.

At least it's dry, he thought. He probably needed time for his body to warm up. Time for heat to permeate his bones.

The fierce wind was doing its best to stop them in their tracks. The cab was buffeted by wild gusts. Sometimes it swerved alarmingly and Jeremy, again, wished he hadn't been hit with the late shift for a week. Four more nights. The wipers whined on their diagonal up–and–down sweeps, brown leaf remnants caught between rubber and glass.

There weren't many other vehicles around. What could you expect at this time, in the middle of a stormy winter's night? He shivered and looked forward to sleeping in tomorrow. That was one good thing about the night work. Except Rosemary had to get up and go to work at the normal time. Maybe she could take a sickie. Stay home. Sleep in with him.

That'd be nice. He shut his eyes and tried to doze. The erratic movements of the cab kept him awake, but at least he rested his eyes.

Suddenly, he flew sideways in his seat as the cab swung around a corner too fast and the driver hit the brakes and almost lost control of the car.

"Hey. Better slow down a bit, mate," Jeremy said. "Not a good night for going fast."

The driver turned his skinny face towards Jeremy and smiled.

"Don't worry, sir. Is all good."

"There's no rush for me to get home," Jeremy lied. He wanted to get there as quickly as possible. But in one piece.

"Don't be concerned, sir. All okay."

The driver turned his full face and grinned at Jeremy for so long that Jeremy gestured to the road ahead. He estimated the driver was about forty, maybe a bit older, light-brown, wrinkled skin. Lot of black hair that clung wetly to his forehead. Must have been out in the rain, too.

The car sped through the rain with the driver still looking intently at Jeremy, who could see an intersection approaching fast. Aghast, he waved his hands vigorously.

"Look, look."

The driver turned to look ahead again. The car bounced as it hit a pothole and the driver over-corrected. The cab skidded a few metres and then steadied.

"All okay, sir. No worry." He smiled.

The man couldn't stop smiling. Not just smiling when he looked at Jeremy. The grin never left his face, whether he was staring ahead or turning to look at his passenger.

It had been a long time since Jeremy felt like smiling. Bloody long time. And here, inside this cold, dark cab, he was feeling less and less happy as the minutes passed. He felt resentment building towards this inexplicably cheery cab driver.

He knew this wasn't fair. Not the driver's fault – not the rain, cold, late hour, short-staffing. Not even the driver's fault if he was congenitally driven to smile no matter what was happening around him. Since when was it a crime to be cheery?

Jeremy turned to the driver.

"When does your shift end?"

Smile.

"Oh, not for long time. Just started." He turned and grinned. "No worry. All okay."

Jeremy was still sure the car was going too fast for the conditions. Again, it swerved suddenly, and then swung back with a wild tilt of the steering wheel. Then, another scary wobble splashed water up from a wide puddle. Jeremy threw his hands up and yelped.

"Steady on. Please slow down before you kill us."

"Not yet, sir."

"I'm asking you to slow down a bit."

"All okay. Soon be somewhere."

"Somewhere? Where's that? I want to get home. My place. Not just somewhere."

The driver didn't answer. Just grinned at Jeremy before turning back to face the front.

Jeremy stared out the window trying to see where they were. Should be halfway home by now. He couldn't recognise any landmarks and wished he'd been paying more attention. Instead of sitting back with his eyes closed for part of the trip.

"Where are we, driver?"

"We here, sir. All okay." He smiled even more widely.

"You're going the wrong way. This isn't the right way home."

"Is just this way, sir. Rest for while."

Jeremy couldn't believe this. After waiting all that time for a cab, he gets one driven by a lunatic. A smiling loony.

"Turn around, driver. Use your GPS and get back on track."

"Not now, sir. Best we go this way."

Jeremy pointed across in front of the driver towards the GPS unit mounted in a holder on the dashboard near the driver's door.

"There. There. Use that. Kentville," he said loudly.

The driver smiled at him, then turned to the front.

"Can't use it, sir."

"Yes. Give it to me. I'll get us back to the right way." This was ridiculous.

The driver pulled the GPS unit off the dashboard and held it in his right hand for a moment before dropping it into his lap.

"Good man," Jeremy said.

The driver smiled at Jeremy and opened his window. Rain flicked across the interior. He picked up the unit and threw it out.

"What, are you mad, man? Why did you…"

"See, sir? Like I said. Can't use GPS." He smiled widely, showing more teeth and closed the window.

Jeremy slumped back into his seat, stunned by the driver's action.

"Soon be there, sir."

"Where?" Wearily.

"Somewhere, sir."

"Look, just let me out here. I'll get home somehow from wherever it is we are now."

The driver turned to Jeremy and gave him a big grin.

"Not possible yet, sir."

Suddenly, the driver spun the wheel and the cab bounced around a sharp corner, throwing Jeremy into the door.

"Shit. Just…"

"Please don't swear, sir. Not nice."

The driver put his foot down and the cab accelerated. Then he hit the brakes and it slowed suddenly. Jeremy pitched forward and back as the vehicle bounced.

He jumped when something flopped onto his right hip. Reflexively, he pushed at it to get rid of whatever it was. His startled movement caused the thing to slither into the back again. Jeremy shook with fright. What was it? A snake? It looked like… an arm? A hand? Cold, grey. And slimy… wet or muddy.

He thought he heard a groan. What the hell was he in the middle of? Whatever, he had to get out.

He looked at the driver, who didn't appear to have seen what had happened, but he turned his face to Jeremy again and smiled. His teeth glistened, multi-coloured, in the reflected light from the instruments.

"All okay, sir?"

Jeremy nodded, dumbly. He didn't dare say anything. What could he do? He was trapped in a cab with a madman who had a body in the back – or at least someone in bad shape. He could ring someone... But not if the mad driver could hear... Text. Send a text to...

He pulled his phone from his jacket pocket. Looked at the dark screen. Pressed the home button and it lit up. Tap. Tap. Text screen. He'd send a text to Rosemary. She could get... He didn't know where he was. He tried the driver again.

"Where are we?"

Grin. Chuckle.

"We just here, sir. Always here."

Chuckle. Grin. Eyes squeezed shut then popped open. He looked at the phone in Jeremy's hand.

"What you got there, sir? That not good."

Jeremy held it up. No point trying to hide it. Only make this crazy man suspicious.

"Just my phone. Got to ring my wife and..."

The driver suddenly lunged, swinging his open hand at the phone, knocking it to the floor at the driver's feet.

"Why did you do that? I need to make a call. My wife will be worried..."

"Of course she will, sir." Grin. "So she should be."

White teeth.

"Why? Let me try to get it off the floor. Ignore me. You just concentrate on your driving."

Jeremy leant down, right arm outstretched. His fingers touched the phone just as the driver stamped down. Jeremy yelped and pulled away, rubbing his fingers.

"Shit, man. You could have broken my fingers." He pulled the glove off and gingerly massaged his fingers. "I think one's broken. Stop now and let me out."

"Can't stop now. Too wet outside for you. Please not to swear in my cab, sir."

"Bugger the rain. Better out there than in here with a mad man and a..."

"And what, sir?"

"How did you get a licence to drive, let alone to drive a cab?"

The man smiled at Jeremy.

"Always wanted to be a cab driver, sir. My ambition all my life. They wouldn't let me."

"Who wouldn't?"

"People, sir." Smile.

Jeremy considered pulling the door open and jumping out. Going too fast. Probably be killed. He put his glove back on hoping the little bit of warmth would ease the pain.

"How long have you been a cab driver?"

The man looked at Jeremy, face wrinkled with happiness.

"Just tonight. Just started tonight, sir. How am I doing?"

Bloody awful, Jeremy thought. He said, "Is this your cab? You the owner?"

"I am now, sir." The driver beamed. Obviously happy.

"Where's the man who owned it before you?"

The driver laughed.

"You'll see soon, sir. We all soon be together."

"No. Let me out. I haven't got time to meet anyb... one."

"We be quick. Time not matter, sir."

The driver swung the wheel to the right and the cab crossed the bitumen road and went into a side street. The cab rattled and bounced along. Jeremy reckoned they were on a dirt road. There were no lights around them now. Ahead, the headlights sprayed through the rain to show bushes lining the road.

The driver had slowed on the rough surface and Jeremy saw this was his best chance. Dive out into bushes. He should survive that. Better chance than if he stayed in this mobile chamber of horrors.

Now! He flexed his legs for the jump and pulled at the door handle. It didn't move. It was locked.

"You still safe, sir? Good we have the childproof locks on. Save you from falling out." The man kept smiling. Jeremy felt tears of frustration run down his cheeks.

"Please, let me go. I won't tell anyone. I just want to go home. Please." He shook the door handle to no avail.

"We'll see, sir. I need your help now."

He needs me? Jeremy stared at the driver. To do what?

The driver braked and the cab turned off the dirt road onto a narrow track. Jeremy knew no one would find him tonight. Maybe not ever.

"What's happening? Where..."

"We here now, sir. You just wait a moment."

The driver got out and walked behind the car. Jeremy heard the boot open. The driver had left his door open. Jeremy leant down and crawled towards it. He gritted his teeth as his right knee scraped on the brake lever. He could hear the driver moving something in the boot, could see the bushes so close to the open door. If only he could move fast enough. He would run so bloody fast once he was on his feet again. Just...

"What you doing, sir? Having a rest?"

Jeremy looked up to see the driver looking through the driver's side rear window. He was smiling. Then he slammed the front door.

Jeremy stretched to reach the front door handle, but heard his door open and felt something hard tap his ankle three times.

"Better sit up now, sir."

Jeremy turned and moved back into his seat. His door was open, and the driver was grinning at him. Of course.

He saw what had hit his ankles. The driver was holding a gun. He was waving it at Jeremy like an admonishing forefinger.

"No time for silly nonsense now, sir."

"For God's sake, man, what are you doing? Why have you got a gun?"

"Get out please, sir." He gestured with the gun.

Jeremy kept his eyes on the wobbling gun barrel as he slowly climbed out. He stood, shaking, in the rain, his shoes in light brown mud.

"Come with me, sir. I would value your assistance, please."

He prodded Jeremy ahead of him as they walked around the cab, past the open boot. When they reached the driver's side the man waved his gun at the rear door.

"Open it, please, sir. And pull out previous owner, please."

"Previous…"

"No more question, if you please, sir."

Jeremy opened the door and bent over to look inside. As he had feared, there was a man slumped across the rear floor. His shoes were close to Jeremy's side. They were black, scuffed. He wore black jeans and a blue shirt. Jeremy couldn't see his face. He was lying face down. One arm was drooped onto the floor behind the front passenger seat.

"Pull him out, sir."

"Pull hi… Why? What're you doing?" It was fairly obvious, and Jeremy's mind raced with ideas of escape. Duck, run, scream, jump at the driver…

The gun. That was the idea stopper.

"Too many questions, sir. See. This gun means no more questions. It means just do. Quickly now, sir."

He smiled at Jeremy as if he had just promised him a treat.

Jeremy grabbed the man – or was it just a body now – by the legs and pulled. The man groaned – he was still alive. Jeremy pulled until the unfortunate former cab owner was lying in the mud. He had rolled onto his side and Jeremy saw his face.

He looked about fifty. Balding. Eyes closed. There was a large red stain on his shoulder. Rain was diluting the colour. Jeremy looked behind him at the bushes. Low and scraggly with trees further on behind them. Maybe…

"No time to rest, sir, bring him around here."

"What? Drag him through the…?"

"Not question time, sir. I have been very patient." Smile. "Now is just doing time."

The driver waved the gun. Jeremy dragged the man by his legs, his head bobbing on the wet grass. Once, his head bounced on a small rock bringing a low groan from the man. Jeremy's damaged hand hurt, and his grip was loose. He slipped, fell backwards and lay, panting. How would this nightmare end? What was the...

"No playing silly games, sir. Plenty of time to rest later. Plenty." He waved the gun and grinned widely.

Jeremy got to his knees, and then to his feet. He began pulling the unconscious man. It was hard work. Eventually, they made it to the other side of the cab.

"Put him over there, sir. Out of the way."

Jeremy pulled the man again and let his feet drop from his grasp when they were about three metres from the car.

"Fine. Good job, sir."

"Okay. Good. Can we go now? Take me home?" Jeremy asked with false optimism. How could he get out of this?

He could always get the police to come back here. Ambulance first. As soon as he got home. Home. He ached to be in his house so much. With Rosemary. She must be worried sick by now. Or maybe sound asleep unaware of the time.

Every second with this lunatic made it seem less likely he would survive the night.

"Sorry, sir. We can't leave Mr Owner here by himself. Too lonely for him." He smiled broadly at Jeremy.

"But he won't know."

"Don't be unkind, sir. Better you stay here with him."

"But... but... it's cold and wet and..."

"But you won't know, sir."

Jeremy froze inside. The driver smiled again and raised his gun towards Jeremy.

"No. No. Just leave me here. And. Wait. I haven't paid you for the fare. I owe you some money..."

"Doesn't matter, sir."

"But… you want to be a cab driver. Don't you want to operate the taxi meter? Like a real cab driver." Jeremy grasped the only straw in sight. He knew the driver was crazy.

The driver lowered his gun and smiled at Jeremy. He walked backwards a few steps, eyes – and grin – fixed on Jeremy.

"You are right, sir. I must do the job properly. Let me see how to get fare reading. Just stay, sir."

He pointed the gun at Jeremy to emphasise his command. Then, smiling broadly, he turned and walked quickly to the driver's door. He swung the door open and leaned in.

Jeremy saw he had a brief chance. Be quick. He backed away from the cab towards the thicker bush. He could see the driver intently poking at the meter. Jeremy stepped back again. Twice. The driver looked through the window. Maybe in the dark he hadn't realised that Jeremy had moved.

"Sir. I have the amount you owe, now. You said you wanted to pay. Hey…"

Squinting through the passenger window the driver saw something was amiss. Jeremy had moved away, towards the bushes.

Jeremy half turned and ran. The driver stood and fired over the cab roof.

"No," Jeremy cried out and he heard another shot go over his head as he fell full length. "Shit!"

He heard the driver shouting but couldn't make out what he was saying. Luckily the driver was as bad a shot as he was a cab driver. But maybe not from point-blank range.

Jeremy rolled away from the body he'd tripped on. Now on the other side of the body, he kept rolling. Over and over. More shots. He heard the sound of bullets hitting trees. He knew he was going to be killed. In this dark, wet nowhere.

"Ah ha, there you are, sir. You had me worried for a while."

Jeremy looked up and saw the driver smiling down at him. He had stepped over the cab owner. The gun was aimed at Jeremy's head. Rosemary might never know what had happened to him.

"You were trying to skip off without paying the fare, weren't you, sir? Naughty. Naughty. But don't worry, sir. I can get it from your wallet later."

The bastard was still smiling. He was going to kill him in cold blood with a grin on his ugly face.

"Sorry, sir. I must go now. Maybe time to pick up more passengers. Such fun."

Jeremy turned his face and tried to get up. His feet slipped in mud. Hopeless. He flinched at the sound of the shot. But something odd was happening. Somebody was falling.

"No. No," the driver screamed.

He was on the ground. The wounded owner was pulling on his left leg. He was conscious again. Just. His grip was slipping as the driver kicked out and tried to bring his gun to bear on his head.

Jeremy scrambled over the other man and grabbed at the driver's gun hand. He punched downwards, hitting him full in the face. The driver screamed. Jeremy grasped the gun and prised it out of the driver's grip. He banged the butt down on the driver's head.

"No. No, sir. This isn't right."

Another brutal blow with the gun and the driver whimpered and his eyes glazed. He seemed to be unconscious, but Jeremy kept the gun tight in his hand. He turned to thank the other man, but he had passed out again.

He stood up and walked unsteadily to the cab. He opened the front side door and sat sideways on the seat and looked at the dark shapes of the two men lying in the mud. Suddenly, Jeremy was startled when he saw the driver was moving. He stared through the wet darkness and gripped the gun tighter.

173

He relaxed when he realised that the wind which was jostling bushes into erratic dances was whipping at the unconscious – or dead – man's clothing. He dropped the gun into his jacket pocket.

He sighed, suddenly very weary. He'd never been a violent man. Never attacked another person. Never bludgeoned anyone unconscious. But what else could he have done? Now what to do?

Go home, that was what he must do. Soon. Get help for the injured cab owner.

He looked again at the men on the ground and gasped when he saw the white teeth of the driver set in a wide grin, glittering in the headlights. But Jeremy knew the driver wasn't conscious. He'd hit him very hard with the gun butt. If he was alive, he would surely be out for a long time. Jeremy shivered and closed his eyes. He took several deep breaths. He knew he had to get out of that place but found it hard to move.

After a while he went to the other side of the cab and got in the driver's seat. He picked his phone up off the floor and tried to switch it on. But it was busted, and nothing happened. He dropped it into his top coat pocket.

He sat for several minutes, eyes closed, gathering strength. He could hardly believe he'd got out of that nightmare.

The keys were still in the ignition. He started the engine and turned the lights on. Slowly, he reversed and turned the cab to get back on the track.

He drove slowly, his fear screaming for more speed, but he knew he could easily career off the narrow track. Maybe wreck his only means of escape. He could only see blackness to the sides and ahead beyond the headlights' gleam.

Soon, another turn in the track took him onto the dirt road. It was wider but still deserted; no house or other light. But he felt safe enough to speed up a bit.

And he knew that a bitumen surface and suburban streets were at the end of this road. He was still shaking but thought he could safely consider his nightmare was over. How long now before he could be in Rosemary's arms again? Dry, warm, safe.

He squinted through the windscreen and was sure there were lights in the distance. Civilisation! Surely the tiny glowing specks promised the end of his night of terror? Just a few more kilometres and he'd be out of this dark desolation.

Suddenly, there was a bang and the cab wobbled and then skidded towards the trees on the side of the road. Jeremy braked gently, wrestled with the wheel and got control back. The cab stopped just metres from a tree, shining white in the headlights.

He sat shaking at the wheel, and then turned and peered up the black road. Could the driver have caught up? No way, he told himself. He had driven slowly along the track, but nobody could have run fast enough to keep up. Certainly not a wounded man, last seen lying in mud.

He got out and looked around. Nobody here. He walked around the front of the cab and along the side. He saw the cause of his latest fright. The front passenger side tyre was flat. Burst.

"Damn!" he exclaimed, kicking the tyre. "Will nothing go right tonight?"

He knew he had no real option other than to change the tyre as fast as possible. The lunatic could still be alive and even now trotting along the track towards him. He shuddered at the thought of the man's grinning, bloodied face staring down the track as he ran to get him.

Spurred by the new fear, unlikely as it was, Jeremy went to the driver's side and pressed the lever to open the boot. He hoped this cursed vehicle carried a spare tyre, jack and tyre lever.

He went to the back of the cab and pushed the boot lid up. It lifted easily because somebody inside pushed it up.

"There you are, sir. I am so happy to meet you again."

Jeremy stepped backwards in shock. The driver was sitting in the boot, left hand holding the lid up. His wide grin cracked dried blood on his cheeks. He held a tyre lever in his right hand.

"How…" Jeremy felt it was no use trying to escape after all. This man would always be there, in his face, smiling. Chilling him with polite conversation that hid murderous intent.

"Bad mistake by a cab driver, sir. Leaving the boot open before driving off. Not good for a driver to do." He smiled widely. Jeremy stood helplessly.

"Now, sir, we must change places. It is uncomfortable in here. And air gets bad."

Jeremy thought of Rosemary waiting for him at home, probably awake by now, worried sick to find him not there beside her. He must get there!

He reached into his jacket and drew out the gun. The driver saw it and shoved himself down and further back in the boot.

"Not nice, sir, to shoot your driver."

His voice was whining, and he looked terrified. He had stopped smiling.

Jeremy aimed at the cowering figure and pulled the trigger but nothing happened. He didn't understand these things. Was there a safety catch – or something? What about his safety? Damn.

He jumped across to the boot, grasped the lid and forced it down before the alarmed driver could raise his hand to stop it. Jeremy banged it down hard and heard it click. Locked. He heard the driver yelling something and banging at the lid.

He went to the driver's seat and started the engine. He drove slowly into the bush, scraping past the trees. When he felt it was hidden from the road he switched off.

He looked down and saw the meter was still running. The red figures kept ticking over – now $245.60. He reached down and switched it off.

"I think tonight's journey should be on the house. I deserve that at least," he said to himself. "I'll walk the rest of the way," he said.

Jeremy set off, striding in the rain, smiling.

THE END

> To survive, you must tell stories.
> -*Umberto Eco*

CHAPTER 16

Cleary had some files on other cases to go through, so he gave Peter the morning off to compensate for the nights he had spent reading the manuscript. When he had asked Jan why she wasn't going to work, she had only said she was going after lunch. To her annoyance, he sat down at the table and used the 'free time' to continue reading the manuscript.

He began reading.

>hello

>hello whos that

>what did you say George don't you recognise your own brother you have only got one

of course I recognise you Stephen I was just thinking about something else when the phone rang a story I was writing but I'll stop that now its good to hear you been a week or so and I've been wondering how youre going

as I have about you are you keeping well

oh I guess Im okay taking me a long time learning how to be blind I mean physical aspect of that went ahead without any effort on my part but learning how to live in this world that I have been in for more years than I like to remember is more difficult

not made any easier by some people around you I worry about you George sometimes when I go there I can almost smell the toxicity of the place you know just...

I know what youre saying but Stephen I cope and some other things that happen around here give me great story ideas so it helps my productivity

well thats really making lemonade out of lemons

I gotta meet this deadline to get my next book published

yes I know that of course howre you managing changing style from novels to short stories

Ill just say its different –

but will they sell as well make you as much money as before

I could go on at a greater length but you didn't ring to hear that sort of stuff

Im always interested in what you're doing you've made a great success of your life mate... more than I have and well getting back to your needs George are you getting good support from organisations like Vision Australia and Guide Dogs

yes they are helpful people as you know I've learnt how to use the long white cane and I can get around pretty well with that now it can't help me press a lift button or even find the one I want for example or find public toilets bit risky poking around in a urinal with a cane can be embarrassing

the guide dogs people gave you that cane training can you get an actual guide dog from them

you know Margot she doesn't want to have the worry of a dog in the house and looking after it even though I would have to do it she thinks that would be too much to cope with on top of me

so instead of you getting the guide dog you have to put up with the bitch

well said Stephen anyway a guide dog to my mind wouldnt be able to tell me what lift button to press either or find a disabled toilet... that's not quite right because I know they can be trained to go to places I frequent but in any case Margot's adamant about that and I love my Fido the loveliest cat Ive ever had

you and your Fido

enough about me how are you going down there

not that well I guess you know business is going all right have got some good people working for me including a good new pharmacist for a start shes very good but its an expensive thing

have you got your debts under control yet

all my business would be great if it wasnt for funny business from my ex wife Joan

giving you trouble I thought she was well out of it

problem is she part owns the business about a third and she wants to sell out

she wants you to sell the pharmacy

she wants her money back wants to get rid of it she needs more money to live a good life on the Gold Coast I guess

and you don't have enough to do that Stephen

no nothing like that Ill have to talk to the banks I don't want to lose my business George I built it up took a lot of hard work so hate the idea of losing it I thought I was well rid of her and she was feeling the same about me but its up to her guess I can see why she wants money but it doesn't help me get it

have a talk to the banks as you say maybe there is a solution let me know how you get on

yes I heard you had a bit of a cold a few days ago

who told you that

Nola and that's part of the reason I rang to see if youre over it did you see the doctor

yep I saw him was nothing much gave me antibiotics not sure if I needed them but I took them and Im fine now getting along well as I told you at the beginning of this call

Im very pleased to hear that George I do worry about you it must be hard for you there with the humiliations you have to go through every day both in the house and even when you go on your rare visits to the shops you shouldnt have to put up with that sort of crap

Im used to it all now water off a ducks back its not all bad I cant stand Nagle Margot cant stand me but Nola is such a lovely daughter she helps me a lot

Yes Nola is a lovely girl

she does all my manuscript work transcribing my words from the voice recorder onto a document on the computer and then she revises it edits it and prints it out but only the short stories not the sort of crap Im talking about now shell go back and probably delete most of that if not all of it anything I cant turn into a short story

how are your stories going I guess thats what I asked you before

yes Im going along fine I have to do another well probably five or six before the deadline comes thats going to be a bit tough giving me some stress but I think I will get them done in time and if Im a few weeks late I may be granted latitude when are you coming up here again Stephen any chance of time off in the next few weeks

yes planning to do that and theres someone else I want to see while Im in Katoomba.

someone I know

yes someone you know a bit I think someone Ive been getting to know fairly well over recent months

Im pleased to hear that Stephen anyone in the neighbourhood

yes you could say shes in the neighbourhood

aha she youve given it away a bit there

thats all youre going to get at the moment George

alright Ill wait we will go down to the pub for an hour or so

Id like that yes I'll be up for that goodbye

goodbye

Very interesting, Peter thought, as he went back to reread the phone conversation. He wrote a note for himself in his notebook, then returned to the manuscript.

good afternoon mr Martin nice sunny spot you have there

yes be good to relax for a while away from all the conflict in the house will my lawn mowing disturb you

no carry on Jeremy

so this is where you are George nice sunny spot on the terrace I hope I havent woken you

a bloke cant get any peace and quiet around here even when he tries to hide

sorry George

you dont sound sorry Nagle why are you bothering me and why do you call me George when were alone and mr Martin when were with Margot or Nola

just a couple of mates talking George

don't you just love the smell of new mown grass

yes wafting over me is relaxing especially when someone else is doing the work

bloody hell Nagle did you have to scrape the chair across the terrace like that a bloke cant relax with you making such a racket

only settling down next to you to enjoy the sun with you George

Nagle your unwanted familiarity such as you calling me George is only part of your total lack of respect for me you act like you're running the place

maybe I will one day hey George

its not a laughing matter Nagle I'm serious that'll be over my dead body

do you feel safe sitting there George

what are you getting at should I feel unsafe in my own yard in my own home

even the mower can be dangerous throw up stones that might hit you in the face you wouldn't see it coming would you

Ill take the risk Nagle at least it cant bloody blind me good of you to think of my safety though

I'm very impressed with how you handle your blindness George I'm sure I wouldn't cope as well as you do

mmm

so many things around a big house could hurt you

not much else I can do I'm not going to lie in bed all day or hide in a cupboard no need to be impressed

only the other day you were a lucky boy could have been a bad fall

you talking about the bucket bloody big metal thing crashing down the stairs onto me fortunately I was holding the handrail and I twisted around when it hit my legs but I didn't fall over so bad luck for whoever threw it at me

mustve been a shock to you George you must have wondered what on earth hit you but you avoided it do you really think that someone deliberately dropped it on you

funny wasn't it that nobody yelled out to warn me the bucket seemed to have jumped out of thin air and headed straight for me what do you know about that Nagle

nothing to say are you surprised at my question I would be surprised if you're surprised

it sounds like you suspect me I had nothing to do with it George these things happen does it worry you that unexpected events like a stone from a lawnmower or a bucket on the stairs could harm you

you dont have to worry about me Nagle Im not worried about unexpected objects Im more worried about people around me

what is it Nagle nothing more to say I'm sure you haven't come around to express your concern about my safety

are you leaving or moving your chair away from me

argh what the hell did you dump on my lap

have you seen your cat lately George

why are you asking me about Fido he's always around

what sort of a name is Fido for a cat

what are you getting at

I mean Fido that's a name for a dog

cats dont know what names mean neither do dogs for that matter

why are you blathering oh my god I know what's in this bag

Im afraid I have some bad news George your cat with the dog's name is now a dead cat

dead what are you telling me whats happened

it was an accident I ran over him on the driveway you know how stupid he was sitting there in the sun where cars go a miracle he's lived this long

you bastard Nagle you did this on purpose you don't have the excuse of blindness how could you miss a cat the size of Fido sitting in the path of my car

your car thats right what an unfortunate coincidence your cat killed by your car in your driveway

wipe the smile off your face Nagle

what makes you think Im smiling

I know you are

I cant say how sorry I am that this happened George

I know you cant say how sorry you are theres no sorrow in your voice no remorse

George I can ask Jeremy to dig a grave down the back

yes do that then get out of here Nagle go back to your room or get out of the property altogether

that's not very friendly George

and shut your bloody radio off dont want to listen to your lousy cowboy music

you should pay more attention to it George theres some good lines among the music and good lyrics you know

rubbish just go

Im going leave you on your lonely seat here that song Ive just turned off on my phone by the way not my radio was blue eyes crying in the rain did you hear the words George love is like a dying ember only memories remain is that what you are experiencing George life with only the embers left alright Im going sorry about Fido

we don't believe hes sorry do we Fido

the still body the lovely fur tears on my face

this terrible day has given me an idea for a new story bugger of a way to get inspiration

and that is it I still feel the sun warming my face but I still live in the darkness of night

poor old fido best cat I ever had not that I had many Nagle said he was sorry but remorse is easily acted practising on my cat first then itll be me

at least fido didnt have to suffer the indignity of blindness wouldnt have known what hit him I dont suppose I will either what a bugger I am paranoid they tell me as the comedian said I wasnt paranoid until everyone started talking behind my back whisper whisper whisper all over the house even in the garden

they may plan to get rid of me whoever they might be I have a couple of suspects but I may well surprise them I may get revenge in advance before it happens ha see how they like that

I wont get another cat but Ill have another go at that story about the cat they couldnt put outside serves them both right for not letting a cat be in the house overnight

its been running around in my head for a while I think

Ill call it something like the cat that cried in the night then Ill start with a loving husband and wife sitting at home in the comfort of their lounge room one night she will be reading a magazine in the armchair Ill call him John he will be at the table fiddling around with a dusty rusty old tin box with a lid that he has removed it will have some strange writing on it that he cant decipher it will be a box he found at the back of the garage

Ill make it a box of lots of little bottles with coloured liquids in it most were empty or dried out with a thin film on the bottom he will tell his wife Ill call her Jean that it once belonged to a distant cousin who was a magician

what sort of magician Jean will ask magic tricks with cards an illusionist an escapologist like Houdini so many different types

John will say he was a real magician or so my grandfather said he could change the behaviour of animals apparently not only the pet animals but it seemed to affect the owners as well

Jean will tremble at this and turn to another page in the magazine That's so creepy John why are you fiddling around with that stuff it's so old

then I will have their lovely little cat come in a cat I'll call Freddie that they have owned for several years it is what they call an outside cat didn't sleep in the house it slept on their verandah

that doesn't seem a very nice thing to do to your pet cat sleep outside all night I'm sure you agree with her Nola

John said they had a very comfortable set up nice soft bed warm blanket food & drink they made it a decent place

I'll have Freddie jump up onto Jean's lap and she will pat her Freddie you may have noticed Nola that I will make a female cat I may have to change from Freddie to something more feminine

I can build that into a good scene then I will have John tipping a couple of different coloured liquids into a small plastic jug it will sizzle away and he will be impressed with what is done with the chemicals from that old magicians box grinning like a little boy with a new toy he will take it over to show off to Jean

however Freddie the female cat gets agitated the nearer the gurgling sizzling vessel of coloured chemicals come closer to her then the critical moment Jean will throw her arms up and tell him to take that terrible stuff away because it stinks but her arm inadvertently knocks the arm holding the jug causing the mixed chemicals to come out in a thin black greenie stream yes the colours have now turned into a murky black oily substance and it falls on Jeans arm and on fluff there thats what Ill call Freddie fluffy cat.

get rid of it she shouts

Im sorry Jean John will say but it's no use Jean is well and truly agitated by now

she will jump up hanging onto the cat with one arm and it will be meowing and meowing and yelping that is the most terrible smell I ever smelt she says

John will be delighted at what magical transformation in the liquids he has caused but is not so stupid that he will smile at this he keeps a very set face grim this is indeed very serious his face will say fluffy will jump out of her owners arms and run around the floor Jean will swear some more at John finally screaming at him that he should have known better than to muck around with ancient well past their use by date stuff magic shit I'll make her very angry she goes off to have a shower as she leaves she calls out if this yucky black stuff doesn't come off my skin Ill come back and pour the rest of that container all over you my mate

John is feeling a bit guilty by now he tells his wife not to worry hell wipe fluffy down and then put her out Ill just put her out then there is no reply other than the slamming of the bathroom door

for the next half hour I will have him trying desperately to put that damned cat outside for some reason fluffy refuses to go out this night normally she is very obedient seems to look forward to the whole adventure of a night out there in their own little home but not this night she squeals and screeches jumps up on chairs on the table and then scrambles up to the top of the bookshelf and lands there on all fours she curved her back and hissed at John

to John it seemed that their lovely household pet hated his guts he tries several times to grab her but she always was too quick and got away going from one part of the room to another she knocked over a vase it broke on the floor and the water and flowers went everywhere part of the glass cut John's arm while he was reaching for the cat didn't bleed much but it did put blood on his shirt

I think I will eventually have John throw the cat out he must throw her hard because as soon as she hits the ground she spins around and runs full pelt for the door and he slams it and she bangs into it he sits down breathing heavily he had never experienced such a thing with any sort of animal what the hell has that stuff done to this normally gentle cat meowing has now turned into something very dismal very sad sounding cat he heard the shower stop

he sat waiting for Jean to come out and say good night one of her kisses sometimes extended the time going to bed or their time in it but that night she won't come out again he will hear her still angry slamming and banging things around and then there's quiet he gets up and walks down the hall he thinks he can hear her asleep very quietly he goes into the bathroom down the hall then before he can get undressed and under the water this scratching sound on the wall outside and some gingery furry thing with a terrible stink came hurtling through above his head down onto the basin and then down onto the floor and out the door

what the hell John will admonish himself he had forgotten to close the little sliding bathroom window but fluffy had not forgotten it

she was making a big noise and he was afraid that fluffy would awaken Jean and she would be very angry at him again he tiptoed to the bedroom door and looked in and she was lying there naked on her side quietly sleeping left arm under her head there were still specks of black stuff on her forearm

then there will be another lot of round and round the dining room table and up over the bookshelves and another vase overturned in another corner a chair is tipped over and John wonders if he will ever get that bloody cat outside

all that period of time and incidents with the cat I will spread out in more detail to make it more exciting and more frustrating for poor John

but eventually he will get fluffy out and close the door and after checking and double checking all doors and windows he will go into the bedroom so exhausted he can't even face a shower I will have him lie down full length on the bed alongside his wife who has not bothered to get under the covers of course I will make it a warm night so she will not be bothered by coldness on her nakedness John lies alongside her for some time almost asleep

then I will say John thought it may be better having a shower and get into bed properly at the risk of stirring Jean and making her angry again he will reach over and rub his hand down over her bare shoulder and then ruffle her hair patting it she will purr and open her eyes and look at him with an unknowing gaze from outside comes the mournful cry of the distressed cat

and he will scream and scream and scream

there, I think I can make that into a chilling story with a horrible last line yes that is worth working on well done if I say so myself this is a tribute to poor old Fido maybe or maybe not what do you think Nola I think it will be a damn good story once I get organised properly do you think people will get it that ending when they realise those chemicals have transposed the consciousness of Jean into the cat and the cat into her

yeah sure my readers are very intelligent they know what to expect of me

it is always a great feeling when the plot works out and there is an ending that will put a chill into peoples minds yes George Martin has done it again

but will it be polished in time for the publishers deadline

> Each of us is a book waiting to be written, and that book, if written, results in a person explained.
> -Thomas M. Cirignano, *The Constant Outsider*

CHAPTER 17

At ten o'clock the next morning – the third day after George Martin's death — Inspector Cleary and Detective Sergeant York were sitting in a Katoomba coffee shop discussing progress, or lack of it, so far. As they talked, they drank their coffee and took bites out of their toasties. There weren't many people in the coffee shop. They were tucked into a corner where they could talk more freely without being overheard.

"Tell me, Peter, what have you gleaned from your nightly homework? Has the manuscript changed your mind about any aspect?"

Peter finished chewing on the last of his toastie before answering. "I'm not too sure, Sir, sometimes I'm driven to think one way, and then I read a bit more and I reconsider what I originally had thought."

"Do you think that rough manuscript, that first draft, as you call it, has anything useful to say about George Martin's state of mind?"

With the back of his hand, Peter wiped crumbs from his mouth, before answering.

"He has a bit to say about suicide in his short stories that cleverly are derived from experiences but not directly about him killing himself. He also has a story about a woman who pretends to be blind in order to kill her husband. But you know those things. I have told you about them.

"And I have noticed that his short stories are a lot darker than his novels were, horrifying at times. It seems to me that his mindset was a lot grimmer in his short stories. I think he had a twisted mind. He may always have been inclined that way but perhaps his blindness coming later in life could have contributed to his dark moods."

Cleary swirled a spoon in his coffee mug. He didn't drink.

"We have to allow for that, of course. Going blind within a short period of years would shatter anyone's life. From what you tell me, the thoughts he put on paper were none too happy."

Peter said: "It's also difficult because he is not only dictating the words of a new story, he records his thoughts and lets us listen to what others say to him and what he says to them. He jumps all over the place."

"As you said at the beginning, the whole thing needs a very deep and skilled revision. Proofreading and deleting. Sounds like a big clean-up job for somebody."

"It was supposed to be. Nola worked on the short stories, as we know, but hasn't touched the other stuff so far."

Cleary picked up his mug and took a long drink.

Peter said: "I think fifty percent or more can be ignored. The short stories are a relatively small proportion of the whole manuscript. And there aren't enough stories there to make a book, yet."

"So, in your view," Cleary said, "George Martin had not yet finished what he had set out to do: to write a book of short stories?"

"I don't believe so. I think a decent sized book of short stories would need another..." He paused, "maybe another half a dozen stories which, as we've heard, he had already written."

"Are the stories themselves, in the manuscript you're reading, finished or will they need further revision, perhaps another two or three times? Isn't that the way writers work? The first draft is not the way the writers would want their stories to be presented to the world."

"Yes," Peter said, "I think professional authors say a book is made into a good book in the revision process, never the first draft. I feel a touch sad for Mr Martin for that reason. He put everything into writing them, I believe. But he fully intended to shape them into really good stories. Now he never will."

Cleary spoke to a waitress passing the table and asked for another couple of coffees.

He said to Peter: "If, on the one hand, we say that George Martin hanged himself, we have to consider how he could have done it. He was not young, not particularly fit, and to cap it all, he was blind. I can't imagine how he could have stood on his desk or on a chair and reached up to put a rope around a hook that would have been beyond his reach.

Peter opened his mouth to say something but stopped when Cleary put up his hand to indicate he wasn't finished yet.

"I know you've suggested he might have been able to throw the rope over the hook. But I think you would have to be lucky. I mean, he couldn't see the hook, He could have had to try several times and would have been balanced precariously in the first place and have risked falling. The autopsy didn't indicate any bruises or other marks on his body to show he might have had a fall from a chair or desk."

"I agree, Sir, but I don't think it would have been impossible."

The coffees arrived and both men paused while they drank a little each.

"And we must also allow for the fact, Peter, that he would have been sleepy after taking so many drugs. And if he realised how difficult it would be to throw a rope or place it over that high hook, why would he begin by taking tablets that would make him drowsy, possibly put him to sleep?"

Peter said: "Unless he took them after the rope was hooked up."

"I think those are questions we are not able to answer at this moment."

"You may be right, Sir."

"So, if Mr Martin didn't commit suicide, who made it look like he had? And why?"

Peter put his mug down on the saucer with a rattle. He looked at his senior colleague, as if expecting him to continue. Which he did after a few seconds.

"We know he and his wife didn't get on very well. In fact, she seemed quite alienated from him. We know that she wasn't very sympathetic to his blindness."

"I think from reading the manuscript," Peter said, "that he was very sad about that situation. I believe he still loved his wife and wanted them to be together again. That may have led to severe depression. I think that shows in the manuscript."

"George was also jealous of Mr Nagle, from what you have said and from some of our interviews. He was suspicious of the chauffeur's intentions."

Peter picked up his coffee again and sipped. He put the mug down more quietly this time.

"I think he was paranoid, Sir. He was suspicious of whispers that he heard in other rooms."

Cleary said: "A few whispers is not much to be suspicious of."

"He thought his wife and Nagle were talking to each other in low voices and he didn't think they would do that unless they had secrets that they didn't want heard. And as I said, they stopped talking when he appeared at the doorway of a room such as the lounge room. He couldn't see if there was anyone in the room at all. And he couldn't hear them. So he suspected them of carrying on some sort of affair. Building a relationship. Why else would they stop talking when he appeared in the room? Anyway, that's what he thought."

"I suppose he wouldn't know if there was anyone there or not, unless he went up and reached out at each chair."

Peter said: "No. The poor bloke was lost in the darkness of his house whatever time of day. Whether there was anything going on between Mrs Martin and Nagle, or with any other person or persons he couldn't know."

"Well, how about this Nagle, then? Do you think he hated George Martin?"

"That's confusing. He doesn't seem to like Mr Martin and some of his actions could be construed as conveying a deep dislike, even hatred, of him. For example, he ran over and killed George's beloved cat but confessed this to George explaining it was an accident."

Cleary nodded.

"And yet, there are passages in the manuscript where Nagle comes across as being sympathetic. And in the interview with him as well. He said Mrs Martin was, in his words, 'cruel' to George, and mocked him for some mishaps."

"Yes," Cleary said, "that's confusing. We may have to talk to Mr Nagle once more. I had hoped not to, but we can't work out what the man really thought of George Martin."

"Who else is a possible suspect, Sir? I don't think Nola would have wanted to kill her father. I don't think that embarrassing bedroom incident would have been enough reason."

"That may have been enough reason if her relationship with Jeremy James was forbidden. She may love him more than she's let on. That might be difficult to sort out, also," he said.

Peter said: "She's a strong-willed woman who is unlikely to end a relationship just because her father ordered it."

The detectives paused while they finished their coffee.

Cleary said: "I don't think George had many friends. From what we can gather, his closest friend was his brother, Stephen. It seems they were great mates and that George relied on his support."

"Jeremy James," Peter said.

Cleary seemed a little surprised. "Well, Peter, I don't think Jeremy is a strong suspect for the murder, if that's what it was."

Peter smiled. "No, sir, I mean Jeremy James is here. He's coming to our table."

Jeremy was, indeed, walking towards the detectives with a smile. An older woman was walking with him.

"Hello Inspector and Detective Sergeant," Jeremy said. "Enjoying some local hospitality, I see." Jeremy and the unknown woman stood near the table. Both were smiling at the detectives.

"Hello Mr James, and who is your friend?" Cleary asked.

"This is my mother, Jenny James." They exchanged greetings and Cleary invited them to sit at the table.

"No, no," Jenny said, "we have some … umm more shopping to do."

Cleary said: "Okay, are you getting along alright?"

"We are a happy little household. Happy considering the circumstances we have experienced in the last few years. My husband left me some years ago. And it has been a struggle financially and in other ways as well. It's hard to cope, detectives, being on your own, bringing up a child."

"I am sure it is very difficult, Mrs James," Cleary said. "Do you work in town?"

"I do a few hours at a local hairdresser's. It's not much, but it does help pay the rent. We'll get by, won't we, Jeremy?"

Jeremy nodded and Peter got the impression that Jenny was uncomfortable talking to them. He was sure Jeremy was sorry he came to the table at all.

Mrs James said: "It must be a terrible job for you, investigating such a crime. I am surprised that it is not classed as a suicide. Is there a reason to consider something far more terrible was done to poor Mr Martin?"

"How well did you know Mr Martin?" Peter asked.

"I didn't know him very well." She paused. "But I did love his books, he was a wonderful writer."

Cleary stood alongside her.

"We can't divulge anything more at this stage, Mrs James. We shall soon release the results of our investigation."

Jeremy and his mum said goodbye and walked out into the street.

"Should we interview Mrs James sometime soon?" Peter said.

Cleary didn't reply. He was looking after the James couple as they walked further down the street. He seemed preoccupied with some thought.

"Well, what now, Sir?"

Cleary snapped out of it and looked at Peter. He said: "I would like to talk to Stephen Martin again. It could be difficult to catch him. He seems to be away from his pharmacy almost as much as he is at it. Anyway, we'll give it a try."

"Excuse me, please."

Cleary and Peter were surprised to see a small girl standing near them. She had come so quietly while they were engrossed in conversation that neither had noticed her. She had blonde hair, long enough to curl up when it reached her shoulders. She wore a light blue dress with a white pattern, that, on closer inspection, was revealed as small birds.

Cleary said: "What is your name?"

"Emma. Do you like it?"

Cleary and Peter exchanged glances. Peter said: "It is a lovely name, and your dress is lovely. Can we help you?"

Emma hesitated for a moment before replying.

"I wanted to see Mr Martin who I was talking to the other day. Mummy told me he writes stories. I wanted him to see my dress with his big white stick. Daddy couldn't see it this morning because he is very busy and had to rush off again."

"What does your daddy do?" Peter said.

"He works... a lot. Mummy says he's always too busy." Emma hesitated. "The man's eyes were broken, you see, and I told him a doctor might be able to fix them. I wanted him to see my dress today if he could, and he said he would write a story for me."

"I'm sorry," her mother said, rushing up with a harassed look on her face. "Emma, I told you not to bother these nice men."

"I assure you, Madam," Cleary said, "Emma isn't bothering us at all." He turned his gaze back to the little girl.

"Did you think he would be here at the shops?"

"He was here before. Sometimes he had brown and black shoes... I mean one shoe was black and the other one was brown. Isn't that funny?" She giggled.

"Emma, you mustn't bother these busy detectives." She reached down for her daughter's hand.

Cleary asked her how she knew they were detectives. But as soon as he asked the question, he realised how foolish it was. This was not a big town. A famous writer's death would be known by everybody, and he was sure the presence of two detectives going around interviewing people would be known by half the population. Emma resisted her mother pulling her hand.

"I just wanted to find out if he had fixed his eyes. I mean, that the doctor had fixed his eyes. But coming here in the car, mummy told me Mr Martin was dead."

She looked from one detective to the other. Her face was sad.

Peter said: "Yes, Emma, it is a very sad thing, isn't it?"

"But... but," her face brightened, "My friend Meredith said her cat was dead... I mean, they thought her cat was dead... and they took it to a vet, that's a doctor for animals and the cat was made better and was not dead when they brought him home.

"She was very happy... Meredith was very happy."

Her mother tried once more to pull her away from the table. But Emma shook her arm free and turned again to the two men.

"That was a very happy ending, wasn't it, Emma?" Cleary said.

"Yes. It was, I think. So, you see, I thought... I think maybe that if the writer man went to a person doctor, he could make him not dead again."

She looked hopefully into the detectives' faces. "And he could come home, and we would all be happy again. And if that helped his eyes get better too, he would be able to see how pretty I am."

"We all wish that, too," Cleary said in a voice that was sincere and indicated that he did, indeed, wish for that outcome.

"But, Emma, nobody can fix your writer friend."

"That is sad. Mummy said he made up stories. So, he won't write any more stories, will he?"

Both men shook their heads.

Emma suddenly thought of something else. "Mummy said you are special policeman. I think she said you are defective."

Her mother finally grasped Emma's hand firmly enough to start pulling her away. Peter wanted to hug her but knew he shouldn't do that.

Emma turned back and said: "Goodbye. I am sorry that I disturbed you. Mummy said I shouldn't disturb you, but I wanted to find out if my friend could be helped. Now I know he can't be. Goodbye."

The detectives waved goodbye.

"It's a bugger, sometimes, isn't it, Sir?"

"It is so often a bugger, and it is hard to get through life without sadness after sadness, starting, as we just saw, when we are quite little. I worry about the sadness that my children will face through life.

Peter nodded.

"You and Jan have got all that ahead of you, Peter."

"We are beginning to think that will never happen for us."

After a gloomy silence, they picked up their mugs and saw the coffee was gone. Cleary attracted the attention of the waitress and ordered two flat whites.

Money often costs too much.
-*Ralph Waldo Emerson*

CHAPTER 18

Peter took a deep breath and opened the manuscript, taking advantage of the Inspector being away from the office.

hey its uncle Stephen I didn't know you were in town

I couldnt keep away when I heard my brother was in hospital well I could have but blood is thicker than water as they say and as a bonus I get to see my beautiful niece again

thanks for coming how did you hear

Nola phoned me how are you feeling or perhaps more importantly how are you healing

Im fine I would be a lot finer though if I wasn't stuck in this bloody hospital you wont be here long dad a day or two

got the gist of it George but tell me in some detail but not too much what actually happened you look a mess excuse my frankness heads busted up by the look of all those stitches knee doesnt look too good either all swollen up

its better for me to have my legs uncovered at the moment even the weight of a single blanket hurts like hell

who beat you up

a bloody little toddler did well it was his trike I fell over it in the park

serves you right for chasing the little bugger

you can laugh Nola but it wasnt funny at the time

now and again Margot and I go for a walk in the park we used to do it regularly but we cooled off doing that when she cooled off me the park has a good long smooth concrete pathway that winds in and around the bushes and so on and its usually a safe place to walk

it certainly looks as if it is

these days when we walk Margot heads off and gets a long way in front when I protest she says I walk too slowly for her it doesnt give her enough exercise makes me think Im wasting my time doing it not getting enough exercise she mustve walked around the trike and kept on going without bothering to move it or even warn me so I just

but what about your cane isnt that supposed to let you know when theres something in front of you

he was using it uncle Stephen but we think it must have gone between the wheels and under the seat or something so he didnt notice anything there until he was falling over it poor dad

I went a real cropper I can tell you straight down face and knees hitting concrete path sunglasses smashed I think I broke my thumb although the doctor doesnt agree

Margot heard you hit the ground and came running back for you and

I dont think mum heard anything uncle Stephen

theyre a good pair arent they one blind the other deaf

its nice to hear youre cheering each other up at least

anyway if she did hear it she kept on going wouldnt want to end her exercise too soon would she

she went around the rest of the course and came upon me lying in the middle of a crowd the ambulance came soon thanks to some stranger ringing them

no wonder youre so grumpy

yes he has a reason to be grumpy dont you think

well hes been grumpy a long time over the years I dont know what excuses he had then

thats hardly fair uncle Stephen I can remember times when he wasnt grumpy

you may be right Nola I think there was a time a couple of years ago

you two can laugh about it but I can tell you it hurts like buggery

were just joking with you dad dont take it so seriously although you sure have many reasons to be serious here have a chocolate and would you like some coffee

I would like that I think we could all do with a cup

Ill get that I won't be long I know where the canteen is and I know what each of you have

George while shes away I want a quick chat with you Im upset at the way Margot is treating you I hear bits and pieces from Nola and I see the way she talks to you and ignores you you need a lot of care youve lost your sight she doesnt seem to be aware of what that does to a person

or else she just hates me more than I can bear to think I blame that Nagle fellow we dont need him there are others who can drive us around she is not the person I loved and married all those years ago we were drifting apart before my sight failed

youre the money earner here the one who brings in the cash a successful novelist making more money than most authors do in this country and where is the gratitude

not so successful now but I do what I do because thats what I am

I could have a word with Margot try to get her to see what shes doing to you

I think she is very well aware of what shes doing to me she enjoys it enjoys my discomfort my embarrassment my humiliation my pain

its not fair I might still try to have a chat but I know what you mean

but enough about me Steve how are you travelling from what you told me recently you are in a bit of trouble financially has that improved I thought your shop would do very well I mean a pharmacy everyone needs medication drugs cosmetics all the damn things they sell in pharmacies these days

yes I expected that too but I didnt count on a big franchise opening a glitzy new place in the same street they sell more items they provide more services than I can so it is a bit of a struggle at the moment

when I bought it I thought we would be set for a long time and Ive been struggling but I have been making ends meet now my bloody ex wife wants to sell it up and take her share after all my hard work

you paint a gloomy picture there Steve Im sorry to hear things arent improving ahh heres our coffee thank you dear

I bought some bikkies as well

I see you have a little TV up on the wall there George to keep you company

sorry of course I know you can only hear it

with the rubbish on TV these days it may be better to be blind

dont be so silly dad its never better to be blind but you also have a little radio alongside you

with the stuff we get on radio now I think it would be better to be deaf

this is depressing Im going to take a few chocolates is that okay

live it up while you can better coffee than they bring me on a tray

are you going to be around town much longer

sad to say no I have to get back in the morning in fact Ive got to do some business in town before I go so Ill have to leave you here in the loving care of your daughter

I am going to give you not only a kiss as you leave uncle Stephen but a couple of chocolates

Im off now George

see you again soon I hope Stephen

you sure will I have some plans for the future that
may pan out well for me and someone else

for someone else uncle Stephen tell me more

no too soon youll learn all in good time

    Peter glanced at his watch and decided he could read a bit longer.

are you alright love can I get you anything else

this is my second cup as you might have noticed Im a
slow coffee drinker I like to savour it and this is a nice
quiet place to do so

we do our best yes is very peaceful particularly this
late in the afternoon you sit there love will be open
for another half hour or so

thank you

hello mr Martin do you remember me

I cant see you and I dont recognise your voice who
are you

you might remember me Im Emmas mum weve met
a couple of times

I remember now we first met when she lost touch
with you in the shops somewhere

I dont want to intrude on your privacy mr Martin
but Emma talks about you a lot she's taken a liking to
you and shes insisted that we come over and say hello
I hope you dont mind we wont be very long

I was relaxing in solitude here

mr Martin I am Emma do you remember when you helped me find mummy and then I saw you another time when you had different colour shoes

yes I remember you Emma what are you doing here

mummys been shopping

yes and now we have to go to the pharmacy

can I wait here till you come back mummy

we mustnt disturb mr Martin like that we have to leave him alone hes relaxing with a coffee

please mummy

if its alright with you and with Emma she can sit here on the chair on the other side of the table I wont leave here until you return

is your wife coming soon

yes she could come any minute but as I said I will wait here with your daughter until you get back

you be good now Emma I won't be long only a few minutes

do you like sitting in this cafe mr Martin

yes sometimes

dont you like going into the shops youre always sitting outside somewhere

Im inside now I like to be away from the shops I used to enjoy going shopping in certain types of shops but now I block peoples way and I cant see whats on the shelves

I could go with you and tell you whats on the shelves I could help you find things

can you read

only some words some little words like cat and dog not a lot of words but I can recognise chocolates and bikkies and drinks there are lots of things I could help you find in the supermarket even though I cant read everything

very nice of you Emma but I don't need to do any shopping in there today and my wife who will come soon to take me home is doing all that anyway youre a kind girl

dad is kind sometimes too

Im sure he is

are you still writing stories

yes I am I have to finish writing stories for a book

I would like it if you could write a story for me sometime

when I finish all the stories for my book I will write a story for you I might even make it about you

thats making you giggle

its making me happy Ive never had a story about me

it wont be soon because I have to finish these ones or my book wont get done

I will wait I can wait very easily I have to wait a lot Im waiting now but its fun because youre talking to me

George Ive finished now Marks just gone to get the car from the back of the carpark hell drive to the front to make it easier

we will just have to wait a little while.

I cant wait havent you had enough of waiting

I promised Emmas mother that I would stay here until she comes back from the pharmacy I cant leave her by herself.

George why do you keep picking up little girls when I leave you sitting outside the shops

Im being very quiet were just talking a little bit I said I would help mr Martin do some shopping but he said you were doing it all you have some big bags there

yes yes you dont need to help him shop because I have done that

I told her that Margot

our car has just come around to the front Mark will be sitting there tapping his feet if we dont go now

if he wants to dance in our time let him he is getting paid for it its unsatisfactory George Emma will be all right sitting here

Margot once I promise something I keep that promise Im not going to leave a little girl sitting alone in a cafe you know thats not the right thing to do

its okay my mummy is over there she can see me and is waving to me I will walk straight across to her and I wont get lost thank you mr Martin and thank you mrs Martin

now we can go come on

goodbye Emma

Peter heard Cleary opening the office door and he quickly closed the manuscript and stood.

> It's not what they say about you
> it's what they whisper.
> -Errol Flynn

CHAPTER 19

Peter was about to leave Inspector Cleary's office when there was a knock at the door.

"Will I get that for you sir?" He paused with his hand on the doorknob.

Cleary looked annoyed. "Damn nuisance, better find out who it is."

He opened the door. "It's Constable Janice Holesworth, she says there is a Mrs Cawthorne wanting to see you."

"Never heard of her. Why does she want to see me?"

Constable Holesworth said: "She says it's to do with the murder in her street." If the constable thought that this would attract some extra points from her boss, she was disappointed.

"Well? What bloody murder is she talking about? Did you ask her that question?"

Hesitantly, the constable said: "I did do that, Sir. It's about the famous author's death. The man who hanged... I mean, was hanged."

Cleary sighed. "Better show her in, then." He looked at Peter. "Stay here, Peter."

"It might be the wife of the man I interviewed at his home the other day," Peter said.

Cleary nodded.

Mrs Cawthorne was a small woman, with auburn hair. She wore a blue dress and matching blue shoes. Cleary had never seen her before; he was sure of that.

He looked at the woman, who seemed awestruck to be in the office of a senior police detective. After a few moments of staring at each other, she said: "I am sorry to disturb you, sir. I thought... I thought this might be important."

"Please sit down. Mrs –"

"Cawthorne," she offered. She moved into the room and sat in the hardback chair opposite the inspector.

Peter remained standing at the window.

"I understand you have something to tell me, Mrs Cawthorne. Something that may be of interest to me regarding a certain crime?"

"It might, Sir. I can't be sure, but I thought I should bring this information to you. People are saying it's all fixed up now, that you know who did it and that some people will soon be charged."

Peter didn't know how this information could have been going out around the mountains. He thought if Cleary was annoyed, he hid it well.

Cleary asked: "What is it you have to tell me?"

"I live almost opposite the home of Mr and Mrs Martin, and I," she paused, "well, my husband was interviewed by one of your detectives a few days ago. Fred said he told the detective that he saw someone going down the street and in the gate late the other night."

"Yes, yes, my sergeant told me that." He waited patiently and then the woman spoke again.

"Well, I was feeling so sad about what happened over there that I made a casserole." Peter wondered if she had come here to tell them about a meal she cooked. Cleary sighed.

"I made it for Margot and Nola. I thought it might save them cooking …" Her voice trailed off. She saw the Inspector's eyes fixed on her, appeared to steel herself and continued.

"Well, sir, I took the casserole over to them the other night."

"What night was this, Mrs…?"

"Cawthorne," Peter said.

Cleary's glare told Peter that he didn't need prompting.

"It was two nights after poor Mr Martin died."

"What time was this?"

"About 11, possibly 11:15.

"I know it was very late, but their front door was open, and I… well, it was forward of me, I know, Sir, but I thought I was doing a nice gesture and I… I just walked in with the casserole wrapped up in a tea towel. I didn't want to spill it, so I was walking slowly."

Cleary picked up some papers and started sifting through them as though these were more important than the words he was hearing. Peter hoped she would get to the point soon if there was one.

"I knew where the kitchen was because I had been there some time ago. I heard voices…whispers…coming from down the hall."

Cleary looked up. "And what were these whispers, saying, Mrs Cawthorne?"

"I stood for a few minutes wondering whether I should knock or shout out or anything, but then I heard what they were saying, and I kept quiet…"

Cleary dropped the papers on the desk and looked intently at Mrs Cawthorne.

"They were whispering in an angry sort of way. You know when people are really wanting to shout, but they know they have to keep quiet. Sort of, like, shouted whispers... If you know what I mean, Sir."

He said he did.

"I couldn't tell who was talking. I didn't recognise their voices. It was a man and a woman. And they were saying something about a recorder."

Peter stopped leaning against the window and leant forward.

"A recorder?" Cleary said.

"Yes. A recorder. I think it was a tiny hand recorder. By the way they described it. They said... That is, the woman said, 'Why is that so important?' then the man said, 'We must find it. We absolutely must'."

"The man said that it was important that they find this recorder?" Cleary asked. He was sitting up now straighter, paying full attention to what she was saying.

"Yes. I've got it right, I'm sure. The woman was agitated because it sounded like she couldn't understand why the man was so angry... worried about a simple little recorder. He kept saying, 'We must get it.'

"But the woman said, 'No, we must get out of here quickly.'"

"The man said that they must get the recorder, but the woman only wanted to get away."

"I could tell it was very important to them. And I thought about this for some time, Sir, before I came in here. Fred told me it might be important. But we did wonder why two people would be arguing or so agitated about a voice recorder. I just, well, Sir, I just thought you might like to have this information."

Apparently satisfied that she had said what she had come to say, she stood without being asked to leave and turned towards the door. Cleary opened the door for her and thanked her for being a good citizen by coming to them with information that might help them in their inquiries.

He beckoned for Constable Holesworth to show Mrs Cawthorne the way out.

"What do you make of that, Peter?"

"I think we've got a few men and women to choose from as possible suspects."

Cleary said, "You're right there. Seems we are not the only ones interested in that recorder. It's a mystery where it got to - our guys didn't find it even though they went over the house with a fine-tooth comb."

"It still hasn't been found. It is important, and from the agitation in those two mystery people I'm not the only one to think that. It could have some –"

Cleary interrupted with obvious impatience. It seemed he was annoyed at the whole world now. "I thought we were close to cracking the case."

"But George Martin wouldn't have had time to hide it if he was being hanged against his wishes."

Cleary clicked his tongue. "Of course it would be against his wishes. Dammit."

Peter said: "I understand, Sir. I will talk to the guys who searched for it.

"We'll get them, Peter."

> I will love the light for it shows me the way. Yet I will endure the darkness for it shows me the stars.
> -OG Mandino

CHAPTER 20

Peter placed a bookmark on the page he was reading and closed the manuscript. He stretched his arms and groaned. Time for coffee, he said to himself. As if reading his thoughts, Jan walked out of the lounge room and into the kitchen. He heard the kettle click on. He closed his eyes and thought about what he had read so far.

"Here you are, darling," Jan said, walking in with a mug in each hand. She placed one on a coaster in front of Peter and sat alongside him at the table. Peter grinned and said: "Good timing, I was about to get one."

"How's it going?"

Peter shook his head. "It's good reading, but I don't know if it will help our investigation into this particular case. Jan frowned.

She said: "I don't know, of course, what you are investigating. I sort of do but I know you can't talk about it."

"It's a complicated thing," Peter said, "I know what I thought at the beginning and what I think now are two different things. I'm looking at all the signs reading about what this man ... well, I won't bore you with all that detail."

Jan sipped her coffee and put it down. She patted his arm. "I'm sure you'll get the right answer, Peter."

"I hope so," he said, "Cleary is expecting a lot of me, I believe, but as you know, I'm new to plain clothes detective work."

Jan didn't answer straight away. There was a short silence. Then she said: "Yes, you may well see something that will solve the case." She paused. "Even though you often miss other signs around you."

Peter looked surprised. "What do you mean? Is there something around here that could help me? Signs, clues -"

"Possibly... signs, clues that could have helped you in another matter."

"What are you talking about, Jan? I don't understand."

"I'm sure you don't," Jan said. "You see there are signs that you seem to have missed."

Peter lifted the mug to his lips but held it there without drinking. "For example?"

"Aww, darling," Jan said. She gently pushed his arm down until the mug was on the coaster again. "For example, my sickness in the mornings over recent weeks while you headed off to work as usual."

"You told me that you would be alright and not to worry."

"I didn't want to hold you back. I've been sick in the mornings, and there are other signs ..." She patted her stomach.

Peter heard her voice complaining but saw her lips smiling.

"Yes, Darling, you're going to be a father."

Peter face changed from one of puzzlement to excitement and even joy.

He stood so quickly that the manuscript dropped to the floor. He started to bend down to pick it up but stopped abruptly and embraced Jan as she rose to hug him. They hugged and kissed some more until laughter broke their lips apart.

She said: "You'd better get back to your other investigation."

"No, there's so much that I want to know. When –"

"I'll tell you more when we're in bed but finish your work first."

Peter sat again and opened the manuscript. He forced himself to concentrate on the matter in hand.

> I have always liked sitting out the back looking around my garden and up at the stars now I cant tell whether its dark or the middle of the day but I often feel that night time vibe perhaps its the coolness slight breeze or something I just feel it somehow
>
> I love it too dad I love the stars I always have I remember way back when we took holidays out in the bush the stars were spectacular
>
> they were werent they out there without any distraction from the city lights we could see the full glory of the stars as Clancy said the everlasting beauty of the neverending stars or perhaps it was the neverending beauty of the everlasting stars either way it was awesome
>
> I love that you remember it so well dad that time it was lovely for all of us you me and even mum then
>
> now if I was being serious as I too often am nowadays I would have to query the never ending or the everlasting bits when I look up

because you cant see them now the sky still looks beautiful

Nola you also remember looking through my big telescope looking around at the sky especially the planets as a little girl you were ecstatic looking at the moon

yes yes yes I do remember that where is that telescope now I haven't seen it for years

your mum sold it on ebay when I found out afterwards she said there was no point in a blind man having a telescope and the money would come in useful

thats a pity

do you ever think about the universe that will go on long after all human beings have left or died out on this planet

thats a very deep thought yes I do think of that sometimes when there are no people left to watch the sky all the planets and stars comets asteroids the whole damn caboodle will go on about its business circling spinning orbiting flashing across the universe none of that wonderful cosmic machinery will care less that there are no living beings around

it gives me the creeps shivers down my spine when I think too much about it how odd none of that out there needs us at all

no but just think of this Nola they were all going through the various mechanisms holding each other to each other expanding spreading out when there were no people around from the beginning many billions of years ago and I know when any of us disappears from the earth all of its people will continue to go about their business day after day without needing us at all

its all too hard to imagine dad its hard enough here on earth now

dad I know youre concerned about your manuscript

yes I am a bit its the deadline you know

I am working on your printed manuscript now its slow going Im cleaning it up bit by bit concentrating on the short stories first I promise I will complete them and Ill work on the conversations as and if needed

I know you will dear but be warned there are more stories running around in my head

more for another manuscript

no no there is only that one the printout of my recording sometimes I talk directly into the laptop and the text appears on the screen

oh I didnt know that was there another job for me then

a little job its not my main source of material thats the transcript from the voice recorder the laptop dictation is a bit funny at times the other day when I was talking into the computer I was distracted when your mum came in and asked me how long it would be before I could sit down and eat I told her of course the computer read out the full conversation its very sensitive and so easy to get alien material in the midst of my stories

those alien bits as you call them get into your voice recorder stuff as well

a lot of it does the difference is that the recorder has the various voices of the speakers male or female young or old however dictation into a computer appears as plain text on the screen without any indication of who said what I have to be careful I wish I had the eyes to clean this stuff up myself it is so much more difficult dictating stories and sorting through recorded bits than tapping away on a computer keyboard

dad I am doing the revisions now and I am doing a bloody good job

thanks dear I know you are I didn't mean to harass you

lets go inside now Ill make some coffee or would you rather a cup of tea at this hour

lets leave the sky to go about its business its been a long time since Ive been able to see it I am secure in the knowledge that for my lifetime at least it will keep on working a lot longer than I will I think I would rather tea now

SOLITARY ECLIPSE
A SHORT STORY BY GEORGE MARTIN

> note for you Nola we may have to leave this as it is for the moment I have to do more research into the science of this and I know you have problems about some aspects so I think before you continue revising this further we better talk after my further research however time is pressing in on me and I know I have less than two weeks to get all these stories to my publisher we can only do what we can do

So hot again. Might as well say it's day again. Black lumps –once crows–lie still across the brown grass under our tree. Another disposing-of-the-bodies chore. I weary of it. Probably no need for it. Look around. Not anymore.

Sometimes, when I shade my eyes with my hand and look towards the hill, I think Abla is staring down at me. Trick of light but gives me a start. He's silhouetted in the sun's giant disc. I know he is facing the other way. Into the valley where the once-wide -and-deep river forced its way past us, arrogantly free and darkly wild. Now dry and cracked, its only water shimmers meekly in rivulets and impotent pools. No longer a danger to a small girl; no longer a destroyer of a father's hopes. Never again will it uncover a brother's cowardice.

It's stinking hot– literally– on the hill. No shelter. I'm sweating here under the shade cloth; even sweating inside my insulated hut. I didn't think all the people would go. I mean die out.

Our... my star is bloated with age, running out of life-sustaining fuel. Even at night– once was called night– when it is on the other side of the planet, its orange tentacles flare around the edges. Like living in a halo–a dying giant's smirk at me: my two angels are buried in the valley. Seldom any darkness at night; only when black, smoggy clouds engulf us... me... me. The Moon cops more heat now and glows like a bank of interrogation lamps. I'd confess to anything if it would reduce my sentence. Ha. Nobody to scoff at my attempts at humour. As happens here.

I miss gazing at a sky sparkling with millions of stars. Now sparse; a sad expanse of white, spotted like dandruff on my good shirt. One of those Eva scrounged from Wilson's Menswear–he was long gone.
Of course, they told us. Warned us. They knew the universe was expanding at a fearful speed, accelerating away from us minute-by-minute. So fast. But we didn't feel it. Then, eventually, we began to see the gaps between galaxies. The stars were leaving us. So many warnings. Some fanatics even set up camps on hills and preached that the end of the world was coming. Did that millions of years ago. Closer to the truth now, but not alive to see it happen. If there was a god, who could love one so vindictive?
We listened to the scientists, but what could we do? Not superheroes. Nor were they.
Those misguided thousands who set off in several interstellar shiploads to settle new worlds all perished. Even if they had survived, they would be dying with the universe as much as I am.

Funny how I miss true neighbours when I look up at night. Still some there, of course but they're going, disappearing into the unimaginable infinity. Some say that one day— whatever a day might be then —it will all come rushing back after another Big Bang.

There are more of some things: red dwarfs, white dwarfs, quasar black holes. Many of them. Our final destiny. Before then, for me, goodness knows what.

Goodness. Who knows what goodness is anymore? I don't, and I'm the only 'who' existing. Last of an endangered species.

I should go into town again. Just in case there's something there I missed, some food. A tool I might now find useful. Shouldn't have thrown my hammer away. I could have washed the blood off.

Yes, shop foraging tomorrow…We used to go into town and do that a lot. Me and Eva. Such fun. She loved dressing up. She looked beautiful. Like a fine lady, I said. Which she was. She always scoffed and told me to open my eyes wider. But she always smiled and turned away.

Eva was like a child in a lolly shop at those times. She used to try on one outfit after another, and dance how she felt about each one. I remember happiness.

She'd kick off her shoes, pull the skirt above her knees and jig around the shop floor, smooth brown legs, hopping over and between discarded clothes. Often deftly balancing on the tips of her toes.

Sometimes, Eva would stop abruptly, poised mid-dance like a figure in a frozen stream, purple skirt hitched high, smiling at me in that pretend-shy way I loved. If I suggested, in my pretend-shy way that she never believed, that we visit the bedding department, she would nod, and I'd take her hand and we would rush towards the internal doorway. Sometimes… times gone… As ……

Once I saw Abla watching Eva dancing, through the shop window. He stared at her from the footpath. He turned away when he realised I was looking at him. He quickly walked away as if caught with his hand in the lolly jar. Eva didn't notice.

I was uneasy; but I never mentioned it to either of them. I should have told Eva. Might have saved ... No.

My favourite place in that desolate, decaying town was the Biblio Knowledge Centre. What a treasure trove of thoughts, creativity, dreams, research, criticisms, history, wishes, warnings–and most revealing of all: the thrill and romance of page-Clearys, screen-flickers, recounting ancient human dramas. At heart, so much like us, despite appearances. The predictions from millennia ago made us laugh. So many pronouncements of coming catastrophes. How wrong they were. Mostly. Eva and I laughed at them. One day she suppressed a giggle, looked at me with a serious face and said: "Are we dead?" I touched her lips and said she felt very much alive, and we kissed.

They said we were all doomed. The whole damn human race. Yet there we were billions of years later. Now, I face my lone eclipse. Anger replaced laughter.

Way back, close to the dawn of civilisation, a poet called Thomas Dylan, or perhaps the other way around–those ancient names were a bit odd–once advised us to "Rage, rage against the dying of the light". I think it was about dying old. Our Sun is older than any human ever was and taking many human lifetimes. And I have raged. How I raged as the future dawned on me, and people I loved died around me, and the universe deserted us.

They –those who are all dead now– hadn't factored in our intelligence, ingenuity and our resilience. They didn't know then that science and technology would step in to give evolution a helping hand – more than hands, of course. Few would see that we would become part human, part devices. Now miniaturised robots run around in our blood, repairing us before we know we're broken. Technology hand-in-hand with evolution.

They said we could live on and on and on. But the joke was on us: On the verge of immortality, we realised our life source in the sky was dying.

My greatest pleasure at the Biblio was the fiction: through uncounted centuries, it was more real to me–more human– than the works of non-fiction.

Me and Eva loved 'made-up' stuff: long stories, short stories, poems, songs in myriad forms, in a tiny patch of a doomed planet circling its dying star.

We delved into the minds of men and women over millennia. Eva and me stood like dwarfs before giants, in the massive central room of towering, old-fashioned, scruffy-fronted bookshelves.

But outside that cultural treasury, galaxies were rushing away from the Milky Way; from each other.

We knew we lived on a beautiful planet. One more beautiful than any other in our system, or the galaxy for that matter. A planet covered by a multi-coloured, crazy patchwork of oceans and mountains and lakes, rivers, forests, jungles, towns and cities and farmland. Once were ice caps.

About a year ago, a group of us went on a grand tour of our continent — a sort of farewell tour. It was that. We enjoyed our time together. We had long been friends. All too frequently, conversations, laughter were silenced instantly as if by a Radov set switch and we stood, hands reaching for others, staring mutely at another part of our lost heritage, another piece of our dying home. The change shocked those who'd visited those sites. It was like visiting a beautiful young woman and finding, when she opened the door, she had turned a hundred since you last saw her.

And everywhere there were bodies. And the eyes of the soon-to-be-bodies watching from windows, rooftops, trees and bushes.

We walked hesitantly along streets of once bustling cities, awesome in their immensity, depressing in their quiet emptiness. We trod carefully, holding our breath as much as possible, looking all around, up and down, as if we expected a monster to roar out of a doorway. Eva was especially nervous when we passed the gaping entrance to a carpark.

It could have been a dream holiday: no tourists. No living residents at all made it a nightmare.

We didn't hang around. It was a terrible journey home. Death everywhere. It was overwhelming. At some places we were the only ones alive.

Then, death struck us also. Ja-Neel collapsed, coughing, choking in the thick greyness that enveloped us. Abla was inconsolable and cried a lot when Ja-Neel died the next day. We all did. She was pretty, bright, always cheery–and Abla loved her.

For a while, I thought Abla wouldn't continue with us. Better if he had stayed there. If only Eva — and others – hadn't implored my brother to come home. Too late for 'if onlys'.

Our grand tour became a trail of tears. More of us died; many more around us.

We passed bodies every day; human and animal–birds fell on us, suddenly dropping out of the clouded sky. Too many dead people to consider burying.

We saw huge fires to the east. Another behind us. We hurried on.

Just we three made it back.

Nobody here when we returned. Those who farewelled us. They were... No one to embrace the prodigal sons and daughter. The only 'fatted lamb' was grotesquely swollen, long dead, in the lower paddock.

I hovered between life and death for days. I awoke late one night to Eva's glowing smile lighting her beautiful face.

We were warned, but what could we do? No power on piddling, insignificant Earth could hold back the Universe's inexorable progress to infinity.

Stars flare up, explode, die, black holes form, voraciously, silently, sucking in anything that wanders near, like a giant invisible vacuum cleaner.

There are black holes in our neighbourhood. Long after I've gone, the solar system will probably be sucked in. Or maybe not. Before that, all the bits of the universal engine will have spun out of sight of each other– not that there will be any eyes left to see. A race where the winner loses any which way.

No matter to me. I won't be around. I'm glad Eva, too, won't suffer through that cataclysmic finale. She saw enough as it was.

Always on my mind. Could I have done anything to prevent it? To save Eva?

Helpless on all fronts: from the human level up to the astronomical.

I didn't save Eva that day. Right here, close, on the same soil. So what chance did I or the entire human race have? We could only watch as the Sun devoured Mercury and licked at Venus with flicking, flaming tongues. Earth next...

Helpless, doomed spectators, cooked by the Sun's rays, buffeted by solar winds.

Our medium-size star will keep on growing and growing at the centre of the solar system whether we are here to see it or not.

That gives me a shiver down my back. It is so eerie to think of the Universe going on about its business without anyone to look out at the moon and the planets, and far, far beyond.

They will keep on going and going and going, doing what they will do.

It may all disappear into an infinitively tiny spot. And then, some said, it might all reverse, starting with another Big Bang. Don't know why it bothers.

Funny in the end. I guess this is the end or soon will be.

I am lonely, looking out there up into the vast, unfriendly expanse.

I miss Eva. And my precious little Eva-ly. I go to their grave and stand and wail and fall to my knees.

It's a steep slope there now, of course.

Then the river was wild and rushing. And hot. We trusted Alba to keep her safe. He said he was distracted when she slipped into the frothing water. He just stood watching. Said he couldn't swim. I ran down when I heard the screams, but I was too late.

Our legs are not built for running. Evolution didn't always get it right. I won't have to worry any more.

Hard to dig graves with short fingers. Can't get a good grip around the shovel handle, as thin as it is.

I must move my thoughts from that afternoon. Focus on memories of the great library, of the ancient books with their fragile stiffness, pages webbed with crinkles and zig-zagging cracks.

Somehow real and unreal, comforting and disturbing. We owed so much to the men and women who preserved these treasures over the aeons.

Now nothing can save them. The loss of them is more heartbreaking than my impending destruction.

The words, sentences, thoughts often took my breath away. Sometimes shocking, sometimes sublime, always... uniquely human. Unbelievable to modern minds. Our brains, taken over by so-called thinking cap implants, version-by-version, upgrade-by-upgrade, lost their essential humanness.

We no longer needed to think–we had miniature computers always on hand, stepping in before our poor brains knew there was a problem to solve.

So glad Charles Dickens, Margaret Atwood, Milton, Shakespeare, Jules Verne and ... all those... had to rely on their natural abilities.

And yet. What does it matter now?

But no creativity, little imagination or inspiration. Our literature is robotic; music like kids playing with saucepans and big spoons; our songs trash.

They promised to add the missing 'spark' to the TJC v326.86 update. A promise that won't be kept. "Doh", as some idiot cartoon character once said. How can such inanities last for billions of years?

Millions of years without great literature – or anything creative, not even clever toys. Except those invented by kids too young to have thinking caps.

Shakespeare was wonderful – despite his wall-like name — what he did with the English language. Blind John Milton's beautiful poetry... unhampered by loss of sight or lack of thinking cap.

That Lord fellow–name or rank, I don't know. I have read in places that once people prayed to Lords. I read in places that fellow Tenny something wrote wonderful poetry... "O for the touch of a vanished hand...", Eva's hug, Eva-ly's little fingers grasping mine... gone... "The sound of a voice that is stilled." I sit in silence... at their haven under the hill.

I also spent hours engrossed in lives of kings and queens and presidents and prime ministers, explorers of a world so different from now, a world where the oceans weren't boiling and rivers rushed, bursting with life, a world where green and blue were dominant, not brown and grey and black. Enough...

It's weird, sad, to realise no one will ever read, hear, or see them again. They'll lie there ignored by the Universe as it dies around them, its components spinning and spinning and being sucked into black holes.

Earth will probably be vaporised before that by the ravenous flames of a gigantic sun at the centre of what's left of the solar system.

It breaks my heart when I think of that. Every trace of human existence in the Universe will disappear. All those... I haven't contributed to anything for posterity. Can there be a posterity if there are no people?

I regret what happened, I reacted badly. Could I have done anything else? Perhaps...

Nobody to ask; nobody to accuse me. But I had to help Eva. Didn't I? Who am I asking?

I couldn't control my emotions. That's it. Plain and simple.

I ran as fast as I could up from the river bed when I heard Eva shouting for me. Screaming: "Kai-na. Kai-na".

It could have been another snake. But where was Abla? They were both in the shed. He was wrestling with Eva, trying to push her to the ground. Her shirt was ripped. He was pulling at her skirt with his left hand. I lost it.

Grabbing the hammer from the bench, I shouted: "Get away from her," or something weak like that.

Eva twisted her head to see me rushing at them. Her eyes wide with fear. I might have seen a spark of hope in them. I blink that instant of the scene away. I can't bear that seeing me gave my little Eva hope at that moment. It was a false hope.

He turned to face me, pushing Eva away. She rushed back at him, furiously punching him. He grabbed her right shoulder, spun her around and flung her away. Her feet scrabbled in the dirt floor as she tried to regain balance. Desperately, I tried to grab her. Just out of reach. She staggered, fell towards the bench.

I saw, as if in slow motion–slower in tormented dreams–her body topple, heard the thud of her head, the whisper-quiet groan.

A little yellow shoe slid, stopped at my feet.

I yelled for her to get back. Before she could move, Abla violently shoved her away.

Before I could get to her to staunch the blood flow, Abla hit me from behind. My legs buckled but fury drove me back up. I turned, swung the hammer wildly. It slammed into the side of his face. He grunted and punched my upper arm. I almost dropped the hammer, but I knew death waited there.

Blood ran from his left ear. It spattered when my second blow struck. He swore and kicked my legs, but I could see he was badly hurt. I was past caring. I swung again and he crumpled to the ground.

I knew my brother was dead.

So was Eva.

I buried Eva on the hillside, next to our Eva-ly's tiny plot. I tried to say appropriate words but only managed "I love you, Eva" before tears flowed, my lips trembled, and I couldn't continue. I think she would understand.

Sometimes when I shade my eyes from the glaring sun, and I gaze at the top of the hill, I fancy Abla is waving to me. But it's the wind blowing his free arm away from the post, wriggling like a thick snake struggling to escape tree traps.

He'll stay there, staring into the river valley but see nothing. I should have buried him, I suppose. But I wanted a reminder on the hill of what he did. And what I did. I'm keeping my brother.

I think I will close my eyes and lie here until morning. I don't want to look at the sky around my poor planet, my doomed home. I can't stand the memories of what can never be again.

That fellow, billions of years ago, Shakespeare, he wrote 'To be or not to be, that is the question'. I don't recall the answer – if there was one. But, I know, here, now. Helpless under the heat of the star consuming the last of its hydrogen, turning it into helium, here, now tonight, for the last man… last murderer, on earth, it is 'not to be'.

THE END

When Peter read the last sentence of Solitary Eclipse and then re-read it, his shout of "Got it!" brought Jan running to the dining room door. Her face morphed from alarm to surprise. She looked around the room as if expecting something unusual to have suddenly arrived there, like a bag of gold or…she didn't know what. Peter was still sitting at the same place at the end of the table. The manuscript was still lying in front of him folded back. There were two biscuits left on the plate and his coffee mug was almost drained. He looked up at her, his excitement apparent.

"Sorry, Jan, I interrupted your program. More good news. I think I see something clear-cut here. What's the time?"

"It's about ten. Why?"

"It's a bit late, isn't it?"

"It's the same time on your watch."

"I want to phone. I want to contact Mr Cleary. This story, the final one, I think it means something important to our investigations."

"What is it?" she asked, taking a step into the room.

"I wish I could tell you right now. I want to tell somebody. But I'm not supposed to."

"Does this mean the end of your nightly homework?"

He nodded. "It may be."

She turned back into the living room calling out over her shoulder: "I'll get back to my whodunnit. I want to know who the culprit is in this little mystery on TV."

Peter couldn't resist it. He picked up his phone and called Detective Inspector Cleary.

"Hello, Sir, it's me –"

"I can tell it's you, Peter. I hope you have a good reason for calling me at home at this hour."

"I think so, Sir. I have just read the last story in the manuscript –"

"That's pleasing for you, but is that why you rang me sometime after ten?"

This last story, Solitary Eclipse, is the first I have read where George Martin actually writes that his life is about to end. I think it might mean suicide was on his mind, Sir."

"If that is so, if it is as clear-cut as you seem to think, we may well close it up and move on to some other business. But I want to read what you have read and come to my own conclusion. I think I would rather do this tomorrow morning in my office. After all, if it's shows that George Martin killed himself, the killer won't get away overnight, will he?"

Peter felt a bit squashed, enthusiasm dampened by his superior's response.

"You're right, Sir, it can wait till the morning. I am sorry for disturbing you. I will see you in the morning. Good night and good night to Sandra."

> The why of murder always fascinates
> me so much more than the how.
> -*Ann Rule*

CHAPTER
21

Peter tried to not watch Inspector Cleary read the last pages of the manuscript. He knew Cleary hated being watched while he read any sort of paperwork. They were sitting across the desk from each other in Cleary's office. Peter looked up at the calendar on the side wall wondering what some of the circles and marks and words and dates meant. He probably knew because he was kept up to date with everything but he just couldn't read them from across the room. He looked at the clock on the other wall. It was mid-morning. He looked back at Cleary. He tried to note any sign of excitement in his boss's demeanour. At last, Cleary closed the manuscript, turned it upside down on the desk in front of him.

"What do you think, Sir?"

Cleary looked at him with no sign of what he thought on his face.

"I can see what you are excited about, Sergeant,"

"It seems to point to Martin contemplating suicide. But I think what Martin wrote here could point in other directions than the one you have gone down."

Peter was dismayed. He thought it was obvious. George Martin didn't expect to go on living for much longer.

"But, sir, his last words indicate he soon won't be existing. That he won't, as he says, 'be' anymore.

"George Martin was a creative writer. He made up all sorts of stories. And we are looking at— or hearing— a man who perhaps several months earlier had been given a death sentence by the doctors."

Peter thumped the top of the desk. He put his hand back on his lap following a disapproving look from Cleary.

"I forgot that he had a terminal disease. What an idiot. I shouldn't be a detective."

Peter hoped that Cleary would contradict him. But he waited in vain.

"Yes, Sir, I do know that he had prostate cancer and…"

"And he was told he didn't have very long to live."

"So… so, he wouldn't have had any reason to kill himself, then?"

Cleary said: "Unless he was afraid of dying in hospital, possibly in great pain. He had been a very independent man, so I think the idea of being in a terminal condition in a hospital bed to be waited on and treated with all sorts of medications and goodness knows what, would be enough reason for a man to commit suicide. Don't you think, Peter?"

Peter saw that he had no other way than to agree, Cleary had come to the same conclusion as he had, but from a different direction. He thought it wiser not to point that out to his boss.

"So, we are no further ahead than where we started a couple of days ago."

Now, Peter just wanted to give up on the whole thing. Call it suicide. Give Margot Martin and Nagle and perhaps even Nola, what they wanted to hear: death by suicide. Died by his own hands. Perhaps while of unsound mind.

"Where to now, Inspector?"

Cleary patted the manuscript and said: "This unfinished manuscript may yet help us in some way. But for now we will consider it a closed book." Peter had a downcast look.

"But there is something else we should do. Something that may help us further than the manuscript so far has done."

Peter hoped so. He hoped they would get something out of this. If George Martin had been killed, it was essential that they caught his killer or killers. It was not the time to give up on this.

"What can we do?" Peter asked.

Cleary briefly held up the manuscript and dropped it again, "This may not be the whole George Martin story. I'm not satisfied that it has revealed the way the man was feeling. How do you see that, other than that short story? Has the manuscript helped?"

"Well, as far as we know, he dictated almost everything he saw and heard. Sorry, didn't dictate what he heard. I know that. I mean the recorder gives us his thoughts and thoughts of other people who at times showed they didn't like Martin. Some outspoken people paint a clear picture of the man. But –"

"Yes, but here's the thing." He looked at Peter. Peter perked up.

"Of course. He also dictated at the desk. Meaning he may have other parts of his story recorded on the screen. Did the tech guys bring the computer back here?" Peter said.

Cleary got up and went over to the cupboard behind him. He unlocked the door and pulled out a laptop computer case. "They have returned this and cracked the password. They reckon we'll be interested in what's on it."

He unzipped the case and took out the computer. A MacBook Pro.

"I suggest we have a look at the last few things that were recorded in the manuscript on the computer. I am assuming that the printout is from the recorded material being transcribed into the printed manuscript text. But he may well have said some other things after the manuscript was printed out."

Peter got up. He was excited now. He went over and almost pushed his superior aside. Gently, but firmly.

"Let me have a go. I know this machine. I use it at home. Do you mind if I have a look?"

Cleary stood back. "Sit in my chair. Here's the password IT figured out." He handed Peter a slip of paper.

"Oh," Peter said, reading it. "It's 'Margot'. Such an easy password to guess if you knew the man." He sighed. He would bet good money that Margot's password was not 'George'.

For some time, Peter tapped furiously, then sitting with finger poised above the keyboard, stared at the screen. Cleary stood on the other side of the desk watching but not knowing what was happening on the computer. He didn't interrupt Peter's thoughts. Let him concentrate on the task.

Then Peter exclaimed: "I have it. It is stuff that appears to be written after the last page of the printed manuscript. You were right."

"What does he tell us?" Cleary asked moving slightly around the desk, trying to see the screen.

Peter didn't answer. He was concentrating on reading. He gasped, then said "Oh my God". More silence.

Cleary bent over, hoping to see what was causing Peter's silence.

"What is it? Is it of any use to us?"

No answer. Peter worked quickly, scrolling down the page and back up, then reading down again. At last, he looked up, his face glowing.

"This settles it, Inspector. This is conclusive proof that George Martin was murdered. He did not hang himself. Others did it."

Peter got out of his boss's chair and gestured for Cleary to sit.

"You read it. I'm sure you will agree with me this time." Peter was, indeed, sure that the Inspector would read it the way he did. Would see what he meant. Would come to the same conclusion.

Cleary did come to the same conclusion. "This changes everything, Sergeant, this seals their fate. We have them."

Cleary switched the computer off and closed the lid, put it in the case again. He stood and took the computer to the cupboard, closed it and locked the door.

It's very easy to kill—so long as no one suspects you
-Agatha Christie

CHAPTER 22

Text read from George Martin's laptop:
hello george how are you going working away at this late hour

I might ask what you are doing here nagle scared the life out of me just bursting in like that what have you got there

I thought you might like a cup of coffee I think you have been at it for longer than usual look at the time I think I have made the coffee the way you like it margot helped me with that

I am sure you will like it george

margot I thought youd be in bed by now and you also Nagle what is going on?

look george "we are trying to be nice I know you have had a rough trot lately and I would like you to relax. Give yourself ten minutes break. relax sure you will then restart your writing refreshed all right okay thank you nagle and you, too, margot

That's the way I'll come back in ten minutes to take the mug out of your way can't have you knocking anything over your computer can we?

finished it now, George?"

"I... I... think so it was a big mug you gave me and I drank more than I usually do.

well, the more the better, I would have thought, darling

darling? are you talking to me, margot

well I think I should start again and call you darling while I can... all that coffee should have refreshed you and cleared your mind ready for the next bit of writing

to tell... the... truth, margot... I think that it... strangely... has made me sleepy

Mr Nagle said that is strange isn't it George

yes... must rest a little while... longer... wake up a bit more

maybe you could stand up walk around the office a little bit to stretch your legs. get your circulation moving again "what do you think Mark"

No and I am... so...tired I think I should probably...go to... bed I may need help to get there this is very strange I have been working... too hard I guess."

probably true. George we can help you.

Good. Good... Thank

I think he is asleep now Mark.

"We must be sure. We don't want him shouting out Help or something like that.

"Look at him. He can't shout. He can't even whisper anymore. That is ironic, isn't it?

You are right. I'll put the rope over the hook now. It shouldn't be too difficult if I stand on the desk. You keep an eye on him. Make sure he doesn't get a fresh burst of energy.

"I will look after him. After all, he is my husband. I should care for him. And I will care for him till death us do part. That's a good one, isn't it, Mark?"

It's fast and tight enough up here I'll come down now and help get the rope around George's neck and both of us will haul him up until he is sitting on the edge of the desk.

"It won't be easy, Mark. He is pretty big and heavy.

And I am very strong, Margot. Why are you giggling?

"This this is all so exciting. I just realised I'm in the middle of creating a murder mystery. We both are."

Bugger that. None of that fancy stuff. Just get the job done and you will be free and I will be free to

"to do what we want to do from now on, with lots of money.

Swing low Sweet George Martin novelist. Short story writer.

Right. Just check around everywhere. Margot make sure we are not leaving any clues here. It is important that the cops think this is what it looks like: a suicide.

Well done, Mark, we did it. See how he swings so easily. If I push him.

What a great way to start a new day, a new life.

You go now Margot. I'll have a couple of hours sleep and then wait for you to come in and 'discover' the body. When I hear you I'll come running. That's our story.

Thanks Mark, you are good at odd jobs. I'll go and get into my nightie.

"All right, Peter," Cleary said, speaking firmly as if he had made a decision that required instant action. "I agree, that does sound a lot like they did it." We will go now and talk with Mrs Martin and Mr Nagle. Let's see what they have to say."

Margot and Nagle entered the lounge room in the Martin home, each appearing both surprised and annoyed at their summons. Cleary nodded at them and waved them to the long lounge. Nagle plopped himself down on one end. Margot stood for a moment, then sat at the other, leaving a space between her and the chauffeur.

"What is the meaning of this?" she asked. Peter noticed the anger in her voice. But there didn't seem to be any concern. If they were the murderers, he would have expected anxiety, suspicion even. He did not appear worried. They were cool customers he thought.

Cleary said: "We have obtained some more evidence that implicates both of you in the murder of Mr George Martin." Both suspects cried out.

Margot said: "Preposterous. You have overreached yourself, this time, Inspector."

Nagle had leapt to his feet, shouting: "It's a bloody frame-up. You can't possibly have any evidence of that sort."

"Please sit down. Both of you, please. You must listen to what we have to say. Then you will have the opportunity to speak about what you have heard."

Margot and Nagle looked at each other. Nagle sat down. Peter thought that despite their outrage, they were curious to hear what was coming.

Cleary said: "I have here a recording of the last words that were dictated, apparently inadvertently, into Mr Martin's laptop computer. Please listen to it in its entirety before interrupting."

He placed the laptop on the coffee table, opened it, and logged on.

"This was the last thing recorded on this laptop. It seems Mr Martin may have been interrupted while dictating a story. This time he was dictating it directly onto the computer, as, I believe you will be aware, he sometimes did. As you know he most often transcribed his stories and other information from his voice recorder onto the computer. That is what made all those pages of what we have called his manuscript. This part that you are about to hear is what was recorded in his last moments."

Margot clasped her hands together and stared at the laptop as if someone had placed a bomb in the room. Nagle slumped back and folded his arms across his chest.

"Detective Sergeant York has read the entire printed manuscript –"

"Just rubbish," Margot shouted.

"He read it to the very end, but we didn't know that there was a further recording. Please listen to the final scene in Mr George Martin's life."

He highlighted the section on the computer and started Siri reading it out.

Peter watched the two on the lounge. Their reaction seemed to be one of disbelief. They looked at each other, the detectives and the computer with wide eyes. Several times Nagle grunted. Margot was biting her bottom lip. But, to Peter, disappointingly, they did not look like killers, who had been confronted with the evidence that would put them away. Very cool guys.

Cleary closed the lid of the laptop when the recording ended. He waited for a response from the two suspects.

Margot began to rise. Nagle followed suit.

"That's all spurious, Inspector," she said. She sounded amused. "If that is all the so-called evidence you have, then you might as well erase it right now, delete it. We were not there in the room when my husband killed himself. None of that conversation occurred."

Nagle said: "That is a lie – all of it. It's a stitch-up. Margot... Mrs Martin is telling the truth. As I am also. I didn't say any of those things. I didn't do any of those things. I would never do those things. And I know Margot did not say any of those things."

"So, detectives," Margot said, "where the hell has that come from? The computer read it to us. Some people say, a computer doesn't lie. Well, that, in itself, is a great big lie. I am afraid that you will have to go back to the drawing board, fellows, because you have not solved this case. In fact, as we have said from the beginning, there is no case here. Nobody killed George. He killed himself. The sooner you all agree that is the way things were, the sooner we can all go back to what is left of our lives."

Her voice was shaky. Towards the end of that statement Peter saw that her eyes were watery, but no tears ran down her face.

"We will want to talk further with you down at the station. I will give you half an hour to do whatever you need to do before accompanying us there."

Margot stomped to the door and slammed it just before Nagle reached it. He looked at the closed door, turned back to the detectives, smiled, opened the door and went out. He closed it more quietly than Margot had done.

Peter had gone to the laptop and picked it up to place it in the case. Cleary had been looking thoughtful and he raised his hand to stop Peter continuing. He took the laptop from Peter and sat on the lounge with it. He opened it and reread what they had played just moments before.

Peter said: "I'm ready to go whenever you say so, sir."

Cleary raised his arm. His other hand still on the laptop. Peter could see that he was scrolling down through the text, then back up and back down again. He felt a tad uneasy. What was the Inspector looking at? Cleary gazed at Peter.

"Peter, I think we may have been a bit premature."

Peter's heart sank. Had he stuffed up this evidence? How could he have? Text was there on the computer just as it had been recorded faithfully, without any human intervention. He looked at Cleary, waiting for further elucidation.

"There was something about all that text," Cleary said, "and I was wondering what it was that had struck me. I am not great at technology. I know the basics and can get by, so I didn't at first realise what was wrong."

Peter felt his boss was, by implication, and between the lines, saying that he, as a skilled computer user, should have seen something. He waited for Cleary to continue.

"Come, look at this, Peter." He handed the laptop to Peter who sat down with it on his knees.

"What is it, sir, that I am looking for?"

"Just look at it all." Peter shook his head, but turned his eyes back onto the screen, at the black letters on the white background. He was about to query his boss again when he saw it. His face went pale.

"Oh, shit. How did I not see that? I'm sorry."

"We both missed it. As obvious as it is, we didn't see what was staring us in the face. I think we were too eager to get somebody for this."

"We will have to apologise to Mrs Martin and Mr Nagle, now." Peter gulped.

Cleary said: "Yes. This so-called murder scene appears to have been staged. Possibly set up by George Martin to frame them."

Peter was embarrassed that his non-computer buff boss had spotted what he, the 'expert', had missed.

Cleary clarified his thoughts. "Yes. When you are dictating to a computer, it records everything it hears perfectly but unless the person speaking announces punctuation such as quotation marks, capital letters and such, it won't appear on the screen as it did in this case where we have such anomalies like 'Mr Nagle said' and the word 'period 'denoting the speaker wanted a full stop at the end of a sentence. This is supposed to have been sitting on the desk recording the exact words of Mrs Martin and her accomplice Mr Nagle. So those two, intent on their murderous task, would not have said 'start quotes, end quotes' or even 'ellipsis', for goodness sake.

"Sorry, sir, I stuffed up. Another thing I noticed at the top right of the screen when I turned the laptop on. There was a warning that a USB drive had not been ejected properly."

Cleary swore. "So, Sergeant, someone pre-recorded that so-called murder scene and copied it into the laptop for the bloody dumb cops to think they had cracked the case."

Peter slammed the lid of the laptop. He stuffed it into the case and zipped it up. Both men sighed.

'What do you make of it," Cleary said, "Do you think that George Martin dictated all that with the intent of framing his wife and the chauffeur? Do you think he was that cunning?"

Peter thought about that for a moment, then said: "He may have done that. At one stage in the manuscript, he said that if they killed him, as he feared, he would get them. Did he go to his grave, content in the knowledge that wife and chauffeur would be going to jail?"

"I've never heard of such a thing."

"Neither have I." Both men sat on the lounge in silence for a few minutes. Cleary broke the silence.

"Of course, there is another scenario. "He may not have intended to punish them in this way, just wanted them to be inconvenienced and embarrassed for a little while. When we rushed in and took them to be interviewed... interrogated... for a crime they didn't commit. Maybe he wanted to get his own back in a way that wouldn't send them to prison."

"Or," Peter said, "that may have been written by somebody else. It may have been written by somebody who did kill George Martin."

"That's also possible. What we have to find out is if someone else had access to the laptop after Martin's body was discovered."

Peter stood and walked around the coffee table. He said it would not have been Nagle or Margot who typed it because it would send them to prison.

"Who would have so inexpertly typed that with the intent of framing two innocent people?"

As they went out of the room to break the embarrassing news to Margot and Nagle, they were both of the same mind that George Martin had written the scenario deliberately to get the police thinking that his death, about to be caused by himself, would, for a while, point the finger at his wife and Nagle. But he had done it in such a fashion that he knew his ploy would eventually be discovered and neither would be charged.

"He must've had a lot of faith in the cops spotting deliberate errors," Peter said.

Cleary nodded. "The cops were a bit slow in spotting that, but fortunately we did see it before we made fools of ourselves. Can you imagine what a lawyer in court would make of that?" Neither wanted to imagine that situation.

They went up and broke the news to Margot first. She surprised them by not railing at them about their stupidity. To the contrary, she thanked them for their astuteness in not being tricked by what she saw as George's attempt to frame them. Nagle wasn't so understanding, but beneath his grudging acceptance of their apology, he was obviously relieved.

> It strikes me profoundly that the world is more often than not a bad and cruel place.
> -Bret Easton Ellis, *American Psycho*

CHAPTER 23

Peter shivered when he and Cleary walked into Jeremy's vegetable garden. He wasn't sure whether it was the coolness in the pre-dawn mist that still hung in the air or shadowy figures dimly seen among the tomato stakes. The doctor was there, not to heal, but to report on the manner and time of the woman's death. They were shocked at this unexpected murder of the woman they had only recently chatted with at the shopping centre. This was another mystery to them. But in this case, it wasn't a mystery of whether it was self-inflicted or murder.

"Sir, did I misunderstand? I thought they said she was dead."

Cleary turned away from the scene in the garden and looked at Peter. "You heard right, Sergeant."

"She seems to be standing... or at least upright. I guess it..."

Cleary touched Peter's shoulder. "Let's go and have a closer look. It is strange, even bizarre. I agree."

Peter hadn't said anything to be agreed with. But it was more than bizarre. It was chilling. Mrs James was upright and appeared to be looking further down into the garden, her head bent forward. Her arms were stretched out, on either side of her body. The detectives went closer, nodding to the scene-of-crime officer and Doctor Gaston. Peter gasped when he saw why she was in such a posture. Jenny James's wrists were tied to tomato stakes with dark green twine. Her feet were barely touching the ground. Peter walked between some small tomato bushes and looked at Jenny who was strung so horribly on tomato stakes in her son's garden. He looked at her face, her eyes open, and Peter knew they were not seeing him or anything in the yard. The last thing they had seen was probably her killer. The person who had put a rope around her throat and strangled her.

Peter shivered again, and he knew now that it wasn't the coolness of the unseasonal weather.

"Peter," Cleary said, "where do we begin to find even one suspect for this seemingly," he paused, as if lost for words, "seemingly inexplicable killing?"

Peter didn't have an answer for that, he just shook his head.

Cleary spoke to the uniformed officers who were assiduously searching, lifting leaves, every plant and bush, as well as the rows between the garden beds. They shook their heads. Nothing so far.

Doctor Gaston was bent close to Jenny's neck, turning his head as he peered at her from all angles. He didn't touch her. That would come later. In even greater detail. The scene of crime detective motioned with his head for Cleary to come to where he was standing near the tomato stake that Jenny's right hand was tied to.

"What have you got, Matt?"

In reply Matt pointed to a dark brown stain near the top of the stake. Cleary peered at it. Peter got as close as he could without treading on something or somebody.

"Blood?" he said looking up.

"Yep," Matt said.

Peter took a step closer, squashing a tomato under his foot as he did so. He shook his shoe and rubbed it on the grass to the horror of the others at the scene. He was pleased that at least his shoes were covered with the required bootees.

"Sorry, so sorry. It was just a reflex action. I trod on a tomato."

Matt said: "So that's the end of that tomato then as a DNA check."

Peter reddened – not quite as much as the tomatoes, but they might have seen him as a blood brother. He began to stammer an apology, but saw that Cleary was smiling at Matt.

"It's okay, Sergeant, we've checked the ground all around here and I don't think your clumsy action will affect the investigation. I think the blood on this splinter will help us much more than the squashed tomato."

Peter was relieved but annoyed at the allusion to his clumsiness. He knew they were right.

Cleary said: "It looks as if the person who did this might have been caught on a splinter."

Matt nodded. "Yes. And I think forensics might find some more DNA under her fingernails. There appears to be a little bit of skin."

Cleary looked around the yard. He glanced down at the squashed tomato and looked up at Peter, who blushed again. Peter wanted to ask whether it was possible to trace DNA from one tomato to another. Could tomato residue on the killer's shoe be matched with a squashed tomato near the victim? He wasn't game to ask that question. Probably ridiculous.

Cleary said: "Okay, we'll leave you experts to it. Get your reports to me as soon as possible, please."

The experts were too busy to say anything other than a brief "Okay", "Fine", etc.

"Let's go talk to Jeremy now, Peter. Poor bloke will be distraught."

"Coming across your mother like that would be absolutely horrifying," Peter said. He wasn't looking forward to this at all.

They went in the back door. There were several officers already in the house examining this part of the crime scene.

They found Jeremy sitting at the dining room table, arms in front of him, palms down, head resting on his hands. He was sobbing quietly. Peter asked him if he would like a drink of some sort. He said: "No thanks".

Peter made coffee for each of them, anyway. He placed a mug before Jeremy who lifted his head at the sound of the movement on the coaster. He looked up at Peter and then Cleary.

"You guys are doing this all the time, aren't you? Murder, I mean. Can you help me understand why people do this to other people? Please? Two people who have not offended or hurt anyone. Poor Mum. She was so looking forward to the future."

Cleary said: "It is often hard to understand, Mr James. I am sorry... for your tragic loss. I would have liked to have known your mother for longer."

Jeremy wiped his eyes with the back of his hand. "She was. Very friendly. And... Well... I don't understand it. If only I had been here tonight instead of..."

Peter said, "Don't be hard on yourself, Mr James. We all have to go on doing the things we do day by day. We can't stop and sit, doing nothing on the off chance that some crazy person could shatter our lives. We can't do that. We have to continue –"

"But these things shouldn't happen. Not to real people... Well... You know what I mean."

"We must ask you some questions, Mr James," Cleary said. "I know that is the last thing you might want."

Jeremy spoke, louder than he had before: "The first thing I want is to get the mongrel who did this. And if that means I must answer questions, then go ahead. I will help all I can."

"Where were you tonight?" Cleary said.

"I should have been here. Not over there. Not doing..."

"Whoever did this, Mr James, may have waited until another day or night when you weren't here for some other reason. We don't know why he killed your mother... or she, for that matter. But if it was for some crazy reason, then it was only a matter of time, perhaps."

Jeremy looked at Cleary without speaking for a minute or so. Peter broke the silence.

"Have you spoken to Nola yet?

Jeremy paused, then said: "She was here, but had to go home to check on something. She's very upset. She'll be back later."

Cleary said: "Can you tell me the time you were absent, and where you were and what you have been doing?"

Peter wondered if Jeremy would want to talk about what he had been doing. But he knew they had to ask these things.

"I was with Nola at her home. We were..." He trailed off.

"What time did you come home?"

Jeremy studied his watch as if that might help with the answer. He looked up. "It was about 4:30." He blinked a tear away. "All the lights in the house were on but Mum wasn't anywhere. I found her in the garden as you know."

"Were you with Nola all the time that you were at the Martin house?"

Jeremy picked up his coffee mug. He took a deep drink. "I was in her room all the time I was there. I didn't see anyone else." He paused. "As far as I know, nobody saw me either."

Peter knew the early estimate of Mrs James's death was sometime around 3am.

Cleary said: "Did you – or Nola – hear anything while you were –"

"No. I mean I can only speak for myself. I didn't hear anything. The Martin house was very quiet. So, if there was a lot of noise of any sort happening at our place, I think I would have heard."

Peter thought murder didn't always make a lot of noise.

"And Nola, she didn't?"

Jeremy shook his head, took another sip of coffee. "I think she would have told me if she heard my mother being killed. Don't you?"

The detectives watched him drink. He looked at them over the top of the mug, blinking at intervals between the sips.

"A preliminary estimate of the time of your mother's death," Cleary said, "was about 3am. It could be placed a bit earlier or later. We will know more precisely in a day or so. What time did you go to see Nola and when did you return?"

Jeremy didn't seem to notice he had already answered that in another form. "I went there about ten o'clock. I said goodbye to Mum and said I would be back in time for breakfast. I came back a bit earlier than I expected. Well, it was four thirty or so, I think."

"Did you leave Nola earlier than you thought you would for any special reason?"

"No, I… We just thought we had better get some rest before we had to go to work."

That wouldn't have left much time for sleep before work, Peter thought.

"Is it possible, Mr James, that you left here a bit later than you just said?"

Jeremy appeared to be calculating various times involved. "I can't be sure. I didn't expect to have to keep track of all my times to allow for a murderer's timetable."

"Mr James, do you know of anyone who may have wanted to harm your Mum?"

He shook his head. "Nobody. I think she was loved by anyone and everyone she knew. It seemed that way to me."

Peter said: "She worked part-time at one of the local beauty salons, didn't she?"

"It's not a beauty salon, Inspector, I mean Sergeant, it is a hairdresser. She worked there two days a week."

"Did she ever have an altercation or a disagreement with any customers? Or other staff that you know of?" Peter couldn't imagine anyone who was so angry about the colour, tone, or the cut that they would kill the hairdresser. However, he waited for Jeremy's answer, which was a definite no.

Cleary said: "Are all the neighbours a friendly lot? Anyone around here angry with anyone else in the neighbourhood?"

Jeremy thought, rubbing his eyes and wiping his wet knuckles on his shirt. "Mostly, I think, we just get on with our lives without interacting much at all." He paused and looked at Cleary. "There was a fellow across the road a few weeks ago… I think his name is Cawthorne. He's a big man."

Peter was sure that this was the man who told him about the late-night visitor to the Martin home.

"What happened? Did he have an argument with you?"

"Not with me. With Mum. She caught him one night in the back garden, stealing tomatoes and other stuff. She threatened him with a garden stake."

"Did you see this happen?" Cleary said.

He shook his head. "No, I had gone down to the shops. Mum told me about it when I got back. But she was laughing about it. She thought it was funny."

Cleary said: "Did he threaten your mother?"

"He wasn't very happy, but I think he's harmless. He sometimes threatens people. He says he's going to get them. He drinks a bit, you know." He paused and appeared to be thinking of what they had just discussed. "This morning when I went into the garden, I thought Mum was looking at someone or something. It could've been him, but I didn't see or hear him."

Peter wondered if he might be having second thoughts about the man across the street as a potential murderer.

Jeremy reached into his shirt pocket and pulled out a crumpled piece of paper. He handed it to Cleary. "I found this note stuck to the fridge. It's from Mum."

Cleary read the note. It was handwritten. "Jeremy, I have done something very wrong. I'm going away tonight for a little while. If you don't hear from me by tomorrow afternoon, don't forget to fertilise Mr Martin's lawn. He has already paid you for it. Check the bag of lawn food. You may need to re order. I'm sorry. Love you. Mum."

Cleary handed the note to Peter and said: "Jeremy, what do you make of this?"

"It's quite odd, Inspector. I don't know what she's done wrong or why she planned to go away. And Mr Martin hasn't paid me. Mum knew he always paid me after I finished each job. And it's an almost full bag of lawn food. I think she would've known that."

Cleary said: "Do you have any idea where your mother would go? Or with whom, if anyone?"

Jeremy shook his head. "No. I don't know. She has never suddenly gone away overnight before." He paused and took a deep breath. "Obviously she didn't go this time, either."

Peter looked up from the note. "Sir, there is something in this note that Mrs James might have wanted Jeremy to know."

"But it's all confusing."

Peter gave the note back to Cleary. "See that space in the word 're order'?"

Cleary nodded but looked at Peter as if to say, "So what?"

Peter continued excitedly: "It might be that the hyphen is missing," he paused dramatically and looked at his audience of two, "but it could be that the 'c' is missing. Deliberately."

Cleary said: "Recorder. You may have something, Sergeant."

"You think Mum was giving me a message about the missing recorder?"

Cleary stood and told Peter to go to the shed and check it out. If the recorder was there, he was to bring it back and if it wasn't there, wait for him in the house. He said he would look around there a bit longer and then join Peter at the Martin house. He added: "We will talk later to Mrs Martin, Nola, Nagle and people at the hairdressing salon."

As the detectives walked into the hall, Peter turned back to Jeremy and said: "Jeremy, did you show that note to Nola when she was here?"

Jeremy nodded. "She was intrigued by it, too."

Cleary and Peter looked at each other. "I think you'd better get over there quickly." Peter hurried off.

> Murderers are not monsters, they're men. And that's the most frightening thing about them.
> -Alice Sebold, *The Lovely Bones*

CHAPTER 24

Ten minutes later, in the shed, Peter's fears were confirmed. A large part of the fertiliser bag's contents was strewn around the floor. Someone had beaten him to it.

Despite the evidence, he pushed his hands into the bag, feeling around for the recorder, spilling more lawn food in the process. Nothing.

Had it ever been there? If it had been, who has it? Peter wondered whether he should report this to Inspector Cleary. No, his instructions were explicit. If the recorder wasn't in the bag, he was to go to the Martin house and wait. Peter decided he would look there for Nola: the one most likely to have it. He folded down the top of the bag, roughly sealing it with hand pressure. A clear case of shutting the stable door too late.

He went into the house through the side door, coming out near the stairs. To the right of him past the stairs was the kitchen. He checked to see if Nola was in there. She wasn't. The house was silent. He thought someone had said, at some stage during this shocking morning, that Mrs Martin and the chauffeur were out. She had gone to have her hair done. Peter wondered if it might be at Jenny James's workplace. Surely not.

Peter headed up the stairs to look for Nola. She wasn't in any of the bedrooms, so he went to the office. She wasn't there either. Had she left the house altogether?

Peter stood near the desk in the centre of the late George Martin's office. He scratched his head as he looked around, and up-and-down, hoping to spot the voice recorder. He didn't like his chances of finding it after so many others had searched for it including a dangerous person or persons who were very anxious to get the recorder back. Peter knew that it offered the best chance of proving one way or the other whether the author had killed himself or been killed. More likely, the killer, if there was one, had found it and disposed of it. Could that be Nola? He pushed the thought from his mind but nevertheless decided to look for her again downstairs.

He heard a door slam downstairs. Peter had left the door of the office ajar, and now he thought he heard someone coming up the stairs. He stayed where he was. No need to go out until he knew who it was. Who knows, he may hear something to his advantage – to the advantage of the investigation.

He soon found out who it was. Nola.

"What are you doing here?"

Peter was about to answer when someone else did it for him. "Not unusual for me to be here, Nola."

"I'm sorry. Course it isn't. Gave me a bit of a fright. I didn't think there was anybody here."

"Where is everybody?"

Peter hoped he wouldn't give her another fright when he popped out of the office. If he did. For now, he sat in the office chair and waited. The new voice was familiar. Yes. He thought he knew who it was.

"Everybody is only a small number of people. Mum is at the hairdressers, and Nagle is waiting to drive her back, I suppose. She may be out a little longer. Is it important for you to see her?"

"No. You may do just as well."

"I'll help you if I can, Uncle Stephen."

Stephen Martin. That's who it is, Peter thought. He wondered what he was doing coming into an empty house. But then, Nola's uncle might have more right than a detective.

"I've been looking around some of the rooms."

"What are you looking for in our house?"

"It's obvious isn't it, Nola? I'm looking for the recorder. Your Dad's recorder. I think it's important. I know the police want it. It might solve the mystery of your father's death. My brother's. I'm just trying to help them."

Good of him, Peter thought.

"You think it may solve the mystery of Dad's death?" Nola said.

"Yes, it may do that indeed," Stephen said.

"I am... I... I suppose it will turn up sooner or later." She sounded hesitant to Peter.

Stephen said: "It's very important, Nola. If you have that recorder, I want you to hand it to me. Don't buggerise around."

"You're making me nervous, Uncle Stephen. Please stay back. Don't come too close. It's just –"

Stephen laughed. "Are you worried?"

"Being up here at the top of the stairs. I don't want to –"

"Want to overbalance? Don't want to fall down onto the hard tiles way down there? Just because I take a step towards you, my dear niece, you don't have to take one back. That's putting yourself in danger of falling down the stairs. Stay put."

"I don't have your bloody recorder... my Dad's recorder, I mean. I don't have it. Now I have to go and do something in my room. Can you get yourself a cup of coffee downstairs?"

"I don't want coffee at the moment dear. I only want the recorder. You wouldn't be this nervous – or is it afraid – if you didn't have it. So why not give it to me to save any possibility of an accident."

Things are getting a bit scary out there, Peter thought. He put his hand on the doorknob ready to go out if anything further developed. Suddenly, Nola screamed. "Let me go."

In his rush to get out the door, Peter pulled hard on the doorknob before his head was out of the way and he felt the bump, staggered backwards into the office chair again. For a moment his vision was blurred. He shook his head. Outside, the struggle had deteriorated into a dangerous situation for Nola.

"Don't push me over the railing. That won't help you get the recorder. Please –"

"You should take me seriously, Nola. Look down there. See the floor. All hard tiles. It won't do your pretty face much good if you slam down onto them."

Peter shook his head again and stood up. This time he opened the door carefully and strode onto the landing.

"Hey, what the hell are you doing, Mr Martin?" he shouted.

Stephen was holding his niece upside down over the balustrade. He was holding both her jeans-clad legs and shaking her. She tried to grab a railing with her right hand. Her left hand was pulling the recorder from her jacket pocket.

Stephen turned a shocked face towards Peter but didn't loosen his grip. The detective told him to back off.

Stephen said: "You haven't got anything on me, detective, so butt out. This is a family squabble. Nothing to do with the police."

Peter spoke quietly, more calmly than he felt. "That recorder is police business."

"Yes." Her voice was shaking. "I'm waiting for the Inspector to come and get it after he's finished with Jeremy. His mother was killed last night or do you know that already?"

"I'm telling you again, move away and let Nola go."

Stephen gave a hoarse laugh. "You're joking, right? Why don't you go back to playing detective somewhere else? All I want is something that Nola has."

Peter said: "If you're talking about the recorder, then that is something I want. And it seems strange that you have such a strong desire for it. Why is it so important to you?"

"For god's sake, let me go. You don't know what you're doing. I could fall, could be killed."

"That is all in your control. You just move your hand back up here, let me have the recorder and I'll settle you back down on the floor."

Peter had moved close to the top of the stairs near the balustrade. He was a metre away from Nola, who was wobbling dangerously upside down, legs in the air in Stephen's grasp.

"I don't know why the recorder is of such importance to you, Mr Martin. This is a police matter, and I am calling on you to let your niece go.".

Nola screamed. Stephen laughed and let one of her legs go. She was dangling, held now by one leg.

"Let her go, you bastard," Jeremy shouted, bursting in through the side door.

Nola screamed: "Don't tell him to let me go."

Peter groaned inwardly. What the hell could he do?

Nola shouted: "Jeremy, I'm going to drop the recorder. Catch it. Don't let it break."

Jeremy ran across the room as the device fell from Nola's hand. Four sets of eyes watched the little device spin through the air. The owner of one pair of eyes grabbed at it. Caught it.

"Good on you, Jeremy," Nola said.

Peter was amazed that she could think and speak so matter-of-factly when she was being held by one leg over the edge of the balustrade.

Stephen said: "Listen son, put that recorder down on the bottom step or your girlfriend will join you down there."

"I'll catch you, Nola. Don't worry, I'll get you."

Great, thought Peter, while Jeremy's grabbing Nola, Stephen will be running down to grab the recorder and be off. Damn. Where's Inspector Cleary? I'm a new boy. Why is he leaving it to me? Peter rushed towards the upside-down Nola and grabbed her other leg. For a few moments the two men tugged her legs as if pulling on a giant wishbone.

Stephen suddenly let go of Nola's leg leaving her hanging by the other leg.

"Don't worry Ms Martin, I won't let you go. Hold still while I lift you up over the railing. You're safe now."

"But he's going to get away with it. Jeremy, pick it up."

Jeremy backed away from the stairs, apparently believing Nola was in safe hands as she was gradually sliding up over the balustrade. He ran towards the bottom of the stairs and bent over to pick up the recorder. As he did so, Stephen barrelled into him, knocking him to the floor. Jeremy still held the small device. But not for long. Stephen, quick as lightning, snatched it from his hand and ran for the side door. Peter placed Nola on the carpet and ran in a desperate attempt to catch Stephen before he got out the door. Jeremy, now on his feet, joined the chase.

Stephen reached for the side doorknob when he was suddenly knocked off his feet in a flying tackle.

Peter ran and fell on top of the sprawled Stephen Martin. He quickly took the recorder and handcuffed Stephen. He looked up as Cleary got to his feet.

"I haven't lost my touch. That's as good a tackle as I ever made in my rugby days."

Peter pulled Martin to his feet and nodded. "Yes sir, it was a bloody good one."

Jeremy and Nola embraced at the bottom of the stairs and walked towards the three men near the side door. Nola's face was pale, and she was shaking, but she said, with a smile at Cleary: "I hope this was all worth it, Inspector."

Cleary bounced the little recorder in the palm of his hand. "I guess we'll soon find out, won't we?"

> Where is your brother, he asked, and Cain
> responded with another question.
> Am I my brother's keeper? You killed him. Yes, I did.

CHAPTER 25

Transcribed from George Martin's recorder
"Hello George."

"Steve, what on earth are you doing here at this hour of the morning? I think I'm the only one in the house who is awake. I'm finishing a story."

"I wanted to have a yarn with you George to see how you're going. So, first, how are you going?"

"For a start, my mood has been improved by seeing you, my favourite brother, coming in and sitting in my office."

"Ha, your only brother, your only sibling. But thanks for letting me know that."

"I could do with a coffee. How about you? I can make coffee fairly well on our machine downstairs. Will you be staying long enough to have coffee with me?"

"I'll be here for as long as it takes so a coffee would be nice."

"Right, wait a sec and I'll get one for you."

"No need. Sit right there George. I've arranged for coffee already."

"Have you got a personal coffee delivery service? You've always been quite ingenious in doing things and getting things."

"Yes, we'll soon have a coffee together. Let's have a chat now."

"Goodo. I could do with a short break. I've been grappling with this story Solitary Eclipse. Too much science involved. Needs more research."

"I have been worried about you George. Last time we met you were very depressed. The way you spoke about some of the stories you are writing indicated that suicide could be on your mind."

"There is a difference between what I think and what I write - a big gap between what I do and what I write. You must understand that, Steve. It's been my living for decades now. I have a great imagination as you know."

"I know, I know, a very successful career you've had. But it must've cut you deeply when your last book was well, I suppose you use the same term, a flop."

"I don't use that term. It just didn't sell as well as my earlier books. If it had been my first book I would have been quite satisfied with the number of sales."

"Yes but it was a big downturn in sales from your most recent books over the past five or ten years. Now you are trying to resurrect your career with short stories. That must depress you George."

"The only thing that depresses me is my blindness. It is bloody difficult coping with a lack of sight. It's not until you experience it that you know how very very difficult nearly impossible it is to live normally."

"I do understand that George. I think your life must be hell and it has affected your marriage, hasn't it?"

"I know it's useless for me to deny that. I think Margot really hates me now."

"I don't think it's gone as deeply as hate. She can't cope with your inability to do the things in the house and around the garden you used to do and that she now has to do."

"I can't even tell what colour shoes I have on or what colour clothes I am wearing. I can't even be sure I'm wearing the correct shoes on each foot. I can't see what I have on my plate. I can't cut it carefully enough. I eat like a slob according to Margot.

I'm a proud man, Steve, as you know. Going back almost to childhood in so many ways, makes life almost untenable for me."

"I am so very sorry about your situation. It brings a tear to my eye whenever I think about it or we discuss it and I think that - Here's our coffee. Come on in.

"I hope this will be to your liking Mr Martin or I suppose that's plural isn't it, Mr Martins?"

"Who's that talking? Who have you brought into my house at this hour?"

"I thought you would recognise her voice. This is your neighbour, Jenny."

"Oh, Jenny, Jeremys Mum.

"Yes, Mr Martin, I thought you might like a hot cup of coffee to help you finish your work. I hope you don't mind me interrupting this discussion with your brother. Let me know if it is not to your liking, I can easily make another one.

"I am surprised by your sudden appearance, Jenny. Are you a friend of Stephen's?"

"We are very good friends George. I hope you are happy for us."

"The night is full of surprises. The coffee is good. Jenny. Thank you."

"Take your time George and try to relax."

"I don't know if a blind person can relax, not really. I have to concentrate on everything I do."

"That must be hard for you Mr Martin."

Even simple things like when I reach out in the kitchen for some item, I gotta be careful of the height of my hand that I'm not sweeping across to knock over a glass or bottle or boiling kettle. I must think very carefully when I'm going down the stairs - this step, that step, this step, that step. I have to think about everything I do to ensure I don't tread on something in my path, to make sure I sit on the correct side of the armrest in a chair. I have had my share of accidents because I was mindlessly relaxing and –"

"We know, we know. I've heard all that before and I'm truly sorry for you."

"I apologise for whingeing so much I shouldn't load my sorrows onto others. there are many thousands who cope better with being blind than I do."

"It is so terrible for you Mr Martin. I don't know how you manage to do all that wonderful writing. I am so impressed that you have kept at it."

"Only by dictating. I wouldn't be able to finish this book of short stories without Nola's help."

"What about Margot?"

"I had hoped for that, Jenny, but she is too preoccupied with other things to help me or so she says."

"You're looking a bit weary George. I thought the coffee would refresh you. Spark your brain into action again."

"I think he might be falling asleep, Steve."

"I am not falling anywhere asleep. A bit tired is all. You can leave me if you like. You seem impatient."

"We wouldn't think of leaving you, would we, Jenny?"

"Certainly not. We are here to the bitter end."

"What do you say to that, George? George, George."

"Steve, I don't think he can hear us. I think he might be asleep. I put enough in the coffee. I hope nobody wakes up and comes in."

"Someone's whispering, can you hear whispers?"

"Don't worry. This office is out of normal earshot of the other rooms, the bedrooms. I agree with you. I'm sure he is asleep now. I'm going to stand up there to put the rope over the hook. We'll put the noose around his neck and between us pull him up to an upright position and stand him on the edge of his desk like we talked about."

"I know we did but now doing it it's different. I am very scared and sorry that we are doing this."

"Calm down Jenny, this is a way for us to have a new life together with no financial worries. George is a very wealthy man so we will benefit from all his hard work. Thank you, George. The rope is right and the noose, too, I'm sure. Now, if you can balance him, hold him like that. Yes, I will start hauling on the rope and yes, yes, he is going up. Let go of his shoulders now."

"Do you need me to help pull?"

"Yes please, now. That's right, that's right, good on you. He's standing up there on the desk."

"Do you think he knows what we're doing?"

"Calm down Jenny. I'm sure my brother is completely out of it. He won't know anything anymore. Now he is balanced on the edge of the desk, the noose tight around his neck and the rope taut up to the hook and the loose end round the desk leg. I'll push him off the edge. There he goes."

"This is so terrible, Steve. I've been dreading it. Now it's worse than I ever thought. Too late to go back."

"For god's sake, Jenny, we can't change anything now. We have thrown the dice. My poor brother won't suffer the humiliation and pain he has been through over recent years. His reputation will not go down any further. He will be remembered as a fine novelist, not as a failed writer of short stories. And you and I will have a secure financial future together. I love you Jenny."

"Do you really? I hope so and I love you too Stephen. I just hate with all my heart doing this to a man I admired for so long and felt sorry for him in his blindness.

"You'll get over it. Take those coffee mugs and wash them in the sink very quietly. We must get out of here through the back door and up through the driveway, the way we came."

"You took a long time coming. I was waiting in the shadows outside and beginning to wonder if you had given up on the whole idea. Now, I wish you had."

"This is no time for second thoughts Jenny. It's done. We're in it together."

"What are you doing with the laptop and the USB drive?"

"I added a special file to the computer while you were washing the mugs. Let's go. Have you got the recorder?"

"No, I haven't seen it."

"What? We must get it. He had it. Did you check his pockets?"

"Of course, I did."

"It can't have disappeared. Bloody hell."

"Could he have thrown it out the window, it's half open."

"He couldn't have done that with us here."

"I was distracted, sorry. Did you hear that, Stephen? Someone's awake I think."

"Oh shit. I'll come back to look for it later. Quick, quick. There's nothing here to incriminate us. Our gloves have left no fingerprints of course and the coffee is gone and any remnants of a drug are washed away in the sink. This is a perfect murder that will be accepted as a perfect suicide if there is such a thing. Come on my darling.

> Nobody's ever been arrested for a murder; they have only ever been arrested for not planning properly.
> -Terry Hayes

CHAPTER 26

Stephen Martin sat quietly in the interview room, facing Detective Inspector Cleary and Detective Sergeant York. There was a tape recorder to their left. He was a lot quieter now than he had been when taken into the room half an hour ago. He sat in the chair, his hands down by his side, grasping the edges of his seat. Constable Brandon stood behind him near the closed door. He had said nothing for several minutes. Earlier he had been shouting, accusing police of setting him up, threatening lawsuits, miscarriages of justice. Throughout that outburst the detectives had sat quietly until he seemed to have understood that it was all to no avail. They had him. His shoulders slumped and he sat staring at them.

Cleary said: "Mr Martin, despite what you have been telling us and claiming, it is plain by the evidence that you killed your brother, assisted by Mrs Jennifer James."

Martin started to protest but Cleary's raised hand quietened him again. "You will agree, I am sure, that the voice on the recording we have played to you is yours. In that recording you identify yourself as George Martin's brother and Mrs James addresses you as Stephen." Cleary paused for a second before continuing. "You have been careless, Mr Martin."

"We found a packet of sleeping tablets in the glovebox of your car and you left in your wallet the USB drive that contains the file purporting to be a recording of the murder of George Martin. That fake recording in the computer, we believe, was typed by you, in an attempt to frame two other people for the crime."

Martin began to bluster again but Cleary would not be silenced and continued more loudly.

"Even here, Mr Martin, you made mistakes. I won't go into the technicalities, but there's no way that could have been produced by recording a conversation. And also, that fake scene you created happened to be a close replica of how you and Mrs James carried out the murder, as we have just heard.

"And in your hurry to get away from the crime scene, you pulled the USB drive from the computer without ejecting it properly. When we turned the laptop on, the message on the screen alerted us to the fact that a USB drive had not been ejected."

Martin stared at the detectives in silence, shaking his head as if embarrassed by his blunders.

Cleary said: "I think I know why you recorded that scene. You realised that a killer cannot inherit anything from his victim. So you set up that scenario to ensure somebody else was blamed if suicide wasn't found to be the cause of death.

Peter said: "Why did you choose to frame Mrs Martin and Mr Nagle in the fake recorded murder scene? Was it because you thought he was having an affair with your brother's wife?

Stephen snorted. "No, they were not having an affair. You detectives are not as smart as you think you are. Nagle is gay. Cleary and Peter looked at each other without saying anything. Then Peter said: "Oh, I see. So George Martin wasted a lot paranoia?"

"He did. Although Nola suspected him of carelessly leaving the bucket at the top of the stairs. And Mr Nagle won't be seen around the home for much longer. As you will find out, among the few people inheriting from George, Nola does very well, including her father's car. She won't require a chauffeur any more. As for me, for reasons well known to you and the legal profession, I won't get a cent."

"Are you sure you don't want your lawyer here?"
Martin shook his head and looked at his hands. Cleary asked him to say it aloud for the tape.
"No I don't."
"We are also going to charge you with the murder of Mrs Jennifer James, whom we know you killed in her garden."
"You can't prove that," Martin shouted, raising his hands and banging his right fist on the desk.
"Careful now, Mr Martin, you might open up that wound under the Band-Aid on your thumb."
Martin said: "So what? I did it at work. It's only a little cut."
Big enough, Peter thought, for DNA to prove his guilt.
Cleary said: "Unfortunately for you, it left a few spots of blood on the tomato stake that Mrs James' body was tied to. It was a splinter, wasn't it?"

The Inspector gazed at Martin for a minute, then said, "Tell me, Mr Martin, why did you kill your partner in this crime?"

Martin stared at Cleary for a long time. He reached into his trouser pocket and took out a handkerchief. He slowly wiped the sweat off his brow and returned the handkerchief to the pocket. He turned his head, looking around the room. Peter thought he looked like a trapped animal.

"OK. I made a mistake in trusting her because I loved her. I realised too late she was the weak link. As you heard, she was having second thoughts. It was in the middle of it, for god's sake. We discussed this at length. She knew all about it before we went into the office. She agreed." He paused and reached for his handkerchief again but changed his mind and continued talking. "And she deceived me by hiding the recorder."

Cleary said: "Where did Mrs James find the recorder?"

"She said it was on the floor under the window, partly behind the filing cabinet. She told me that George probably tried to flick it out the window while I was at the laptop. It didn't go far enough. Jenny saw it and dropped it into her pocket.'

"And she didn't tell you this at the time?"

Martin shrugged. "No. I reckon now that she was lying to me and that she had taken it from George's hand without me noticing.

"She told me later that she couldn't bear the thought of George's stories being lost. She planned to delete the recording of our crime, leaving George's work intact."

"She considered that more important than keeping the man himself alive and intact?"

Martin gave a wry smile. "I know. I can't work out the morality of that. I tried to persuade her to tell me where it was."

Peter thought 'persuade' was a mild word for what Martin had done. Martin was silent for a moment then said: "A killer can't have compassion. Simple as that. She went along with it until reality hit her. It wrecked everything."

After another pause he said: "I was desperate for the money, you see. My ex-wife was forcing me to sell my business, after all the years of work I had put into building it up. George had a lot of money. I had almost none. He knew my plight but didn't offer to help me. He expected me to wait until he died."

He looked at the detectives as if expecting sympathy. He got none. "The joke's on me, isn't it? I didn't know that he was going to die soon. I jumped the gun." He paused for a moment before saying: "I will take up that offer of a lawyer."

Peter thought his lawyer wouldn't be impressed with such a frank statement. Cleary told Martin that they would return him to his cell until his lawyer could be contacted but then added: "Tell me before you go, Mr Martin, did you put that hook up in the ceiling?"

"I might as well confess to that also. I told George it would brighten his office to have a hanging plant there. Margot was happy with that."

Later, back in Cleary's office, the detectives debriefed with coffee. Cleary smiled at his young colleague and said: "Good work, Peter, you deserve some time off after all those nights of reading. Take a couple of days off with Jan."

"Thank you, Sir, we'll like that."

Cleary said with a straight face: "Considering her condition, I'm sure she'll enjoy the break."

Peter almost fell off his chair. "What do you mean... how do you know?"

Cleary smiled. "I'm a detective, son."

EPILOGUE

TWO MONTHS LATER

Nola was slightly annoyed as she walked down the hall to answer a knock at the door. No one she knew would be knocking at this hour on a Sunday morning. She wasn't expecting any visitors. She sighed, probably Jehovah Witnesses or …

She opened the door and saw a woman in her thirties dressed in a yellow shirt and jeans and a small girl in a pale blue dress. They both looked nervous.

"Can I help you?" Nola said.

The woman said, "I'm sorry to disturb you, Ms Martin, so soon after your tragedy, but Emma wants to give you something."

Puzzled, Nola said, "This pretty little girl is Emma, then?"

"Tell the lady what you have done for her."

Emma looked up at her mother and hesitated as if she was having second thoughts. Her mother squeezed her hand.

"I made this picture of the man, Mr Martin, I met at the shops. I thought you might like to put it on your wall."

Nola squatted to be on Emma's level and smiled at her. Emma smiled and held up the picture which was on an A4 sheet of paper. Nola took it from her and studied it. Emma watched her face and waited.

"This is a lovely picture, Emma, and you did this all by yourself?"

"Yes, I did. I talked to Mr Martin at the shops. He wrote stories." She paused and looked up at her Mum and then back at Nola.

"Was he your Daddy?"

"Yes, he was."

More confident now, Emma stepped forward and said: "I made him standing up because it was easier. See the big stick."

Nola nodded.

"I couldn't see his eyes very well. I made them open here and I thought blue would be a nice colour. I think he was a sad man so I gave him a smile."

"That is so lovely, Emma."

"And... and I made his shoes the same, you see."

Nola smiled at her and said: "I do see that." She didn't understand what that meant. She stood and thanked Emma's Mum for bringing her daughter with that lovely picture.

"We will have it framed and hang it on the wall." She turned and gestured at the wall behind her, "just there, where everyone will see my Dad."

She bent and kissed Emma on the forehead.

"You have made Emma very happy. Thank you so much."

"No, all the thanks are from me. You are very kind."

They turned and left. Nola watched for a moment and went inside. She was surprised to see her mother watching.

"Who was that, Nola? What did they want?"

Nola handed her the painting. Her mother looked at it for a few minutes and handed it back. She burst into tears and walked down the hall.

TEN MONTHS LATER

Peter was enjoying the sun on the patio when Jan walked out of the house holding a small package. He didn't stir at first. He was lying back on the sunlounge, an open newspaper on his chest.

"It's present time, Daddy." Peter sat up so quickly that the paper fell onto the tiles. Jan walked up to him, putting her foot on the paper to stop it blowing away. She held out the gift-wrapped present.

"What's this about?' His smile indicated that he had an idea of what it was.

"Happy first Father's Day." Peter slowly unwrapped the gift. It was a book, always a welcome present. He turned it over and read from the front cover:

"Murmurs in the Darkness. A collection of short stories by George Martin."

He looked up at Jan and said: "Wow. This is incredible. So Nola has done her Dad proud. Where did you get it?"

"I saw it online. Booktopia. I knew it was from that manuscript. I suppose you've read all the stories anyway."

Peter got up and kissed her. Giving her a big hug, he said: "I can enjoy them now. I won't be looking for a murderer in every line."

"Phoebe thought you'd love it."

"Did she? Such a bright baby."

He paused, "Oh, should I have waited to open it in front of Phoebe?"

He smiled at Jan and she said: "Just thank her next time you see her."

THE END

ACKNOWLEDGEMENTS

Writing a book when you are blind is not easy. That you are holding this book now is due to the unstinting help of a wonderful bunch of people. It would not have been possible for me to complete this novel without them. My amazing and patient wife, Helen, read every word, sentence, paragraph in the book, at least twice, waiting patiently while I verbally revised it. Her sharp eyes and knowledge of grammar, punctuation etc often interrupted my thoughts to make sensible suggestions about things I had missed. My daughter, Rebecca Davis, also read many parts of this book over the phone while I did the same revision task. Her sister Emily Maguire interrupted her own novel writing to copy edit my book. My son, Ben Pobjie, transcribed my words from voice recorder to laptop and assisted in other ways. My youngest, Alice Pobjie, used her technological know-how to clear the way for publication. I owe thanks to Penny Sara for her sharp-eyed proofreading of the entire book and to Kylie Mason for her astute structural editing.

All these talented professionals made this a better book. Beyond their practical help, their encouragement kept me going when this task became more difficult than I had expected. Any mistakes within this book are entirely mine.

(I must add that my wife Helen bears no resemblance to Margot who is entirely fictional.)